Taken in Isolation

DIANA GREENBIRD

ISBN: 9798665800783

Cover Illustration by FreePik

AUTHOR'S NOTE

Whilst this book is set in a small fictional town in North Dakota, the spelling, punctuation, and grammar of the novel are in UK English, rather than US English.

ACKNOWLEDGMENTS

First, thank you to my fiancé for keeping me company during our self-isolation and for all the research help. You've always supported my writing; giving me time and space, working so hard for us to pay the bills whilst I sit down at my desk and write.

To my family for the tri-weekly video chats/games nights/quizzes: thank you! You kept me sane with each of your particular brand of insanity.

For Phoebe and James, thank you for proofreading my book. I can become so blind after hours of sitting at the desk immersed in Lilac and Dawson's heads it becomes easy to miss the fatal flaws a reader always picks up and remembers.

Thank you to all the key-support workers and staff for working in this crisis. For our NHS in England, the care staff looking after our elderly and any volunteer out there who gave up your own time and safety to help others.

And, finally, thank you to the arts industry – film makers, actors and most of all writers. Your entertainment made the time isolated not so lonely, and I would have gone stir crazy without the steady stream of e-books available to me and easy-access TV with *Netflix* and *Disney+*.

MARCH

1

LILAC

Three years ago, when I saw myself graduating, there were a few things that I never imagined. Daddy not being alive for it was one of them. The second was a global pandemic. But just like that unsuspecting human who somehow carried the first case of COVID-19 to the next: there are a lot of things that we can't foresee. And there are more things out of our control than we could imagine.

'Sweetie – I just don't see how I can fly all the way over there. The US is almost at 3000 coronavirus cases. *3000.*'

Mama's voice was a quiver over the phone. I'd put her on speaker as soon as she'd called, hoping to fill the house with some form of noise besides the whirring of the heating trying to combat the cold North Dakota air.

'You promised.' I tried not to sound like an insolent child, but the whine couldn't help but escape from my mouth.

'Lilac, sweetie, I know. I know I did. I don't like the idea of you being there all on your lonesome. But this is *serious.*'

'I can wait to pack up the house until you can fly, then.

I'll come back-'

'We shouldn't travel. Either of us – who knows who's coming back from China or those cruise ships! Going to an airport is the last place we need to be. It's simply a haven for the virus and infected.'

'Mama, I'm wanting to get *home*. It's not like I'm asking to spend spring break in China.'

'Lilac,' the low timbre of my stepdaddy's voice filled the speakers. 'Don't see this isolation as a burden or something keeping you from life. You would have been staying the next week anyway to go through the house, and you already talked to college about having a while before your exams for your grieving period.'

'Phil, *no* one is quarantining. Only a few states have declared this as a public health emergency, neither of them being-'

'If they did your daddy wouldn't be dead!' Mama interrupted. 'Sweetie, I simply won't listen to you pitch a hissy fit about this. The sports are suspending their games; colleges are moving to online classes, and the CDC just announced that any events including over fifty people should be cancelled.

'At least if you're at the Manor, I know you're safe. Lord knows that town ain't likely to catch the virus what with it being in a bubble an' all.'

The Manor was the name of daddy's house: our old home from when I was five to fourteen before their divorce. Since mama had gotten full custody, I'd never been back in the six years since I'd left. On holidays, daddy had come to visit me on campus, or he'd fly down to Texas if I were staying at home with mama.

'I think the news is exaggerating everything out of proportion,' I told them. 'And if I want to go home I-'

'I forbid you,' mama said.

'You *what?*'

'Helen, dear, is that really-?'

Mama's voice interrupted him. 'I *forbid* you. Steve already died to this gods-awful plague and I'm not risking my only daughter because she believes she knows better than government officials!

'You're to stay in your daddy's house and pack up his things like we planned and you're to stay there until we get the say so from President Trump that it's okay for you to return back to college.'

'Trump doesn't even think the pandemic is a big deal,' I groaned into the receiver.

Mama chose not to listen to me. 'Sweetie. Stay safe.'

When the call disconnected, I was stunned once again by the gaping chasm of silence that surrounded me.

I wondered if this was what daddy felt all the time. Was it this weird for him when we'd left?

I remembered when I'd grown up here there was always noise in the house: the TV on, mama and daddy talking (shouting… arguing), the radio, Kitty, our golden retriever, barking. When we'd left, we'd taken the noise with us.

'What had daddy done to fill the silence?' I asked myself, aloud. Had he talked to himself like I was now doing?

A pang hit me deep in the chest. I would never hear daddy's voice again. Not alive, not unrecorded. I could never ask a question and expect it to be answered by that quiet, unassuming voice he'd always had.

The last time I'd spoken to daddy, had been before he was admitted to hospital in Washington. He spent most his time flitting between here and his apartment there; though since I'd gone to college, he'd seemed to spend more time in Washington than North Dakota.

It had been our monthly catch-up. Mostly, we'd speculated about what was going on with the whole pandemic thing – whether it'd hit the US, how China was coping. He'd visited me at Christmas, so there hadn't been much to say about what was going on in the present we hadn't already discussed.

We'd gone onto ideas for my spring break; how my final dissertation and exams were going. I only had a couple more exams and had already finished my last paper. He hadn't even mentioned feeling ill. He'd been well enough to joke about paying my ex a visit for breaking up with me on Valentine's Day.

His cremated ashes were still in Washington. After the funeral, I hadn't known what to do with them. I had been in a daze, getting back to his empty apartment.

He'd bought his WA apartment as-is, only buying a few linens, and a computer for work. His personal assistant, Lisa, had already cleared it of anything "personal" (most of it just office stuff) and was ready to put it up for sale as soon as she got my "okay".

It was a bare place. Monochrome and unfeeling. More like an office than a home. I could see why he never sold our old house in Grand Yutu – even though there was no one to return home to with me and mama gone. Though most of his business was in Washington now, I'd want to escape back to the Manor if that apartment was the only "home" I had, too.

He was still sat on the kitchen table, in a polished silver urn. Alone in that bleak apartment. My daddy.

I probably should have brought him here. It's what he would have wanted. Possibly. Probably. He hadn't mentioned what he wanted to do with his ashes in the will. I was going to scatter them. I couldn't carry that urn with me for the rest of my life. Sixty years of shuffling that silver pot from one house to the other. But then I'd have to pick the right spot.

I rubbed my temples, feeling a stress headache come on. I'd already popped a couple pills an hour ago – not that they were helping.

I downed another glass of water – keeping hydrated couldn't exactly hurt.

I'd arrived in Grand Yutu several hours ago, exhausted. As soon as I'd walked into the Manor, I felt as though I'd been transported back in time. Daddy hadn't changed a thing in six years.

I'd planned on the drive over here exactly how I was going to tackle packing away the house. I hadn't thought about how difficult that would be until I realised it would be like packing away *him. Us.*

The walls were lined with pictures of us as a happy family, smiling for the camera. Picture perfect, American-dream team. In the quick walk around that I'd done of the house, the only changes I'd seen had been in his office. I wondered if mama knew how the Manor remained as a time capsule.

Is that why she didn't want to fly over? She realised helping me sort through daddy's things would be like opening the wound to a time before her divorce, back when she was Mrs Montgomery.

Instead, I was left alone to self-inflict the damage of those long-lost childhood memories. Remember each moment I used to spend with daddy – seeing him every time I came home, knowing that I was never going to see him again.

After a sad dinner of the rest of the *Subway* sandwich I'd gotten at a rest stop on my drive from the airport to the Manor, I found myself in the library.

The one thing I knew I could tackle was daddy's collection of books. He'd been an avid reader since he was a young teenager and had detested the idea of an e-book. He finished a book a week, never borrowing them from a library, always buying them fresh from the store.

At Christmas, or for his birthday, mama and I had always bought him at least five books. Over the years he'd amassed enough that one room in the house had become his library. There was the "Lilac Wing" which was a bookcase of five shelves with all the books I'd read in middle-school, but the rest were daddy's. Mama had never been much of a reader.

I'd always been astounded by the collection and thought it odd his desire to keep hold of them. I'd never known him to re-read a book. It seemed silly for us to have an entire room dedicated to things in the past that would never be touched again.

Even at twelve, when I used to spend an hour after school in the library, I'd realised how better suited those books would be to someone who could get another use out of them. It had been easy to decide I was going to donate them to the local library. They were always hurting for funds and with daddy's expansive collection, from crime best-sellers to the odd rare classic, it would be a massive boost.

It helped that Edie Dawson, the town librarian, had been my mama's best friend back when we lived here.

It was six o'clock. The library didn't shut until seven, so I pulled up the number on my phone and called. No time like the present and all that.

The number rang out. I tried it once more – it was possible that Edie was busy helping someone. Once more, the call wasn't answered.

I went online to the library's website. The opening hours had been amended since I'd moved. It was now only open Monday to Thursday 12-4. They'd always struggled with funding – or perhaps Edie had decided to take on some reduced hours?

For the next half an hour I took cardboard boxes from my rental and packed up the books in daddy's library. I kept a box for myself, the rest sorted into genre so it would be easy once they were donated to get put on the community library's shelves.

With so many books, it was possible that there wouldn't be enough shelf space. I would have to talk to Edie about donating a few of the bookcases around the Manor, too, so that they wouldn't have to go into their annual budget to pay for the new storage.

701-555-6743.

I grinned to myself as Edie's home number came back to me. It was a trick I'd used a lot during my years trying to recall facts for finals. If I thought about something else, and kept busy, my mind would eventually sort through the information and allow what I wanted to know to come back to me naturally. Intently focusing on an answer and trying to force myself to remember never worked.

Along with the Manor's number, the Dawson's house had been the only one I'd ever had to memorise. When mama and daddy worked late, Edie would take me home with her. It had started off only once a week for the first couple of years, then gradually became several nights until I was eleven and I'd practically been round their house every night.

When I was younger, I'd always felt like I was imposing, until she'd told me she'd always wanted a daughter and me staying over was her little way of playing pretend. Edie had been like an aunt to me throughout my childhood. She was the one thing my mama and I had hated about leaving.

Mama had been so upset when she left. I remembered her crying on the flight to Texas. I thought it was about daddy and the divorce, but she said that when it came to him, she knew she'd made the right decision: they didn't belong together. But Edie… mama hadn't ever been able to make it to the end of that sentence.

I'd never had a friend like mama had Edie. No, that wasn't quite true. I'd had Henry… though could that ever be classed the same considering he'd been years older and more like a big brother to me than just a friend? Ha. *Brother.* Those feelings had sure changed once I'd discovered *boys.*

I rang Edie's home number. Unlike the library, the call was picked up after thirty seconds.

'Hello?' A gruff voice said from the other end of the line.

'Urm, hi? I was wondering if Mrs Dawson still lives at this address,' I asked.

'Who's asking?' the voice practically growled.

'Lilac Montgomery,' I said. 'Edie was a family friend of ours back when I lived here. I tried to get in contact with her through the library, but it was closed.'

'Family friend,' the voice on the other end of the line scoffed. 'Some friends.'

'I'm sorry?' I asked. It sounded as though he was *mocking* me.

'Ha! *Sorry*,' he scoffed again.

'Who is this? Do I have the right number?'

'You're telling me you seriously don't recognise my voice?'

'Mr Dawson?' I guessed.

I'd never seen Edie's husband much when I'd stayed over. He worked in the mines during the day and spent most of his nights with his buddies at the bar, coming home late. Or at least that's what Edie had said to mama when they thought I hadn't been listening.

'*Mr*, so polite *Ms* Montgomery.' His tone was dripping with derision.

If hatred could be physically manifested it would have formed a fist and punched me through my *iPhone.* I had no idea what this man's problem was – whether it was Mr

Dawson or not – but I wasn't my mama. I didn't believe in sticking a smile on and trying to win assholes over with Southern charm. I would be polite, but I would never be a doormat to be walked over.

'Will you please inform me as to whether I have the right number for Edie or not. I'm not really a fan of your attitude,' I said. 'And I would very much like to get in contact with her. I have something she might be interested in.'

He just chuckled, humourlessly.

'Who *are* you?' I asked.

'Dawson,' he said. There was a long pause. I couldn't tell if it was to be dramatic, or whether it was because he realised, I still wasn't certain of who was speaking. 'Henry.'

The breath was physically knocked from me.

Henry Dawson.

The image of the eighteen-year-old boy who'd left to join the army (a year before I'd left this town myself), scruffy dirt brown hair, sharp blue eyes and pretty-boy face with an easy grin popped into my mind unbidden. Edie's only son. My first ever crush. And the boy I'd followed around like a shadow, desperate for him to be my best friend.

'You're back,' I said, my mouth speaking before my brain had okay-ed the words.

'And apparently,' he said in that now deep timber of his I couldn't recognise from the boy I'd once known, 'so are you.'

2

DAWSON

‘They’re closing the school,’ one of the moms said to another.

The kids were still in their skates, with another ten minutes left of their practice. Thankfully, this was a group who had long since gotten past using their sticks as swords to battle one another when things got “boring”.

The mom who was currently talking was Vivian – she had been a couple years ahead of me in high school. Her eldest, Shane, was nine years old and currently skating circles around his friends. She’d almost given birth right in the middle of prom.

Every time I looked at him, I struggled not to picture Roy’s (his dad) face when confronted with either accepting the homecoming king crown or going with Viv to the hospital. It was pretty obvious long before that moment that he was a prick. Shane and his brothers were better off without him.

‘How long?’ the other mom asked.

‘All of next week. I have no idea what I’m going to do with them. Shane drives me up the wall as it is – and he’s started picking fights with Arnie. They broke the coffee table last night. The *coffee* table!’

Viv's three-year-old was currently trying to climb into the sin bin. I skated over quickly before the kid could brain himself.

'Here you go, tyke,' I said, scooping him up and popping him down on the bench in the penalty box. Arnie and Shane skated over, to me and their youngest brother.

'Where's Mitch?' Shane asked.

I looked over to where Viv was still talking. The five-year-old was nowhere to be seen. 'Fuck,' I swore. It wasn't enough that I had to watch the kids I was coaching, I now had to babysit the spectators, too?

'Hey Viv! Control your brood!' I shouted to her, getting her attention.

Her eyes widened as she saw Kean in the box with me, Shane and Arnie pushing each other on the ice. I got them to quit it and skate back to the others, passing over Kean to Viv.

'Mitch!' she shouted, loud enough that a few of the kids on the ice whipped their heads around, their skates spraying ice as they skidded to a halt. They knew the sound of a mom calling her kid for an ass-whooping well enough to immediately stop what they were doing. Even if it weren't their mom calling.

Mitch appeared a minute later from the top of the seats on the away side. He'd somehow gotten one of the spare hockey sticks and was using it as a walking stick as he climbed from one seat to another like an explorer on Everest. He skulked down until he was sullenly stood by his mom's side.

Kean immediately grabbed for the stick Mitch was holding. Mitch pushed him down. Thus, ensued a scrap I tried to extract myself from, only Viv (after telling her boys to quit it) kept me on the edge of the rink.

'Will you be keeping the rink open?'

'What?'

'Next week when the school's shut – are you closing the centre? Or is practice still on. I don't know what I'm going to do if Shane and Arnie don't have somewhere to get all that energy out,' she told me.

'We'll still be open unless I'm told by the Governor himself to close,' I told her.

I managed to skate away then for the last ten minutes of class before the *Nokota Horses,* Grand Yutu's only high school ice hockey team, came for the last practice of the day.

Keeping busy on the ice, coaching the kids, I felt the eyes of my mom watching me in the stands where Viv and her friends currently stood. She wasn't there, but sometimes I felt like I could feel her presence.

I knew it was some deep-rooted psychological bull. All those times I'd been in practice as a kid and she'd been there, watching me. Now that I was back, it stood to reason I'd still feel she was there. There hadn't been a time before I'd left for the army that I'd not been on the ice and she wasn't watching me. Along with my other perpetual shadow. Fuck. Lilac.

The *Nokota Horses* managed to keep me engaged enough that I didn't think much about anything other than the play, their technique and busting up the occasional fight. It took the precise twenty-three minutes I'd nailed it down to like an art to close the centre up and that was that. Coaching was done for the day.

I got into my old truck immediately putting on the heating full blast, not that it did much. The AC had been bust for the past several months, but I didn't have any spare cash to fix it. At least it was March now and getting warmer. December and January had been a killer.

Viv's question burned in the back of my mind. I rested my head on the steering wheel and fought back a groan. It wouldn't be the paycheque that I'd stress about if they decided to close down the athletics centre. It would be the kids. For a lot of them, the athletics centre was the only place that kept them occupied now that the rec centre and cinema had shut down. And that was when they had school to occupy them for most of the day. What an absolute cluster-fuck.

I reversed out of my parking space and towards *Billie's,* the supermarket I worked to stack shelves after coaching hockey practice.

Speaking of cluster-fucks, now that I didn't have coaching to occupy my mind, I thought back to my conversation with Lilac fucking Montgomery last night.

I'd known her dad had died – with an impact that bastard made on this town, we'd practically all celebrated his passing – and had figured it might mean someone would turn up to clear out the Hades McMansion, but it hadn't crossed my mind that it would be *her.*

'Do you- do you remember me?' she'd stuttered after a moment of silence when I'd told her my name.

That fact that she hadn't recognised my voice had pissed me off, probably more than it should have. It wasn't like I'd driven her home from school every day from when she was eleven right up until I left for the army at eighteen. Or that she'd spent practically every second of her childhood with me and my mom in the library or our home.

But what did I expect from a Montgomery bitch? If her mom could easily forget her best friend as soon as she skipped town, why wouldn't her daughter forget the guy she'd sworn with those big puppy dog eyes that if she could choose to spend forever with someone, she would choose me.

Fuck, she'd been thirteen at the time when she'd said it. And her first "boyfriend", if you could even call him that at that age, had just broken up with her and I'd been consoling her tiny teenage broken heart. But still.

'Yeah, I remember you, Texas.'

'Oh, right.'

I didn't know what *that* had meant. But her tone seemed to imply a lot more than just her simple words.

Her voice had gotten a stronger Southern accent since she'd been away. Like how she'd used to speak when she'd first moved here, before the years of living up north had tainted that princess Southern belle.

'Your mama – do you think you could pass me on to her? I really wanted to have a chat about some books I was thinking of donating to the library.'

Clueless. Could she really have been that fucking clueless? 'Mom's not here,' I said.

'When will she be back?'

'Never. She's dead.'

From the sharp gasp she'd given, I knew I'd probably gone a little overboard with the blunt no-fucks answer. But any shits I had left to give wouldn't be wasted on softening the blow that some woman who used to babysit her spoilt ass had passed on in the many years her family had forgotten about her.

'No.'

'Yes.' It wasn't as if I was going to lie about the worst fucking day of my whole life.

'I'm so sorry,' Lilac said.

'I don't need your pity.'

Lilac *hmm*-ed on the other end of the line. 'I understand. A lot of strangers have been telling me they're sorry lately – my daddy passed a few weeks ago.'

She told me like I didn't already know. Like I'd not got black-out drunk in celebration that finally – *finally* – the bastard who actually deserved it was dead.

'But I am sorry, Henry. Edie was like family to me. She was an amazing person. I can't believe that she's gone.'

Mom was the only one who ever called me Henry, bar

Lilac. I hated hearing my name on her tongue.

'I've got to go.'

I couldn't listen to that bitch talk about my mom like she was *family.* What did that girl know about family? *Real* family.

'Wait!'

'What?'

'I was wondering if you'd want to catch up tomorrow?'

I laughed. 'You're not serious?'

'Why wouldn't I be? It would be good to see an old friend. I'm clearing out my daddy's house and it should take a while. It would be nice to have something else to occupy my mind.'

'Yeah, that's not going to happen, Texas. I'm not going to be your distraction.'

She seemed like she was about to argue on the other end.

I didn't give her a chance. 'Anyway, I'm busy tomorrow. But have fun burying the rest of your old man.'

I'd ended the call and tried my best not to throw the phone at the wall. Not that it would have made much of an impact. We'd never moved on to a cordless phone.

3

LILAC

Grand Yutu, the tiny insignificant town in North Dakota, hadn't changed since I'd left. I'd barely seen it since I'd driven in from the airport straight to the Manor, but there wasn't much to see.

What was there to say about Grand Yutu? The first was possibly that there was nothing "grand" about it. Not in size, beauty, or wealth. It was a mostly white population, with the odd Native American or black person thrown in. Nearly everyone was conservative Christian and voted overwhelming Republican. Spending the winter mostly in the minus-degrees, the frozen weather was considered "warm" when we got to anything above twenty degrees.

There was one high school, one small community library with a recreation hall attached, and an athletics centre with a hockey rink and a gym.

One side of the town was perpetually overlooked by the large looming mountain that locals called Miner's Mount. Aptly named as that was where daddy's mine was located. A small, independently run operation that had not only boosted daddy's own income, but the whole town's as well when he'd discovered the untapped potential after getting lost coming home from a business deal in Winnipeg.

Daddy had stumbled across the town in the dead of winter, a snowstorm making it impossible to continue on home. He'd stayed two weeks trapped in this nowhere town, with nothing to do but listen to the locals tell him tales of Grand Yutu.

One story had particularly stuck with him. The mine in the mount the first settlers in Grand Yutu had worked on back in the late 1800s. It had been abandoned towards the end of the Second World War, where the town moved onto agricultural pursuits as the ability to mine coal from the mountain became more difficult. Daddy had come back to the town after the snowstorm with a mining inspector and evaluator who had told him the mine could still be very profitable – and the rest had soon become history.

The other side of town to Miners Mount was nothing but fields and farmland, with one main road twisting and turning for miles on end until it finally found its way to Route 83.

The town was so insignificant, that it was only on maps in the past forty years that Grand Yutu even turned up. Like it had popped out of nowhere. *Nowhere* was where it remained, despite now obtaining a minor nod of acknowledgement from the world.

Even in my early years before puberty I'd known this quiet little town existed in a time warp, outside the *real* America. Mama had either called it the "bubble" or the "time warp".

'Bless her heart, she's never stepped one foot outside the warp,' mama would say, shaking her head in that strong Southern belle accent she never lost even when she'd left Texas.

No one ever really *left* Grand Yutu. Even though the number one complaint by teens and adults alike was that they were *bored,* it was almost as if tiny town life had suffocated their poor minds. That they could just *leave* and find a life outside of Grand Yutu was beyond them.

And just like no one *left,* no one *ever* came from the outside. Edie Dawson had been the first outsider to move to the town for forty years. But she'd been from Bismarck, practically a neighbour to Grand Yutu in comparison to Texas. Me, mama and daddy were *true* outsiders.

From the beginning, everyone found our accents silly, and our sun-tanned skin and summer-kissed hair odd. Like being from the South was actually being from outer-space – or at least that's how I'd felt going into first grade.

Growing up here from a young age, at least I'd been able to mostly lose the accent, but the kids never forgot I wasn't *really* from Grand Yutu. But I didn't matter to me. Daddy and mama were different, too, and different was *good.* Different had changed this town for the better.

I'd always been proud of what daddy had been able to accomplish when he'd first opened the mine. Agriculture had been the main source of income for most of the town, but there was always a risk the crops would fail, and it was a constant struggle to battle the weather. Mining could be done all year round and daddy said the coal supply was almost endless in Miner's Mount.

Montgomery Mines had improved this town. Grand Yutu went from being a place where there was nothing to do, to somewhere that you could go to the small independent cinema (only forty seats, but still); or one of three (not just the one) bars. There was still only the one block of five stores for clothes, accessories, electronics, etcetera, but it was more than the town had had before.

Daddy's successes transforming the town had been what made me major in sociology in college, with a minor in Park and Natural Resource Management. A degree which he'd now never get to see me complete.

The second day back at the Manor I'd decided to get some supplies.

I'd thankfully been saved the hazard of cleaning up spoiled food since daddy spent most of his time in Washington and therefore the house was perishable-free. But it also meant I would starve if I didn't get something in since I was apparently stuck here on mama's orders until Trump's all-clear. So, basically, I'd be stuck here for the rest of my life.

I parked my rental in a empty spot and headed to *Billie's*. The stores on the street were the same, though they looked like twenty years had passed, rather than seven since I'd last been here. The paint was chipped, graffiti marring most of the brick on the sides of the building. The town frozen in time had aged.

Apparently, panic buying had reached Grand Yutu. Darci had shared a few images on our sorority group chat a couple days ago when she'd tried to go shopping and the shelves for toilet paper had literally been empty – like a thousand spaces for loo roll and not a single roll!

I hadn't experienced it yet, what with travelling to Washington for the funeral, then across to Grand Yutu to the Manor – but now I had. Practically every shelf was empty. There were still a few boxes of cereal, milk, bread, and some fruit and veg, but other than that, the cupboards were bare.

'Have you got any more stock in the back?'

'Nah,' the woman at the till answered. 'Had our man stock the shelves full last night. This is all we got.'

I bought as much as I could, hoping that daddy had some backup supplies in the basement. If not, I would be having to order some stuff on *Amazon*. If everyone hadn't already bought out the stocks.

Once I got back to the Manor, after putting away the food in the kitchen, I attempted to finish off boxing the books in the library.

The news that Edie was gone still didn't sit right with me. I didn't know how long ago she'd passed on, or how she'd died – but so soon after finding out daddy was gone, learning another person so close to me was no longer in the world…

I still planned on donating the books to the library, but it meant something different now that Edie no longer worked there. Who had taken her place? Who helped plan the events at the rec centre? Did they like their job as much as Edie had loved hers?

I only managed two boxes before I decided I had to call mama. Surely, she must have known her friend was no longer alive. They'd been best friends for almost a decade. Wouldn't she have wanted to go to the funeral? Shouldn't Mr Dawson have contacted her to invite her?

'Sweetie! You're staying safe, aren't you?'

'Hello, mama,' I said, almost rolling my eyes. 'Yes, I'm safe. I stocked up on some food this morning.'

'Good! You would not believe the craziness that is going on around this town. Shannon Dougherty, hand on my heart, bought sixteen packets of toilet roll and *all* the canned goods from our little shop down the road. Now what does she expect to do with twenty cans of chickpeas? Y'all know that woman can't make hummus to save her life.'

'Mama, I have something to tell you,' I said.

'Lilac – what's that voice? Lord have mercy on my soul do not be telling me you're pregnant in the middle of this crisis.'

'*Mama*, that is *not* the voice I'm using right now.'

'Do I need to be sitting down for this?' Mama asked.

'I- I don't know,' I said honestly. Did she already know? I had to believe that she didn't – couldn't. She would have told me if she did. If she had known and she'd kept it from me, then this was going to turn into a whole different conversation.

'I was packing up daddy's old library and I thought about donating the books to the community library.'

'Oh, sweetie, that's such a good idea. You should really stop by and see Edie. I know how much she loved you, and you were so close to her son, Henry.'

I wanted to remind her that *she* had been the one who was closest to Edie, but I didn't. I suppose that answered my question as to whether she'd known or not.

'Mama, speaking of Henry… I called the Dawson's number last night hoping to talk to her and Henry picked up the phone.'

'He's back from service-?'

'Yes. And he told me Edie passed away.'

'W-what?' Mama's choked word was barely a whisper.

'I don't know how, or when it happened, we didn't really speak for long, but she's gone.'

There was silence from my mama. My mama was never silent. 'Oh, oh lord.' That was the only words I heard before I heard the sobs begin.

Just like when we'd left Texas, the pain of leaving Edie hit mama harder than the pain of leaving daddy. My mama hadn't cried for my daddy at his funeral – but she cried for Edie now.

*

I'd never been the type to drink alone, but daddy's collection of wine wasn't exactly going to go anywhere. I debated between donating it to one of the local bars (there were quite a few vintages here) or saving them for my sorority girls back home. Depending on how long I'd be here would probably give me an answer to that.

I'd already found a red wine from 2016 I was going to

send Darci for her twenty first. It was in two weeks and I was likely going to miss it if things continued to get worse rather than better. Darci considered 2016 her lucky year as it'd been when she'd lost her virginity after being asked by a senior to prom.

I'd made the sad dinner of a microwave Bolognese and was drowning the disgusting taste with a glass of red. Okay, maybe more like a bottle.

Netflix was on in the background, but I didn't even remember what I'd selected to watch.

My phone buzzed on the table. Most of the girls had been chatting non-stop this past week since they'd all had to move out of the house and back home as college was shut. Keeping each other informed of their local drama and trying to one-up each sister had been their way of keeping busy between online classes.

I'd turned into the lurker who read all the messages but never replied. Whenever they talked to me now it was always with that pity tone – expecting me to be in the heart of grief.

The world around us was literally changing, my daddy was gone, and I wanted some rock to hold onto – some shred of normalcy, but my girls didn't know how to be normal around me right now.

I'd tried to explain to Darci that I didn't want them to pretend that they weren't having a laugh or living their lives normally. I didn't expect their worlds to change because mine had, but she hadn't really gotten it. It's why no matter how much I'd wanted to call her and tell her all about Henry, I hadn't.

What sort of person would she think I was that my daddy was dead, but what was on my mind was finding out a woman who *hadn't* given me life had passed on?

I picked up my phone, fully expecting it to be some goofy meme or an image of one of my sorority sister's pets from back home, and instead I opened up an attachment of a half-naked man.

A seriously attractive half-naked man. It was taken from just below his chin (a five o'clock shadow on his face), down to the deep v-cut of his muscles that pointed to his groin just out of the view of the camera.

He had a defined chest, though pale like you'd expected here this far north where the sun barely shone (and if it did it wasn't temps you could be taking your top off in) but certainly not down in Texas. A six-pack, though it could be an eight pack in the right lighting, was well defined and held centre attention. On his left pec was a Celtic cross with the words "death before dishonour" written underneath.

Unknown: WUU2?

The number wasn't saved to my phone, but that didn't mean anything. I rarely saved numbers to my phone: the only ones I had were from my sorority, my mama, daddy or Lisa, daddy's recent PA. My heart clenched at the thought that I had no need to keep daddy's number on there anymore. But I wasn't ready to delete it yet. There were still all our text messages. I wanted to read those again.

My first thought was that perhaps it was a buddy of my ex. I knew from the picture straight up that it wasn't Callum. He'd been defined, yeah, but no six pack. And he had bronzed skin with no tattoos.

I'd deleted his number after I'd found him in bed with his psychology partner. So, there was the potential that it *was* him, messing with me using someone else's picture. It wasn't beyond him. It would be exactly like him to think catfishing his ex would be funny. Though it was more than likely he'd heard through the college grapevine my daddy had passed – and even he wasn't that sick in the head to catfish a *grieving* ex.

My thoughts were interrupted when the next text came in.

Unknown: Sorry. Wrong number. But feel free to enjoy the pic at your own leisure. I'm sure it's good enough for a "distraction" ;)

Henry's words last night came back to me. *I'm not going to be your distraction.* Was that *Henry?*

If it was, then it most certainly was *not* a wrong number because I'd called him on the landline. And that also begged the question how the hell he got my number unless they'd updated their home phone to one with caller ID. I very much doubted that since Edie had been in love with that phone and was extremely technophobic. Getting her to install those three computers in the library had been a nightmare.

I'd tried looking him up on social media a few times in the past, but Henry's opinions on *Facebook* probably hadn't changed much since high school as I'd never been able to find him. But that didn't mean he hadn't looked *me* up. My number could have been posted on any one of my medias. I wasn't exactly "private" on all my accounts.

If this somehow *was* Henry – that meant that *picture* was of… oh, lord. My thirteen-year-old self just did a mental back flip.

From the sharp, defined jawline shaded over in stubble to the extremely toned body, I couldn't recognise the boy I'd known back then here. There was something about the sexy smirk that had a touch of familiarity, but until I saw his nose and eyes I wouldn't be able to know for certain that it was him.

Me: Henry?

I'd typed and sent it before I'd even thought about it.

Unknown: Yes.

I wasn't going to be that idiot simply taking an anonymous stranger's word for it without verification. The last thing I needed was for Callum to be messing me around and then posting screenshots of whatever I said onto *Insta* for a laugh. "*Thirsty bitch in lockdown":* I could already read the comments in my mind.

Me: Prove it.

Five minutes later another picture was sent to my phone. This time, it was the same half naked guy from the photo. On his middle finger (which he was flipping the camera off with) he'd written "Texas". But that wasn't what clued me in. Though his face was mostly blurred, with his finger being in the forefront, now that I could see the profile…Yeah, it was definitely him.

Like the gruff voice I'd heard the other day, it seemed impossible that this was *my* Henry. He'd been attractive at eighteen, but now he was a pantie dropping drop dead gorgeous *man.* He definitely aged well.

Henry: I've shown you mine, Texas.

Was he insinuating that I show him *mine?* Yeah, that was *not* going to happen. I may have been his shadow for a decade, but that was *years* ago. We were veritable strangers now and would probably remain that way considering he'd blown me off when I'd asked if he wanted to catch up with me.

Me: By "accident".

He didn't respond to that.

I cleaned up the living room and turned off *Netflix*, deciding it was probably time I went to bed, even if it was most likely just going to be me staring at the ceiling of my old fourteen-year-old designed room thinking about all the questions I wanted to ask Henry but didn't dare.

How did your mama die?

How did you cope?

Is that why you're such a freakin' grump now?

Does it always hurt like this? Does it get worse? Better?

What did you mean when you scoffed at me calling Edie a family friend?

When did you get back from the army? Are you on leave? Are you going back soon?

How does the army deal with all this pandemic stuff?

I didn't ask any of those questions, though, I just let them all twirl around in my mind, dancing in the silence of the house.

I eventually got to sleep after one in the morning. I hadn't been asleep long when I heard something downstairs. In the emptiness of the house, even the slightest of noises was like a deafening call.

I sat bolt upright in bed.

My room was dark, the curtains closed obscuring the moonlight and the light from the streetlamp outside. I hadn't bothered leaving the landing light on, considering I had my own en-suite and wasn't likely to get up until it was light enough to see in the hallway anyway.

Frozen in my bed, I listened to see if there was any more noise from inside the house. Intently, my ears pricking at any possibility of sound, the intense beating of my heart in my chest felt as though it was going to knock me over.

Then: there. I definitely heard something. What the hell was I going to do? If someone had broken into the house, what would they do if they found me here?

Real freakin' great time to rob the place! Couldn't have chosen the weeks before when there'd been no one in. It wasn't as though my rental was hidden, either. It was clearly parked out front.

Oh, god. That meant that they *knew* I was here, and they didn't care.

Another noise from down below. My heart was still going crazy in my chest. I looked around my room for something to defend myself with. Fourteen-year-old me was freakin' useless. Why couldn't I have been into baseball? No, instead, I'd been interested in *ice skating* because Henry had. And not even ice hockey because I could hardly stay up right even when pucks weren't flying at me.

Though…

As quietly as I could, I made my way to my closet and opened the door, looking for my ice skates. It was awkward to hold, putting the boot on my hand so I could use the blade as a weapon, but it was better than being empty handed.

I crawled the rest of the way into the closet, shutting the door, trapping myself inside. I'd taken my cell with me and made sure it was on silent before calling 911.

'Nine-one-one operator. What is your emergency?' The voice was calm and steady on the other end.

'There's someone in my house,' I whispered.

'Someone has broken into your house?'

'Yes,' I whispered back.

'Where do you live?'

I whispered the address of the Manor.

She relayed the address back to me. 'Is that correct?'

'Yes.'

The operator paused for a moment. 'Are you *sure* there's someone in your house?'

I thought for a moment. I couldn't be certain, but I'd heard a noise. More than one noise, and it'd sounded like there was someone moving through the house.

Just then, that was when the sound of glass breaking began. I screamed. I couldn't help it. It was a gut reaction. The smashing didn't stop. It went on for five minutes. I sobbed, clutching my phone with one hand, my old ice skate in the other.

Eventually everything went quiet downstairs.

'Are you still there?' the operator asked.

'Y-yes,' I managed to say.

'Are you sure there's someone in your house?' she asked again.

'*Yes*,' I said with conviction.

She'd heard me scream. Surely, she should be sending someone over to my house – reassuring me that I was going to be okay and that the cops would be here soon.

'We'll send someone round as soon as possible, ma'am,' she finally said. 'And I'll stay on the line until they get here. Just stay where you are and I'm sure you'll be perfectly fine.'

4

DAWSON

Lilac's break-in spread around town like wildfire. Jane had taken the call and had re-played Lilac's scream for the entire bar to hear on repeat. Each time it got a huge laugh.

Rick Olson, the sheriff, wasn't too fussed about the breech in protocol. Made sense since it was his younger cousin, Lucas, who had broken in last night.

Rick and a couple officers had showed at the Montgomery mansion at six in the morning, after making Lilac wait scared in her bedroom for hours. They'd had a laugh about how it had almost looked like she'd pissed herself waiting in that closet for someone to come save her.

I assumed she'd spend the day unsuccessfully trying to find someone to fix all her broken windows to keep out the cold. Not that she'd find anyone in this town willing to help her.

The one thing I knew for certain was that she'd gone crying to poor mommy dearest about what had happened. I knew because that bitch had the audacity to call me and ask me to check on her.

The town was riled up; ready to run another Montgomery out of town. Last night was just the beginning. Lucas and Trace were all gung-ho about enacting every fucking revenge plot they'd ever considered on those boring nights when there was nothing else to do other than wallow in drink and get high.

I'd had my own share of fantasises about fucking over the Montgomerys, though I was years late to the hate-party by this town's standards.

When Steve Montgomery had been fucking this town in the ass, I'd been across seas on active duty; my first tour in Iraq.

The only hint I'd had that shit had gone down was the mining accident. The one I'd had to go on leave to come home for as my dad had died in it.

"Hint". Like your own dad dying wasn't a big fucking scream from the heavens and hells.

But shit had been different for me in the army. My hometown was put in the back of my mind; put in a place behind walls of protective armour so I could focus on the *there* and *then* of staying alive. I hadn't had time to think about the accident or losing my dad. I hardly thought about my hometown or the person I had been before I'd enlisted at all.

When mom had died, that hadn't been the case. I'd finished my tour and could have gone back home. But just like how I'd joined the army to get out of this small town and try and find a future out there that was more than just becoming a miner or a farmer – I had continued to run away.

I had taken up the army's offer to help me with my college tuition, though fuck knew what I was going to major in. I joined the hockey team, even if I was rusty as shit considering I'd not put my skates on in almost seven years.

After six years of being in the army, I had slowly started to adapt to civilian life again. I started to think about my future and who I wanted to be. What I wanted to do.

I'd eventually begun to realise I missed most aspects of living in a small town, but I didn't know whether I missed them enough to resign myself to the farmer/miner life. I figured I'd have the summer to remind myself of all the stuff I loved about Grand Yutu and three more years of college after that to weigh up the difference.

That had been the plan anyway, until I was packing away the boxes from my campus apartment, ready to go back home for the summer, and I'd gotten the call that mom had been in an accident. She had wrapped her car around a lamppost and died instantly.

I'd returned home thinking I'd been given the middle finger by God. I'd been looking for a sign not to come back to this town, well, now the only person I had left there to go back to was dead.

Go and live your fucking life in the big city, hot shot. You're all alone now.

It had taken mom dying for me to realise the extent of the damage the town had sustained since the mining accident. And I learnt that whilst I'd been living the city life away from home, mom'd been struggling to keep things together, falling down a rabbit hole of depression.

The mine had been shut for good; this town only just clinging on with the farms that had mostly been left abandoned since Montgomery had come to town and re-focused our industry. Tourism was a tainted and dark word now – and I'd become sick after learning the truth of what I'd been oblivious to across seas.

I'd been sorting out the invitations for mom's funeral when I'd learnt who was responsible for all the town's suffering.

'You can't seriously be inviting them,' Carolyn had said to me when I'd asked her to help me to send out the invites. She was always the best at getting around town and was the most up to date with town gossip.

I didn't know who mom's friends had been whilst I'd been away and wanted to make sure that anyone who should be invited came.

'She's mom's best friend,' I'd said – like the ignorant fucker I was.

'Best friend? Helen Montgomery hadn't spoken to your mom since she left this town with her daughter and never looked back. She didn't even call when your dad died in the accident.

'Not that we'd expected her to. The lawsuit Montgomery filed against his own miners almost bankrupted your mom. And all that blood money went right into little Lilac's trust fund.'

I'd stood there, dumbfounded, unable to comprehend what Carolyn was telling me.

'Montgomery killed your dad along with the other fourteen miners. Every bad thing that's happened to this town can be traced back to him. I wouldn't be surprised if your poor mom's accident didn't have some ties to that awful, cursed man.'

That had been the beginning of my dark period before it reached its apex when I found the note my mom had left me. And I realised Carolyn's words were truer than I could have ever imagined.

In my grief, I'd fallen in with Lucas and Trace, two more kids who had lost their dads to the mining accident years ago and still hadn't been able to move past the pain.

Our nights were filled with alcohol and drugs. Getting high and hammered, thinking of insane ways we could get back at the bastard who had fucked this town.

How did we get to Steve fucking Montgomery? He hardly ever came back here anymore, and it wasn't like we could touch him if he did.

It wasn't right that he was still free to roam around and wreck more small towns because no one bothered to put the fucking bastard behind bars. Rich white men could get away with anything. And he'd gotten away with every. Fucking. Thing.

Lucas breaking into the mansion last night reminded me of everything I'd said back then – months ago, now. I'd moved on from that hate since then and hadn't thought about it since. I'd had to.

Mom was never coming back; the town wasn't going to fix itself. I could spend fifty years drinking and wallowing, cursing Montgomery, but that wouldn't solve anything.

I'd quit drinking. Quit fantasising about getting revenge on the Montgomerys who were responsible for not one, but both of my parents' deaths. I'd fuelled my frustration and hatred into plans to turning this town around. Montgomery Mines was closed, but we'd survived without the Montgomerys before and we would again.

I left this town because I'd wanted more than small town life, and in the past year I had become the heart of one. Was that irony? There was never a chance I would leave to go back to college now. I had too many responsibilities here, too much work to be done.

The damage of this town was down to the bone, but unlike the systemic problems of a large city, I knew I could fix this. I knew the people and I knew how resilient they were. I hadn't been there for my mom when she'd needed me, but I would devote my life to making up for abandoning her by sticking by the town she'd loved now.

'Fuck me. Those rich cunts don't have a fucking clue, do they?' Lucas had laughed when he'd found out about Helen messaging me to check on her daughter.

'You're not going to,' Trace said, blowing the smoke from his joint into the air. They didn't do drugs around me – not since they knew how I was trying to clean up this town, but weed never seemed to count even if it was still illegal here for recreational purposes.

'Nah, I'm really not,' I said.

I didn't stick around long enough to shoot the shit with them. I was checking in on Wheat-Locke Farm practically at sunrise in the morning so was heading in for an early night after a day of coaching. But Lilac's scream kept replaying in my mind and Helen's stupid oblivious request.

I thought I'd let go of my revenge plans – and I had. You wouldn't find me breaking into her place like Lucas and Trace. But I hadn't let go of my anger. I didn't give a fuck what Lucas and Trace had planned. Or if the town ran out Montgomery's daughter the same way they'd gotten rid of him.

Shit, I'd even stooped so low as *messaging* the girl; thinking messing her around a little on text wasn't really much in the grand scheme of all I thought about doing in the past.

I hadn't known what I was going to do if she replied. If she'd actually sent me a pic back like I'd requested. I'd just been curious since she'd called me up asking for mom.

What was the heiress like these days? How had she lived since she escaped this small town and the dastardly deeds of her father? Why had she never looked back? Was she now as soulless as her parents?

It was that same curiosity that had me driving automatically towards the mansion, even though I'd laughed at the idea of checking on Lilac like I was at the beck and call of Helen Montgomery's every whim.

Her tiny little car (a rental from the sticker on the back) was parked neatly in the front drive. Unlike the sidewalks around town, her driveway was immaculate, no cracks in the paving or trash littered on the floor. No broken glass, even though from what Rick had said there'd been a shit ton all over the place after what Lucas had done last night.

I surveyed the house. I'd expected to see the smashed-out windows still, but instead, cheap plywood was nailed over the frames. The glass had been swept up.

Someone had helped her. I seethed at the thought, trying to imagine which one of the guys would have helped her out. I could get the answer from Hal at the hardware store since he was the only one who could have supplied them with the wood.

Wanting to know how she'd done it – who she'd managed to get wrapped around her little finger – I found myself out of my truck and walking up the drive to her front door.

I banged my fist on the door, rather than using that precious little doorbell connected to whatever app let you see from the camera out front. Not that she was connected to Montgomery's online security network. Or she would have seen who had been in her house and sent the screenshots to Rick. Like he would have done anything with them.

It took her a few minutes to answer the door. When she did, I didn't know what I was expecting. Perhaps a smaller version of Helen now that she was all grown up? But as she stood there, I was floored. She looked almost exactly like the Lilac I remembered.

Oh, sure she'd grown up. She had tits now, hips and her face had lost most of her puppy-fat. But those big brown eyes framed with delicate eyelashes were still the same. Her cupid-bow of a mouth still looked peach-soft, with that small mole just above her lip making her look like a young Marilyn Monroe.

Her skin was more tanned than it had ever been back when she'd lived here: all freckles and bronze. Her hair was a warm blonde, no doubt with highlights that cost as much as a month's worth of gas for my truck.

She did look like Helen now that she'd grown up, I could see that. But I couldn't look at her and not see *Lilac.*

'Henry?' Lilac asked, her head tilted to the side as though she couldn't be sure that I wasn't a figment of her imagination.

I sucked in a sharp breath, fucking *pissed* that she was calling me that still, but the wind got knocked out of my sails when I saw that her hands were crudely wrapped up in bandages, with blood splattered on them.

'What the fuck happened to your hands?'

Lilac just waved it off. She smiled, showing a row of pearly white teeth. She'd had braces on the last time I'd seen her. They'd clearly been worth the top dollar her dad had paid for her.

'What are you doing here?'

I didn't bother answering her question. I stepped through the threshold. 'What happened to your hands?' I asked again.

Lilac sighed. 'The windows. I wore gloves when I cleaned up the glass, but I took them off to nail the boards to the frames. It was my first time using a hammer: very much a learning experience,' she laughed, self-depreciating.

'*You* fixed the windows?'

There were at least twenty on the first floor. Lucas had smashed them all out with a drywall hammer from work.

'I tried calling to see if there was anyone in town who could do it for me, but all the builders are working construction jobs so were too busy. I looked up some tutorials on *YouTube* and bought the supplies from the hardware store.'

None of the builders in town had any construction jobs going. Tourism was a bust these past two years and no one had any spare money to fix the falling apart town. It had been a brush off. The same way Steve had found his money was no longer good here, this town's particular brand of anti-hospitality was extended to all those with the

Montgomery name.

I could see the tools now lined up next to the front door along with a few spare pieces of plywood. There was quite a bit of blood on them.

'Let me see your hands,' I said.

'What? Why?'

'Because you're still bleeding through the bandages, so you've clearly done a shit job.'

'What are you doing here?'

'Your mom called me, asked me to check in on you.' It wasn't a lie.

'She *did?*'

'Yeah, gave me your phone number, too. She seemed to think we should exchange digits, so you've got a handy local serving boy at your beck and call.'

'You're not a serving boy,' Lilac said, flipping her blonde hair over her shoulder, like she was some model posing for the camera in a summer catalogue.

I half expected to see her in some booty shorts and tank top even though it was the middle of March – but with the windows smashed-out, it was frozen like hell's balls in here.

She was wrapped up in a burgundy sweater with her college name printed across the front. She had on fluffy socks pulled up practically to her knees, her grey sweatpants tucked into them. She should have looked scruffy and like a slob, but she looked cute. I fucking hated her for it.

'Don't I fucking know it,' I said.

I grabbed her sleeve and pulled her into the kitchen. It was open plan so I didn't have much trouble finding my way around. I'd never been inside Grand Yutu's only McMansion before, but it looked like an interior design catalogue for "wholesome and homey".

The first aid stuff was still on the side. I started

unwrapping the bandages from her hands. It was clear she'd never had to take care of herself from the sloppy way she'd wrapped it around her hand. Plus, she hadn't even put anything to separate the wound from the bandage in between. Amateur.

I started from the beginning, cleaning the wound again then putting on the ointment, before putting cotton padding between that and the bandages.

She'd really done a fucking number on her hands. Usually with hammer injuries you got a few bruises, but she'd clearly cut herself on some glass, maybe nicked her fingers with the nail as well.

She didn't wince, though I knew cleaning out the wound must sting – particularly when I had to peel the bandage off her left hand where the blood had clotted to it.

The girl had balls. I'd forgotten that about her. Like nearly all the positive memories I had of Lilac they'd been relegated into the subterranean levels of my mind.

I cleaned her up in silence. I could feel her eyes on me, pressing me with a thousand questions though she didn't say anything. She watched my hands as I wrapped the bandages around hers, tighter than she had done and with more care. She seemed to notice the flecks of scars that marred my skin.

I was still in my jacket – not having taken it off since getting into the house – so it was the only bit of skin available for her to judge. But the rest of me was pretty banged up, too.

Most of the scars I knew she'd be familiar with from back when she'd lived here. Hockey, rock climbing, general fights in high school. I'd been battered and bruised before I went into the army. But my body had changed a lot since she'd last seen me. *I*'d changed a lot.

'All done.'

'Thanks,' she said. She trailed one finger over the

bandages. Only two of her fingers had needed patching up, but I'd simply put a band aid on them. Not attempted to make her hands into little white cotton clubs as she'd done.

'So… how was your date last night?' Lilac asked me.

I furrowed my brow in confusion. *Date?* What was she on about?

'The girl you were supposed to be sending out that booty call message to when you accidentally sent it to me,' Lilac clarified.

'Seems like you had the more interesting night, Texas,' I said, dodging the question, pointing to the windows.

We both knew the message I'd sent her hadn't been an accident. I'd meant to send that message to her. Though I was never going to admit that to her.

'Someone broke in,' she told me.

'Shit,' I said, pretending to sound surprised. 'Did they take anything?'

'No? I don't know really. I've not been here since I was fourteen. I wouldn't know where to begin looking if they did. The TV and everything were still there. The sheriff was convinced no one actually got into the house. They probably just thought the house was abandoned and smashed in the windows.'

Lilac didn't look convinced as she was telling me Rick's excuses.

I heard her scream again from the recording on the dispatch call. Seeing her now in the flesh and blood made things less funny. She wasn't just Helen's mini-me. She was *Lilac.* Fuck how that messed with my head.

'Do you want a drink?' Lilac asked, abruptly.

'Do I want…?'

Lilac went to the fridge. It had a few juices in there, bottled water and a couple beers. 'I've also got a mighty fine whisky and wine collection if you want to take anything with you?'

Lilac led me to the living room where a drinks cabinet displayed an impressive collection of Scottish and American whisky.

'Have at it,' Lilac said.

I didn't move.

'Seriously, take anything you want. I'm probably going to give the rest to one of the bars in town if they can accept it. Or send them off to my friends back home though that'll require a lot more effort and shipping.'

'You're just giving away booze and books?' I asked, recalling how she'd called yesterday to offer her dad's collection to mom's old library.

'What else am I going to do with them?'

I went into the cabinet and pulled out an unopened bottle. I knew from some of my rich silver spoon hockey players on my team back in college this bottle was worth over a couple hundred dollars.

Though I didn't drink anymore, I unscrewed the lid and took a sniff like I was going to take a sip, then just put it back. Couldn't exactly re-sell it with a broken seal now. Lilac didn't seem at all fussed.

'I don't drink,' I told her.

'You can take a few bottles for your friends if you know anyone who'd like them,' Lilac said. 'Seriously, it'll all be going to waste if you don't.'

I wondered what Lucas and Trace would do with alcohol that'd been sent as a gift to them via Montgomery's princess. Though this was good shit, they'd still probably light a rag inside the top and throw it at her house rather than drink anything she'd offered them.

'Texas, no one in this town would drink that stuff if you paid them,' I told her honestly.

'What's that supposed to mean?'

I laughed at her. 'Look, I know you've been gone a long time and your dad just kicked the bucket, but the ignorance game isn't going to work forever. Your dad *ruined* this town. The sooner you get out of here, the better. If you can't take a hint from that-' I pointed at the bordered-up windows. '-You're sure as shit not going to like the next message they send.'

'My dad *saved* this town,' Lilac said, her cheeks blushing a wild red in anger. 'He didn't *ruin* anything.'

'Saved? *Saved?*' I chuckled low in my throat, though there was no humour there. 'Your family was the worst fucking thing that ever happened to this town.' *And me,* though I didn't add that part.

I didn't see the slap coming. It probably would have hurt a fuck load more if it weren't padded by the bandages. As it was, it was just like a dull thump to the side of my face. But the shock of it kept me silent.

'Get out.' Lilac ground the words out. 'Get out of my house.'

'Sure thing, Texas,' I said.

'You don't know a freakin' thing about my daddy,' Lilac said, slamming the door in my face.

'And you do?!' I shouted through the closed door. 'We were the ones living with him here! You're the one who escaped off to Texas! You don't know a fucking thing *princess*!'

I swear I heard her kick the door and swear at me as I walked back into my truck and took off.

5

LILAC

Henry's words re-played in my mind that night as I tried to get to sleep. Every light in the house was on because I couldn't stand the thought of going to sleep in the dark: not after last night. I'd called my mama about the break in – hoping that it would persuade her to let me leave.

I thought as soon as she heard what had happened, she'd be the one booking me a flight home. But I'd been watching the news when I'd been about to call her.

President Trump had issued new guidelines urging people to avoid meeting with more than ten people and had restricted travel to "discretionary" only which meant only going to work if you couldn't work from home, and for grocery shopping or to go to the doctors. Things were getting more serious than I thought and the cases for people testing positive for coronavirus kept rising.

What were the chances that I'd somehow contracted the virus and was now a carrier? Or if I hadn't gotten it, going to the airport would increase my chances of being exposed and bringing it back home with me.

It was likely that if I did get it, I would survive. But would mama? Would Phil? Daddy hadn't. Could I risk being part of the problem simply because I was scared to be alone in my house for a couple weeks until things cooled down?

In the end, I hadn't told her about it. I'd told her about the plans I had for daddy's clothes to be donated to the charity that Darci was working towards starting.

Suit Up, a non-profit for unemployed folk where they could hire out clothes to give the right impression at job interviews. A lot of people who were unemployed didn't have the money to buy a new suit to wear to interviews.

Though it was reasonable for employers to expect that the people who were wanting a job didn't have the current cash to afford the latest outfits to look presentable, instead it just led to a ridiculous bias. The people who needed the jobs most were overlooked for someone who could already afford to dress the part. Darci wanted to eliminate that bias and help people the way she knew best: through fashion.

Daddy's suits would be the perfect start for her business. I'd even managed to get mama to ask around her girlfriends and see if they had any clothes that they'd be willing to donate.

I messaged Darci asking for the address she'd like me to send the suits. She'd not yet found an office space for her business, but her parents had told her that'd help loan her the money to get started once she graduated. Who knows if that would all have to be put on hold with this whole pandemic stuff. But there were probably going to be a lot more people out there in need of her help when everything cleared up. Especially since Trump was now saying we might be heading for another recession.

The night was as quiet as ever, though now that the windows downstairs were nothing more than plywood it was almost as cold inside as it was outside.

Your dad ruined this town.

Henry's words repeated in my head again and again.

Along with the thought that the person who had broken in last night had done so to send me a message. I wasn't safe here.

The hammer I'd used was next to my bed. It was better than an ice skate, but it wasn't exactly premium in protection as weapons went. I'd get myself a gun, but I didn't have a permit and I'd probably end up hurting myself more than protecting myself.

Phil had tried to teach me to shoot. It had been one of our stepdaddy-daughter bonding moments. It hadn't gone well.

Henry had been right about one thing. Me and mama probably hadn't known daddy as well as this town had in these past years. I spoke to him barely twenty times a year for our once a month catch-up and the odd talk in between. Most of the time I ended up speaking to Lisa more than him where we'd try and figure out a time for me to catch him between meetings. But what could he have done that was so bad that would make someone break into our house and scare me?

Ruined this town. That was pretty strong language. The Henry I knew wouldn't have said something so harsh if he hadn't at least thought it was true.

I ended up leaving my bed and wandering around the house with the hammer rather than attempt to go to sleep. My mind wouldn't switch off, scared that if I did, I'd wake up and someone would be standing at the foot of my bed.

Daddy's office was the one place that didn't remind me of my childhood. And with no windows, it was the warmest room in the house and felt the safest. I ran my hand over the bookcases. Most of the stuff in here I'd probably get Lisa to sort through like the work she'd done in his apartment back in Washington.

I sat at his desk, imagining what it would be like for him working here. He had two monitors, a slim keyboard, and a leather notepad to his left. He was left-handed so the right side of his desk was instead where he kept his coaster for a drink, and a photo frame with an image of me from last year when he'd come over to Texas for the weekend to see me before my birthday.

I opened the draws, wanting to look inside for some clue as to who my daddy was now. Or had been, before he died. Not just the image he'd show to his daughter, but the *real* him. One capable of ruining a town…?

In the bottom draw I found four red leather-bound journals. I fought back a yawn as I opened the first one.

December 2011

Our marriage counsellor says that we should each keep a journal of our thoughts. Try to track down where our arguments are stemming from. If we still love each other and are committed to make things work, we need to see where the problems start and how we might be taking out our troubles on each other rather than using our marriage as a soundboard to find solutions and help each other with our issues.

Most of the time she's talking absolute shit, but this might be my last chance to work things out with Helen. The least I can do is write in this fucking thing.

2011. I was twelve. Two years before mama finally got a divorce and left North Dakota and returned to her warm, loving Texas with me.

I hadn't known that they'd tried marriage counselling. It didn't seem like the thing they'd have available here in Grand Yutu. Perhaps they'd driven to the city somewhere for it. 2011: that was when "date night" had begun. Was that code for counselling?

However much daddy had tried, it clearly hadn't worked. Mama had still left.

I leafed through the pages, reading the year from daddy's perspective. Little things he'd say brought me back to my own experiences that year.

It was the year I'd realised I was crushing hard on Henry Dawson. He was seventeen, gorgeous and popular in high school. The captain of the ice hockey team. I'd started to learn to skate when I was eight because Edie had said he was at the rink most of the time he wasn't at school.

I remembered watching him with all his girlfriends who never seemed to last the month, wishing that he'd just look at me.

I had my own diary at the time. There had been an embarrassing amount of love hearts with Lilac Dawson scribbled within like the cliché teenage girl I'd been. I probably still had those diaries somewhere up in my old room. I hadn't taken them with me to Texas after the divorce.

I woke up to the sound of a loud horn as a truck passed by on the road in front of the house. My neck was sore from the awkward angle I'd slept in, my head resting on the desk. My face no doubt had the imprint of daddy's journal.

I got up and stretched, putting the journal back in the desk before leaving to go upstairs and into the shower. I was halfway putting my panties on when I realised I'd started my period.

'Oh, hell,' I swore.

I waddled into the bathroom, but of course there were no tampons. And I hadn't brought any with me because I'd not been thinking about coming on in the midst of travelling up to Washington, then across to North Dakota.

I wadded up a bunch of toilet roll as a make-shift sanitary towel and pulled on some clothes, grabbing my wallet and car keys, making my way to *Billie's*.

'I can't serve you.'

'What? You're kidding. I was only here a day ago,' I said. All I had on the desk in front of me was a box of tampons.

'Yes, that's why I can't serve you. We're protecting ourselves against hoarders. You've already done your weekly supply shop.'

'This is *one* box. I'm not hoarding.'

'It's one box *today.* And tomorrow it will be another, maybe two. And so on.'

'It's a box of tampons,' I said through gritted teeth. 'I just want one box. That's literally it for the *month.* I can promise you I'm not going to come back and buy more. I'll even put it in writing.'

The woman just pointed to the sign that said "we reserve the right to refuse service…" etcetera, etcetera.

I was going to bleed through my panties into my pants. I only had the toilet roll daddy already had in the house and using that as a makeshift protection was going to make me go through that quicker than I'd thought I would.

'Please,' I tried one more time.

The woman just snatched the tampons from the desk and put it behind the counter. I heard a few snickers from behind me. Well, screw you, too.

I stormed out of the store and got back into my car.

You're sure as shit not going to like the next message they send.

It wasn't exactly a one up for breaking and entering – or scaring the living hell out of me in the middle of the night, but it was still a message. I wasn't welcome.

Though it was the same lady who had served me before I had a feeling she was now informed that I was persona non grata.

I'd been half-way home when I stopped off at the biggest of the three bars in town. Though I couldn't buy a box of tampons, that didn't mean I couldn't buy a few. I knew most bars had a vending machine inside the ladies' room. A vending machine couldn't exactly deny my custom. It was worth a shot.

I parked up my car and entered the bar. Though it was midday, there was quite a lot more people than I would have thought to see here.

I avoided the eye contact and ignored the whispers as I weaved my way around the tables to the ladies' room. My sigh of relief when I saw the machine was audible.

I pulled out my wallet and put in as much change as I had on me. I would need to exchange a few more dollars' worth to get any sort of amount I'd need to last out the next five days, but I wasn't sure whether I should alert the barman to what I was up to.

I doubted that this town was as in cahoots as the shop girl at *Billie's* calling everywhere that had tampons and warning them against me going after them, but I'd gotten a little paranoid since Henry's warning.

'They're much cheaper if you buy them from a store you know. Or are you just having a meltdown right now?'

I twirled around to the voice. A woman, around my age with dyed red-black hair cut short into a bob and thick black eyeliner stood in the door. She was dressed in all black with a plunging neckline so low I swear I could almost see her nipples. Though her face was covered in a thick layer of makeup making her look different from the last time I'd seen her, I still recognised her.

'Willa?' I asked.

'Lilac Montgomery as I live and breathe,' she smiled.

We'd been friends back in middle school. I'd never really had a best friend, not like mama and Edie were, but I'd been friendly with most of the girls in my class. Most thought I was still the weird outsider, even if I had grown up with them since kindergarten, the fact that neither of my parents came from here made me the alien.

Willa and I had been in most of the same classes, and shared gossip like the best of them, but we'd still lost touch when I moved back to Texas. Fourteen wasn't exactly a solid age for fighting miles and miles of long distance.

'You're back,' she said.

'For a while. I'm clearing out my daddy's house.'

'Yeah, I heard,' she said. There was no "I'm sorry" condolences, or questions on how I was doing, or how long ago he'd passed. Part of me wondered whether, like Henry's warning, she was part of the "whole" town who hated him. And now hated me by extension.

'What's with the tampon raid?' Willa finally asked.

'I've been prevented from buying any at *Billie's* for fear I'm a feminine hygiene product hoarder,' I said, rolling my eyes at the ridiculousness of it all. 'I came on but didn't bring any tampons with me. Sort of forgot about the whole body-clock thing what with the funeral and the pandemic going on.'

'Yeah, world's gone batshit,' Will said. 'I've got a box in my bag; I can get it you. Come on.'

Willa took me out of the toilets. She went behind the bar to the staff room in the back and handed me a box of tampons when she came back out. I shoved it into my oversized pockets of the ski-coat I was wearing.

'Thanks.'

'Pull up a chair, I'll get you a drink on me. Looks like you need it.'

For the first time since getting here, I wasn't faced with spending the whole day by myself in the house so though I could still feel the angry gaze of everyone around me, I took off my coat and settled into the seat in front of Willa.

'You tend bar?' I asked her.

'During the day whilst Kasey is at school. At night I work at Tit Town, dancing.'

'Tit Town?'

'The strip club that opened up back in 2015. We don't get many tourists around here anymore, but it's pretty much the only entertainment we've got left since the cinema and rec centre closed down.'

'The name's a little on the nose isn't it?' I said. The town no longer had a *cinema,* but it had a strip club? Was this part of what Henry had meant when he'd said the town had been "ruined"? I could hardly imagine how daddy had anything to do with that, though.

Willa shrugged. 'Call's it how it is.'

'Kasey is?'

'My daughter. She's four,' Willa said, pouring me a glass of red wine. I had no idea how she knew that was my drink, but I didn't ask. Perhaps I just looked the type.

I did the math. If Kasey was four, it meant Willa had gotten pregnant back when she was seventeen, still in high school. I knew there was a lot of underage pregnancy here in Grand Yutu, but it was strange to see what that meant for a friend.

It had always been girls years above me back in middle school and they'd always seemed so grown up to me. Though I was only twenty-one now, seventeen seemed so young to be a mom. Even now, I didn't think I would be ready for at least another seven years to consider being a parent. But Willa had a daughter almost old enough to go to school. Insane.

'Who's her daddy?' I asked. I wondered if it was James, the guy Willa had been dating the last I'd known her.

'Some out-of-towner who didn't stick around.'

Willa was about to say something – perhaps ask a question about my own love life – when some guys at the other end of the bar called for her attention. I sipped from my wine glass as she left. I'd never been really the one to day drink, but I didn't want to be rude.

I felt the presence of someone next to me before I saw

them. It was a man, perhaps in his mid-thirties? I couldn't really tell his age, but he looked like time had been hard on him. His stubble was verging on becoming a beard, his hair greasy from being underneath his cap all day. If he washed up, he wouldn't be *unattractive,* but the strong smell of stale beer came off him in waves that physically repulsed me. I tried not to show it on my face.

'Can I help you?' I asked.

'What happened to your hands, princess?' the man asked. Unlike when Henry had asked, this man looked like he took pleasure in asking the question. Like whatever reason would give him satisfaction in sharing my pain.

'I cut them on some glass,' I said, not willing to elaborate.

The man reached out, as if to touch my hand. I pulled back, keeping my hands close to my chest.

'I have a boyfriend.' The words slipped from my lips like a well-practised line. Until a month ago it'd been true.

Callum and I had been dating since the end of freshman year. Whenever a guy had hit on me, I'd been thankful for Callum as a buffer from me and unwanted attention. It was habit to use it again. Not that I was sure this man was hitting on me, but he was creeping me out whatever he was doing.

'Of course, little princess has a boyfriend. Fortune 500 dickhead, is he?'

'Trace: fuck off,' Willa told him. She appeared in front of us, giving him the evil eye.

Trace stared at her pointedly, like he was going to pick a fight with her, but then decided against it.

'A boyfriend, huh? He have a name?' Willa asked. She propped her head up on her hands, as if settling in for a tale.

'Callum,' I said.

I could still feel Trace's eyes on me. I couldn't admit to

Willa we'd broken up without Trace finding out I'd lied to him. And he seemed like the type to take it personally and confront me about it.

'He not make this trip over with you?'

'No.'

'You're all alone in that mansion, then?'

'Like most of the town will be pretty soon enough,' I said. It was only a matter of time before we were given a stay-at-home curfew.

'We're isolated-fucking-central out here,' Willa said. 'Who needs to isolate further when this town is so far off the map corona can't touch us?'

Some of the guys at the table in the back seemed to hear her as they shouted hear-hear and clanked their glasses.

'Not that the Governor sees it that way. Schools are closing next week, and now we're going to have to close up the bar and the athletics centre, too, until April. Fucking nightmare.'

I fiddled with the bandages on my hands, feeling awkward. I didn't belong to this town, but I knew the impact closing the school would have. Kids already got bored during the holidays – and with the cinema and rec centre closed *and* the gym, what exactly were they going to do to occupy their time?

'What happened?' Willa gestured to my hands.

'Cleaning up after the break in to my house.'

Willa winced. 'I heard about that. Sounds like you need to get the hell outta town. We've got some nutters here,' Willa said. Her warning mirrored Henry's.

'Yeah, if it was that easy I probably would,' I said. 'But my mama won't let me come home. She *forbids* it.'

'What happens if you ignore her? She cut you off from your trust fund or something?'

I laughed. 'No. I don't have a trust fund. My daddy was a self-made man and though he loved me more than anything, he wanted me to have a healthy work ethic. If I could live off a trust fund, I'd be nothing more than a mooch for the rest of my life.'

He hadn't factored dying into that plan. I'd inherited everything since he'd never re-married or had another kid. I had no idea what to do with that money. I'd pushed it to the back of my mind for now: focusing on his properties first.

'Then why are you staying? You're an adult. Flights aren't cancelled yet. You could go home.'

'I know…' I sighed. 'But mama's right. Going back home could potentially expose her to the virus. And it's not like I would be much use back home anyway. At least here I have a job to do: packing away daddy's house. Most of my sisters are bored out of their minds now that they've had to move back home with college campus being shut.'

'Sisters?'

'Sorority,' I said.

Willa laughed at me. 'Figures you're in a sorority.' I gave her a pointed stare. 'I'm sorry, you're just a bit of a cliché, you know. You don't exactly help yourself.'

She gestured to my face and hair, probably my accent, too. Since March in North Dakota was practically freezing winter compared to the weather down in the South, I wasn't in my usual outfits, but it was clear that would have gone into her assessment of my "cliché" nature.

'My goal in life isn't to help other people feel more comfortable around me. I am what I am.'

My mama was part of the DAR; my daddy was a self-made millionaire. I was a white, Christian, with a family that could be traced back to the Mayflower on my mama's side. Back home, I lived on a ranch and my mama had bought me a horse for my sixteenth birthday. I was part of a sorority and though daddy was new money and had worked hard to get where he was in life, I was the trophy daughter, born with a silver spoon in my mouth.

If people only wanted to see those things – then they would. They wouldn't look further to see who I was as a person, and I wasn't going to battle to fight against their prejudice. I couldn't control how other people thought about me. I could only control my own actions and thoughts.

'That's a nice philosophy,' Willa said. 'But it's probably not going to go over so well here.'

'College might not look like it's the setting from a Stephen King novel like Grand Yutu, but at least I have something to do here.'

Willa let out a huff. She clearly didn't like me dismissing her warning.

'I doubt this town is going to get any more friendly to me over a long period of exposure. My reception isn't likely to be warmer a few months from now, is it?' I said. 'My daddy's house needs clearing. I do that, and then I'm out of here.'

Hopefully, the virus would have become more manageable by then.

Willa poured herself a shot of some amber liquid.

'Here's to hoping you make it to the sale,' Willa clinked her glass with mine and downed the shot.

6

DAWSON

'Lilac's back in town.'

Willa had caught up to me as I was leaving the rink. It was only a block away from her mom's house: where Kasey spent most of her time when Willa was working either one of her jobs. From the black-on-black ensemble she had going on, I knew she'd just come off a shift from the bar.

She wouldn't have to start work at Tit Town until nine, so she'd spend the rest of the evening with her kid instead of eating and catching up on some sleep like she probably should. But I wasn't one to judge. Willa was a fucking-A mother. She'd do anything for that little girl.

She reminded me of my mom and how hard she'd bust her ass before dad had got the job at the mine to make sure we had a roof over our head and food on the table.

'Yeah, for a few days now.'

'You two were close back in the day if I remember right,' Willa said.

'Ancient history,' I said back. I was at my truck now, but I didn't get in. 'You going anywhere with this?'

'Everyone was laughing about the break in at her place. I know it was your buddies. And now *Billie's* is refusing to serve her. Whatever your vendetta was against her dad you should really try and tell everyone to cool their shit. Steve's dead. He got what was coming to him. Messing with his kid's not going to do anything than hurt an innocent girl.'

Willa talked about Lilac like they weren't the same age. But that's what living in this town did to you. Willa might have been twenty-one, but she was practically forty by the standards of shit that she'd had to go through.

No one in town knew who Kasey's dad was – not everyone believed Willa had exactly enjoyed her kid being conceived – and if that weren't a euphemism for rape what the fuck else could I say? Everyone did know it was an out of towner. With Kasey's birthdate, it was obvious she was conceived just when Steve Montgomery's business buddies had started frequenting the town during summer.

Willa owned one of the shitty apartments near the only park this town had. Worked two jobs and had a kid she could be proud of. She didn't get enough sleep or eat well so her kid could do both.

Willa was the epitome of a good small-town blue-collar person fucked over by a rich white guy who thought he could do whatever the fuck he wanted because he had money and connections. Too many people like Willa had suffered in this town at Montgomery's hand.

'I've kind of got a lot more shit on my mind than some rich girl not getting the welcome parade she wanted,' I said.

We'd been told that we had to close the centre until April – perhaps longer. School being shut for a week was bad enough, but almost a *month* of the kids I coached going without hockey...? Viv's kids weren't the only ones who relied on it to get out that crazy energy that would destroy their houses and their parents' sanity.

I was attempting to put together a plan to secretly open the rink. I could easily stop taking wages – I'd do the work for free. But it was all about risk versus reward. If someone reported us and we were found not to be following the order to close, we could get shut down for good.

'Can't you just… I don't know, tell people to lay off? Quit making things difficult for her. They don't have to be friendly – just not actively be a problem,' Willa said.

'What makes you think me telling anyone anything will make a difference?'

Willa scoffed. 'Because you're like this towns unelected fucking mayor, dickshit. The only one who got out and came back. This past year, you've managed to salvage as much of this town as could be. People look up to you.'

'She's not my problem.' I opened my truck door.

'If Lilac Montgomery is anyone's problem, she's your fucking problem.' Willa grabbed my hand, stopping me from getting in the truck. 'You patched her up.'

'How'd you know it was me?'

'She told me. Just like she told me she was wanting to donate books to your mom's library. And liquor to our bar. She even offered to babysit Kasey for me. She's not a bad person, Dawson.'

'She wants to donate some shit from her dad's mansion: that doesn't make her a saint. Once she sells that place, she'll have another five mil to add to her trust fund.'

'She hasn't got a trust fund.'

'Like fuck she hasn't.'

'She told me she doesn't have one.'

'She lied,' I seethed. 'That's what people like her do: they lie. And if she hasn't, she's just inherited his whole fucking empire now that bastard's kicked the bucket. She could probably buy this whole town twice over and still have change for a two-month vacation in Hawaii.'

I got into my truck and pulled away from Willa. She flipped me off when I checked my rear-view mirror.

Making dinner took no time at all, and I sat at the empty kitchen table trying to work out what the fuck I was going to do to stop this town from falling apart. The Governor's executive order limiting the community's access to state facilities was going to kill us.

Most of the adults only survived through the shit of their average day-to-day life because they got to go to the bar at the end of it. With that closed, more would turn to the drugs Sheriff Olson and I had been battling against since the mine shut down.

More people would lose their jobs. What most people didn't understand is that some people *needed* the next paycheque to live. Missing one month's wage would already put them in debt and could cause them to be treading water, barely keeping their heads above the surface, for years to come. In a town that had already lost so much, this virus was more like a fucking plague ripping into the exposed underbelly I'd been trying to shield this past year I'd been back.

Already I had texts from people all over town stressed out of their minds about what they were going to do from affording rent, to heating, food; what they were going to do with their kids if they weren't in school.

I had out a yellow legal-pad in front of me and was scribbling ideas about how I could try and fix this best I could, what we could get away with without someone finding out we were bending the rules. Every so often, I checked my phone for new messages coming in, adding the problems to my already A4 double-sided list.

I'd been writing the last point down when I got a text from Lilac. I'd saved her number, but I hadn't really ever expected to hear from her since last night. I'd certainly not expected a reply like *that.*

I stared at the image. It was taken at exactly the same

angle as the topless selfie I'd sent her. Though she'd been wearing many layers the last time I'd seen her, I hadn't expected her to have a body like this.

Her stomach was flat, slightly toned, and as bronzed as the rest of her. Freckles dotted the top of her chest, though didn't quite reach the black lace of the bra she was wearing. She hadn't been flat chested when she was a teenager, but she sure hadn't been sporting a D-cup like she had now.

Lilac's hair was wet, curling slightly from the shower. Her skin was flushed from the heat and I could see her nipples poking through the thin lace.

Logic made me realise she wouldn't stay like this. Even with the heating on full blast, with the busted windows downstairs she'd still need to wrap up warm, but I couldn't help but imagine her strutting around that McMansion in nothing but that tiny lace bra and a matching set of black panties, or perhaps a thong.

I couldn't deny that I was turned on at the image.

She's Lilac fucking Montgomery, I told my cock. But he didn't give a shit. All he saw was a perfect set of tits, an amazing body and those cupid lips; wanting nothing more than to have them on my hard cock.

Another text chimed on my phone.

Lilac: Oops. Wrong number.

She thought she was being funny: pulling the same shit that I did. Her way of calling me out of my own bullshit.

The last time she'd spoken to me, she'd slammed the door in my face. I wasn't sure what had changed in the last couple days since I'd seen her, but I figured Willa had something to do with it.

I looked down at the mess of my handwriting, massaging my cramped hand for a moment. My head fucking *ached* like I'd woken up after a bender. I needed a break. And Lilac had given me the perfect distraction.

Instead of texting back or whatever she expected me to do, I called her. She picked up.

I wondered if she'd taken that picture earlier and had only now the guts to send it, or if I'd called her just in time before she'd had a chance to put any clothes on and warm up.

'So, you and this boyfriend are no good together, huh?' I said, in lieu of a hello.

'What?' I heard rustling on the other end, like she was trying to put on clothes one handed. My cock twitched at the image of her struggling to put on sweats over those legs of hers – no doubt as tanned and toned as the rest of her.

'If I remember correctly, first conversation we had since you got back, you asked me out. And now you're making a move on me. If you're that desperate for my attention, clearly your boy isn't giving it to you good.'

She probably hadn't expected Trace to give me the low down on what had gone on at the bar the other day with her – but she didn't know that I was buddies with Trace. We hadn't been back when she was in town. The mining accident had brought a lot of us together who had never crossed paths before despite being in such a small town.

'I'm not making a move,' Lilac scoffed. She was slurring her words a little. Was prissy princess *drunk?* 'I didn't mean to send that to you. I meant to send it to *him* actually.'

'Sure you did, Texas.'

'Yes, just like you meant to send your sexy pic to your booty call – not me!'

'Sexy, huh? You liked what you saw?'

'No.' Lilac dragged on the "oh" like a moan.

'I think you did.'

'You're wrong.'

'I don't think I am, Texas. After all, we both know how much you used to like me back in the day. And I've only got hotter since then.'

I was being a cocky shit and I knew it, but I wasn't lying. I'd had enough puck bunnies after me at college to know even though I didn't see the ice most of the time, I was a catch enough for them. Since I had no cash, and not as much talent as the rest of the team, my looks definitely had to be the draw. It wasn't my charming personality.

Lilac moaned into the phone. It was one of frustration. Like she knew I was right, and she didn't want to admit it. I chuckled to myself. I bet she hadn't wanted me to remember how she'd used to throw herself at me as a kid.

Girls used to think they were so smooth and sneaky with their crushes, but it was the most obvious thing in the world. Mom used to always tell me to "be kind to Lilac" because she knew how it felt to have a crush on someone that age. I'd thought it was cute back then. Before shit hit the fan and her parents ruined everything. Now it was just one more thing to use to my advantage.

'You've also turned into an asshole. Which is not my type, so get over yourself.'

Lilac hung up on me. Fuck. She actually hung up on me. I laughed to myself. A slap, slammed door in my face, and now hanging up on me. Say one thing about the girl, but at least she had some decent self-respect.

That didn't stop me from wanking off at the sight of her tits though. Hey, if she hadn't wanted me to use that image for perverse purposes, she sure as shit shouldn't have sent it. I didn't mind her using the one of me to rub one out.

7

LILAC

'You *don't* have a boyfriend?' Willa asked me.

We were at the Manor, in my old bedroom. The past several days I'd spent packing away more of daddy's things, whilst hanging out with Willa who was now simply brimming with time since the bar had been shut down with all those social distancing orders.

From working two jobs and looking after her four-year-old, Willa hadn't had this much spare time since she was a kid herself. She was still working nights at Tit Town – somehow, they had managed to swing it to stay open, and since there was nowhere else to get a drink, it was packed each night. The tips were keeping her afloat. Until the Governor sorted out the grants from the presidential disaster declaration, it was all she had to go on.

I knew she was worried about money: she worked two jobs to be able to pay the rent on her apartment and feed her and Kasey. I tried to spend as much time as I could distracting her – which had turned to her helping me sort through daddy's stuff and playing with Kasey.

I'd been to her apartment a couple of times and saw that though it was pretty clean, it was also massively bare. Two jobs clearly didn't pay enough for her to furnish her place.

As the only one who'd bothered to speak to me (Henry not included) let alone be kind in this town, I thought offering Willa some of daddy's furniture wouldn't go amiss.

Re-decorating her apartment would help pass the time, and with a place full of new stuff she might not feel the purse strings pinching too hard (since I was offering her anything, she could take as much as she wanted and sell it online for cash if she had to, I didn't care).

Some women might have been too proud, but not Willa. She wasn't going to let pride get in the way of Kasey growing up in a home that had a proper dining table and a comfy sofa and chairs, instead of the cheap-stuff she'd only been able to afford up 'til now.

'No. Well, I did. We broke up on Valentine's Day,' I admitted, answering her question about my fake-boyfriend lie. 'I just wanted that creepy guy to back off.'

'I hear you.' Willa turned to her daughter. 'Kasey, stop jumping on the bed or you'll break your fuckin' neck.'

'Urgh! Nightmare!' Kasey said, stopping jumping.

'Yes, you are my little nightmare!' Willa grabbed Kasey and tickled her under the ribs. Kasey let out a squeal of laughter.

'No, mommy, stop it! Stop it!'

'Do you think you have anyone with a truck big enough to get this stuff to your place?' I asked.

I'd last decorated it as a thirteen-year-old; my room was mostly pinks and purples with white furniture. It was vastly different to what a four going on five-year-old would need, but I thought I'd offer my full room up to Willa and Kasey.

They were designer pieces and weren't likely to deteriorate over time due to wear, so Kasey could grow up with this furniture until she left home, and even then, take it with her. Willa had been more than happy to take it all. Curtains and bedspread included. It wasn't like I needed any of this stuff – and she did. I was only happy to give it to her.

'Yeah, Dawson's truck should fit most of this stuff.'

'Anyone else?' I asked meekly.

'Why? What's your problem with Dawson?'

'I did something really freakin' stupid.'

'What?'

Instead of answering, I just showed her the text thread between me and Henry. It wasn't much. Two pictures, two texts. Whilst she was ogling Henry's bare chest, I summed up the conversation I'd had with him a few nights ago.

'You'd got me drunk: remember!'

'I told you to stop by the Tit Town, I didn't make you drink the place dry.'

'It wasn't exactly an environment I could stay sober in.'

The dancers I hadn't minded. I'd taken a few pole dancing classes back at college: it was an insanely fun and intense workout, but the men were a whole other problem. Not just the type of men that frequented a strip club, but the fact that they were from this town who *seriously* hated me.

I still hadn't worked up the courage to ask either Henry or Willa *why* they thought that my daddy had "ruined" Grand Yutu. With Henry, I didn't want to bring it up because, honestly, he was an asshole most of the time we talked. With Willa it was because I was scared of what she might say.

The longer I stayed in the town, the more I saw how Grand Yutu had deteriorated beyond the point it had been before daddy had opened the mine. The shady strip club, the public drinking – drug deals I'd seen going on with high school kids… If daddy were somehow responsible for this – I wasn't sure what I'd do.

I had spent my life proud of what he had accomplished here. Would my opinion of him change if I realised that he had not only built this town up, but had torn it down in the years I'd not returned… and he hadn't even told me.

I didn't expect him to say "oh, I fucked up the town and now all the businesses are suffering" – like, I didn't even know the extent or the root cause of this all. But I mean, if something bad was going on in my old hometown, I thought he would have at least brought it up.

I was still reading his journals. I was midway through 2012 now. I was going to the ice rink every day. It had been Henry's birthday and I'd gotten daddy to give me the money to buy him some brand-new skates.

It was the journals that were messing with my head if I was being honest – at least when it came to Henry. I'd found my own diaries from back at that age and I'd started reading them alongside daddy's.

I wanted to know what my oblivious little teenage self was doing at that age whilst my dad struggled through his marriage and running the mine as well as his other business over in Washington.

Mostly it was *Henry. Henry Dawson. Henry. Henry. Henry.*

It's why even though he'd grown up to be a complete cocky asshole, I'd still messaged him when I was drunk.

My sober brain would have told me that perfect boy had grown up and disappeared. But my drunk one was just like: girl, back then there was no way a boy like him would have looked twice at you. But now he's a *man* and you're a *woman.* You can *get* him to notice you. And want you – as much as you've always wanted him.

So I'd thought sending a selfie in the only sexy underwear I'd brought with me, fresh out of the shower, and ready to go to bed was an *amazing* idea.

'Why can't I use Dawson's truck again?'

'Did you not listen to a thing I said? I practically sent him a nude!' I hissed.

'He sent you one first. You're both adults. Both

consenting.'

'He thinks I want to get with him – and that I have a boyfriend.'

'But you don't have a boyfriend,' she pointed out.

'And I don't want to get with him.'

'Yeah, sure.'

'I don't.'

'Lilac, every straight woman I know on the planet wants to get with that man. Let's not lie to each other now.' Willa looked down at the image again. 'Mind if I send myself this? He's one fine piece of art,' she winked.

I laughed at her. 'Go right ahead. I'm sure my pic has made its way into the depths of the internet now anyway.'

'He wouldn't share the pic you sent,' Willa said. 'Dawson's not like that. He's a good guy.'

I thought about the way he'd patched my hands up. And came to check on me because my mama had asked him to. Contrary to what he *said,* his actions did speak louder than his words. He might talk like an asshole, but he still acted like the boy I'd known before.

'He can help you move the stuff, I was only being silly,' I said. 'If he'd be willing to come by. I might owe him an apology for calling him an a-s-s-h-o-l-e,' I said, spelling out the last word.

'Ass!' Kasey said.

'Damn,' I said.

'Damn!' Kasey shouted back. How was it that kids knew exactly the right (and in this case *wrong)* words to copy?

Willa didn't mind though, she just laughed.

A few hours later, Henry arrived in his truck.

Willa said he coached ice hockey every day two until ten, helping out at *Billie's* every Tuesday and Thursday ten thirty until two thirty in the morning. He also worked on the farms whenever he could devote his time before practice or on the weekends. But with the government shutting down non-essential businesses, most of his days lately had been taken up with the jobs he *wasn't* paid to do.

He apparently was also the all-around fix it man for the town, running every odd job he could teach himself, helping people out for free who needed it. Like offering his truck to Willa to help move furniture to her apartment.

Everything Willa'd told me reminded me of the boy before. The man who the whole town got to see, apart from me. Instead, I got whatever animosity he was willing to throw my way, between flashes of flirtation and teasing.

'Look what the cat dragged in,' Willa said from the front porch.

'Meow,' Henry winked. 'Hey, Cee,' he said, spotting Kasey who had appeared between me and her mama.

'What's with the bags?'

'Supplies for Texas,' he grunted. 'Since her majesty can't get off her ass to go to the store and get them herself.'

'Wha-what?'

I'd not gone back to *Billie's* since the tampon episode. I'd managed to order a *few* things on *Amazon*, but online deliveries were slower than usual with such a high demand. Everyone and their meemaw were ordering online, trying to save themselves from going outside, minimising the contact and practising social distancing.

'Toilet roll, milk, bread, few cans, *tampons*,' he chuckled putting the groceries on the kitchen countertop.

'You didn't have to get me this,' I said. I quickly went into my wallet and pulled out a fifty. 'Here.'

'I don't want your money.'

'Please, take it.' I couldn't let him be proud. The government might have a few grants here and there to help with the costs of shutting down businesses, but this wasn't a time people should be turning down any money coming their way. Henry had to be hurting for money just like everyone else in the town. One thing I had enough of was cash.

He ground his teeth, but Willa tutted. He took the fifty from my hands, then shoved it into Willa's back pocket and slapped her on the ass. 'There. I took it.'

'Dickshit,' Willa said, slapping him on the ass back. 'You might not wanna get so handsy with me now I know what you're hiding under those jerseys, Dawson. I've been converted into one of your fan girls.'

Henry looked between me and Willa. 'Sharing pictures are we now, Texas?'

'You sent it me,' I said, crossing my arms.

'I recall you sending *me* something back.'

'Oh, it's getting hot in here,' Willa said, fanning herself. She was being dramatic, of course. I'd got the heating on full blast, but it was still chilly what with the windows and all.

'Where's the stuff I need to move?' Henry grunted.

'Upstairs, caveman,' Willa rolled her eyes.

'I can help!' Kasey said, running after Henry who was marching up the stairs like he owned the place.

It took us almost three hours to get the furniture back to Willa's place. Five trips in Henry's truck. I took the soft furnishings like the linens, curtains, a few of the lamps, cork board, string fairy lights and such in my car.

By the end, my old room was bare, except for my closet where I had a few toys Kasey hadn't wanted, my old diaries, and clothes that I had left here and never returned for.

Willa was upstairs in her apartment with Kasey now, sorting through the new furniture. Kasey's room had been set up first, almost looking identical to how I'd laid it out in my room, only it was more cramped considering the small size of Kasey's room compared to mine.

Willa was now just putting the finishing touches on the items she'd selected from around the Manor to go in her kitchenette and living room. I'd let her have whatever appliances she wanted along with furniture.

'Where are you planning on sleeping now you've given your bed away?' Henry asked me.

He hadn't gotten into his truck to drive home, and I hadn't gotten into my car. Instead, we were stood outside, next to our respective cars in the cold March air. More than six foot apart: look at us practising social distancing and all that.

'The guest bedroom has a bed,' I said. Kasey had my bed; Willa had daddy's old one.

'Should have guessed the only mansion in Grand Yutu has more than the two beds.'

'It's got four if you're looking for a new bed. I don't think the guest rooms have ever been slept in,' I said.

'Figures.'

'You can't hate me for my daddy's money,' I said. 'It doesn't work like that. I can't control that daddy was rich.'

Henry ground his teeth.

'I can control what I do with it now that he's gone,' I said. 'Do you object to me giving my things away?'

'No.'

'Then why are you being an asshole about it?'

'I'm not being an asshole.'

I shortened the space between us. 'You don't *act* like one, but there's hardly a sentence that comes out of your mouth that isn't dripping with scorn and I don't like it. I don't think I deserve to be spoken to like that and I want you to know that I think you're better than that.'

'Better than what?'

'Than playing the part of an asshole.'

'I'm not playing.'

I was closer to Henry than I'd been since I came back

to town. He was almost a foot taller than me; he could easily rest his chin on the top of my head. Broad shoulders, narrow hips. I knew exactly what was under that jacket thanks to his selfie and the image was seared into my mind. I couldn't forget it. I couldn't forget how much I wanted to put my hands on him.

I'd wanted him so badly as a young girl. My entire childhood had been me growing up in the shadow of this wonderful boy.

We're not those same kids anymore, I told myself.

He wasn't the boy who kissed me better when Wyatt, my first boyfriend, had broken up with me. He wasn't the boy who'd taught me to skate, pulling me along by my hands whilst he skated backwards like it meant nothing. Not the boy I'd cried for every night for a month when he'd joined the army and all me and Edie had was silence for company as we wondered whether Henry would ever come back to us.

We weren't those kids anymore. We were so much more. And I still wanted him, after all this time. I knew we were strangers; we'd become adults since we'd been apart – but at the same time there was no one that I knew better. And I wanted to know this new man he'd turned into. I just damn straight *wanted* him. I'd been too young for him before, but I wasn't a little girl anymore. I was now old enough to claim him.

I leaned in, standing up on my tiptoes. I thought he was going to kiss me back, until he grabbed the tops of my arms.

'Stop. You have a boyfriend.'

I hadn't expected him to say that.

'I don't. I told that guy from the bar I did because I wanted him to go away. We broke up back in February.'

'Huh,' he grunted.

'Is that your only objection?' I asked. He was still

holding onto me.

'What?'

'Is that your only objection: that I wasn't single, to kissing me?'

Henry didn't answer. I smiled.

Before I knew it, Henry had grabbed the back of my head with his fist, crushing my hair between his fingers, pulling my face towards his. His kiss was all-consuming.

He tasted like mint leaves and lemon, the smell of his shampoo, some eucalyptus-citrus blend that sounded feminine but was oh-so masculine, filled my nose. He enveloped my every sense.

I forgot to breathe as his tongue touched mine. He groaned deep in his throat and I think I moaned in response. His other hand was on my hip, pressing me closer to him. I wrapped my arms around his neck, enjoying the feel of his hard body against mine.

I could feel his erection, his need for me. I moaned once more, thinking about how it would feel to do this minus the clothes, inside, somewhere with a bed. My childhood crush had transformed into raw-hot adult *need*. I craved this man.

Henry broke from the kiss, the hand that had been tangled up in my hair, moving round to my cheek. He touched me, feather-light, with the tips of his callused fingers, tracing my cheekbones down to my chin.

'Fuck me, Texas,' he whispered under his breath.

'Is that an invitation?' I asked suggestively.

Henry chuckled, dropping his hand from my face, and releasing my hip. I hadn't realised how much that hand had stabilised me, pulling me towards him, until it left and I almost physically fell back.

'No, it was a: *fuck* that was some kiss.'

'Doesn't have to stop at one kiss,' I said.

I was never this forward. At least, I didn't think I was. I hadn't been single since before Callum. And only then

I'd gone on a couple dates before getting into a relationship with him. I'd lost my virginity to him, so it wasn't like I was used to propositioning guys for a one-night stand.

And that's exactly what it would be between me and Henry. I was under no illusions. We lived in different worlds and he hated mine with a passion of a thousand suns, even though he kissed me like he was starved for me. After I'd packed up daddy's house and the worst of the pandemic was over, I would be going back to Texas and he would be staying here.

But all that meant nothing. I wanted him like I'd never wanted anyone before in my life. Being with him for one night would be the accumulation of all my childhood dreams. But I couldn't *be* with him like my childhood-self had wanted. Henry Dawson was not the marriage and babies type: at least he wasn't for me. For some small-town Grand Yutu girl he'd be the full package. Spoilt Southern belle? Not his type. But I could be his type for a night.

'Yes, Texas, it really does.'

Henry put a foot of distance between us.

'I'm not a kid anymore, Henry,' I said.

Henry chuckled. 'Yeah, Texas. I've seen.' He shook his head as he got into his truck, putting the key in the ignition. He gave me a solitary salute as he pulled away, leaving me out in the cold.

APRIL

8

DAWSON

Wanking off to Lilac's picture had been the worst fucking mistake I'd made next to showing up at her house to help Willa and then kissing her. It was bad enough that I'd brought her goddamn groceries knowing that she was likely to starve before anyone else in town helped her out – but kissing her? I'd definitely crossed the fucking line. If only because getting caught meant a whole can of worms I seriously didn't need opening right now.

'Madge said she saw you making out with the princess outside Willa's place last week,' Trace said.

Fucking-A. Just what I needed.

'Is that how you're getting access?' Lucas laughed. '*All access pass*. Should have thought about getting her to spread her legs before. But I don't remember much about that in all those plans we'd laid out last summer.'

That had been because the only time I'd enjoyed talking revenge shit with them, I'd seen Lilac as the imaginary figure of the mini-me Helen she would have grown into the years we'd been apart. I'd never known the real adult version of Lilac. Fuck, how would I have even coped back then if I had?

Lilac hadn't turned out like Helen. Still strong-willed,

caring, self-depreciating, but with enough self-respect to know how she deserved to be treated. Her accent might have changed, and she might have physically grown into a woman, but I could still see every bit of the girl I'd loved like family before everything had gone to shit.

I pulled another non-alcoholic beer out from the back of my truck. We were sitting in the carpark at the back of the athletics centre. Me sitting on the bed of my truck, Trace and Lucas on theirs. Usually we caught up once a week at the bar. But the bars were shut. So, the brisk April air had to do us. At least it was dry.

'I wouldn't mind testing out that tight Texas pussy,' Trace laughed to himself.

He was looking at his phone suggestively. For a second, I freaked, scared I'd somehow forwarded the picture Lilac had sent me to him – but then Trace tossed me his phone so I could have a look at what he was viewing.

It was "the Manor" as the Montgomerys always called their stupid mansion.

'What's this?' I asked. It was on some app, live time.

Lucas stood up from his bed, throwing his empty bottle into the back of his truck. Without me there, he would have likely thrown it at the wall, but he knew how I felt about wrecking this town: even if it was just broken glass and litter.

'Get this: Montgomery had the whole house set up with Smart-tech a few years ago. When we broke in, we managed to get access to the gateway and found the passwords. We're basically in full control of her house!' Lucas laughed.

Lucas plucked the phone from my hands and showed me the cameras they could switch on in the house. The front door was the obvious one that I'd seen. But there was also the camera in Steve's study, and the one on the TVs in the living room and game room. They also had access to the blinds, her lighting, the radio – nearly all of the tech in the house. They could even set up her morning coffee, though I knew that's not what they had in mind.

'Watch this,' Trace said. He turned on the speakers, cuing it up to play "Every Breath You Take," by *The Police* in the living room where Lilac was.

It was an on-the-nose choice for them with lyrics about being watched.

Lilac was sitting on the sofa reading from her *Kindle*. She was wrapped up warm, a duvet from upstairs around her legs. When the speakers switched on, she jumped up. She didn't look as surprised as I'd imagined her to.

'How many times have you done this?' I asked.

'Few times a week,' Trace said, 'the song at least.'

She stood up in the middle of the room, leaving her *Kindle* on the couch. I watched as she stood there looking around. She didn't immediately go to turn it off. It was like she was looking for someone.

She said something, but they didn't have audio and that's when Trace cut the lights. With the windows covered by plywood, the blinds rolled down to add another layer of insulation (and probably make her forget that there were no real windows there) the whole room was cast into pitch black. No moonlight or streetlamps able to filter in to stave off complete darkness. I imagined the scream from her dispatch call filling the room.

Lilac was over by the light switch when the lights came on and we had a visual on her again.

'This is the best bit,' Lucas told me.

Lilac went to turn the speakers off, but the front doorbell rang. Not *actually*, he'd simply switched on the front porch light and controlled it all from here.

Lilac went to the door. We couldn't see her from there, but when she left and opened the door – as we *could* see when he swapped to the front door cam, he'd turned off all the lights in the house again.

Lilac shut the front door, turned the lights back on and went back into the living room. That's when the next song played. The *Halloween* theme song by John Carpenter.

Lilac had *hated* horror films as a kid. I'd loved them. She'd managed to sit through a sum total of two, and every time mom would tell me off for months because Helen would call and say that Lilac was having nightmares because of them.

Halloween wasn't one she'd watched, but the theme was freaky enough that she would recognise it: if she hadn't watched it later on in life when she'd grown up.

Lilac's panicked gaze as she looked around the room, searching for something to protect herself with, made Lucas and Trace howl their heads off with laughter. They were enjoying themselves too much and were too high on whatever they'd taken before meeting with me, to notice I wasn't laughing, too.

She'd just grabbed an expensive marble figure, no doubt something she'd use to club whoever was sneaking around her house and toying with her, when Lucas cut the lights again.

Before she had a chance to turn the lights back on once more, Lucas rolled up the blinds. When Lilac managed to flick the switch, the plywood was once more in view. Painted in a red dripping substance the words "Daddy is sorry" and "you will be, too" slashed across the wooden boards.

Lilac's face contorted as she let out a horrific mute scream.

'The bitch thinks the place is haunted,' Trace cackled.

I drove home thinking about the scared, pale face of Lilac.

I'd told myself I'd not thought about her since our kiss.

And that if I did, that it hadn't meant anything, just lust from seeing her in that lacey black bra.

I was too busy to bother wasting any more time on Montgomery's daughter. I'd made sure she didn't starve; Willa was keeping her company and pretty soon she'd be finished packing away her dad's house and she'd leave for Texas for good this time. There'd be nothing to bring her back now.

But it wasn't that simple as ignoring her and convincing myself it was only my cock that was thinking of her. Because Trace and Lucas hadn't let the idea of messing with her go.

I'd warned her that she wouldn't like the next message the town sent to her to get her the fuck out of Grand Yutu – but I'd also done what Willa asked and told the town to not go so far with her as they had done her dad. Pretend she didn't exist had been the order I'd given – but don't actively antagonise her.

Rick hadn't mentioned any more break ins, and Willa hadn't said anything to me about Lilac having any more trouble, but just because I hadn't heard it on the grapevine didn't mean things were all copasetic in Lilac's little world.

I slammed the door of my truck and walked into my house.

Since the kiss, more and more memories had started coming back of growing up with Lilac. Like the mental wall I'd put up back when I was in the army, keeping this town separate from my thoughts, Lilac had somehow been kept apart. Who she had been, and everything she'd meant to me, had been forgotten in the midst of my hatred for her parents. Even in my schemes for revenge, I'd been thinking of Montgomery's heir, not *Lilac.*

That kiss had knocked down whatever dam had been built to keep her in my past and out of my head. I couldn't look at a single room in this house and not be reminded of a time she'd spent here.

Mom had changed the décor a little since Lilac had left, but it was mostly the same. Enough so that there was still the stain on the carpet on the landing upstairs where she'd dropped her hot chocolate at twelve when she'd caught me coming out of the shower in only my towel. Or the holes in the kitchen wall where there'd been a dart board because Lilac couldn't aim for shit, but she'd been too stubborn to give up until she had beat me at least once. (Since it had never happened, mom had been forced to hide it the next time Lilac came round).

Every piece of this fucking house reminded me of Lilac. And how much I'd forgotten about her.

I shouldn't have called her. I was supposed to be keeping my distance. But seeing her on the screen, Lucas and Trace laughing at her fear changed things. I had to talk to her.

'Hello?'

'Hey.'

'I didn't even have to send a topless pic for you to call this time,' Lilac joked.

She didn't sound scared. She sounded normal. If I hadn't seen how shaken up she'd been from the guys messing her about, I would never have guessed it.

'It's the memory of that kiss this time,' I said.

She laughed. 'Oh really?'

I couldn't keep up the flirting knowing that she was putting it on and hiding the fear that she'd been feeling only an hour before – or perhaps only moments before I'd called her. Who knew if Trace and Lucas had stopped messing with her since I'd left them?

'I wanted to check in with you. See how you were doing,' I said.

'That's pretty nice of you,' she hedged.

'I know. Someone I once knew told me that I don't play the part of "asshole" too well. And I never asked how you're doing considering your dad only died a couple months ago.'

'I'm sorry I called you an asshole. I didn't mean it. You're not,' she said. 'I never asked how you're doing considering Edie died…?'

'Last year,' I said. I'd forgotten she never really knew the details. Not that I could blame her. A week ago, if she would have asked, I would have practically snapped her head off rather than answer her.

'How did it happen?' Lilac asked in a small voice. All hints of casual flirtation had gone.

'Car accident,' I admitted.

'I'm really sorry. I wish I'd known. I would have liked to have come to the funeral.'

I wanted to snap and say the last thing this town needed was the Montgomerys faking some sympathy for a woman they'd turned their backs on, but I didn't have it quite in me anymore. The sympathy might have been faked on her parents' part, but Lilac had cared for my mom. I'd known it back then.

I would have thought the years she'd been away, the fact she'd never reached out to my mom meant she didn't care anymore. All my mom used to talk about when I'd managed to call her on the base after we'd catch up with each other was "I wonder what little Lilac is doing now. She'd be this-and-this old now. I wonder if she's doing such-and-such?"

But from what I'd seen of her now, it wasn't like she'd turned into some heartless socialite when she left here.

'Maybe if you'd kept in contact, I would have been able to reach you to send an invite,' I said.

'I'm sorry,' Lilac said. 'I thought mama still spoke to her. I know I could have written – sent over a birthday card or a Christmas card… but I was a teenager. As much as I loved Edie, I got wrapped up in the drama of moving to a new school and starting a new life and mama re-marrying so soon after my parents got divorced…

'They're just excuses, I know they are. The whole "life moves on" bull-crap. But I am sorry. I guess I never realised there wouldn't be a chance to talk to her again.'

'Shit happens,' I said.

I didn't like her excuses. I didn't want to accept them, but without relentless hatred for her parents fuelling me, it was easy to see Lilac as she had been back then. Just a kid, in the middle of her parents' divorce, forced to move back to a state she didn't even remember and get used to a new dad and new life.

Sure, it wasn't like her new life would be a hardship. Helen was loaded from the divorce settlement and Phil was some rich-hot-shot-cowboy type. But it was still difficult for a teenage girl to deal with all that change and then be expected to act like an adult and remember the people she'd left behind rather than just forge ahead and try to make the most of her new life.

Fuck. That kiss had really messed with my fucking head. Things were so much simpler when I could just hate her for her last name.

'Does it ever get easier?' she asked.

I knew she was on about losing a parent. 'No. It's like losing a limb. Sometimes you can still feel the ghost of it, but it's always gone. Time just makes it easier for you to adapt around it.'

'Do you believe?' Lilac asked. 'In ghosts?'

I held back a groan, wanting to throw my phone, or throw a punch at Trace and Lucas for being such assholes.

'No. I believe once you're dead you're gone. All you get is this life.'

Lilac sucked in a breath, it sounded as if she was trying

not to cry. That was the last fucking thing I'd wanted to do with this call.

'I'm really sorry you feel that way, Henry. I wish you had hope there was more out there.'

This girl. This fucking girl. She was trying to comfort *me*.

Lilac was wrong. Wrong about a lot of things, but one main one in particular. I *was* an asshole. I was the worst fucking type of bastard there was. And she didn't deserve that shit.

9

LILAC

I'd spent the day at Willa's place, looking after Kasey.

With how busy Tit Town was getting as the only place open, management had hired two more servers who Willa was having to train to work the bar. Though if anyone found out they were still open, they'd have their licenses revoked and the owners could face jail time, they didn't seem to care. Willa said it was because management were so coked up most of the time, they thought they were invincible. Their motto for keeping open was that the men weren't allowed to touch the merchandise anyway, so Tit Town was practically the poster business for social distancing.

Usually Willa's mama babysat, but her work hours had increased, too. Willa's mama worked part time at the only doctor's practice here in Grand Yutu and with the pandemic, she was busy with all the calls from hypochondriacs who were worried they were carrying COVID-19 along with the usual business. Which meant I'd offered to babysit until Willa's mama got off work and could look after Kasey in the night whilst her mama stripped for the men at Tit Town.

I'd never been around kids much. Before I was

fourteen, I'd never seen my extended family. When mama and I moved back to Texas and mama married Phil, we hadn't seen much of them even then. But babysitting was pretty simple if you followed the sacred rule: don't let the kid kill herself.

It seemed simple enough, but apparently I found that the one thing that little kids *loved* to do is test the boundaries of their extremely mortal bodies. It was sort of the same as when you were the designated driver in college and you were the one responsible for rounding up all your drunk sorority sisters and making sure they all got home safe.

Kasey was like a mini drunk Darci. I'd text her as much. She'd text me back an article about how some people when there was a death in the family had a baby to cope. I'd sent a meme of someone flipping her off. She'd laughed and we'd chatted for a while.

With Kasey to distract me, it was almost easy to forget that I was here because my daddy was dead. I'd spent almost a month here for the sole purpose of packing away the last of daddy's possessions, but strangely enough I didn't think of him as often as I thought I would. Perhaps it was because in the past seven years I'd barely had any contact; him almost already being pushed out of my mind so that most of the time I forgot I even *had* him in my life.

But there were moments where the thought of him sprung up on me. Like when Kasey talked about her granddaddy, and I thought about what it would be like when I had a baby. My daddy would never get to see it; my child would never know their granddaddy.

And then my thoughts would spiral to all the other stuff my daddy would miss. He'd never walk me down the aisle. He'd never get to have "the talk" with the man who wanted to marry me when he came to ask permission.

Since the job of making sure Kasey was alive for when

Willa got back was pretty all consuming, it was easy for me to put those thoughts off, but they returned as soon as I got in my car to drive back to the Manor.

I tried to distract myself with the radio, but instead it was just circling the same news, President Trump announcing that he was going to halt US funding to the WHO; facts and figures of the latest death tolls, more restrictive measures. I turned it off.

Now with more and more states having death tolls in the thousands, Grand Yutu seemed even more like a world apart than usual. Sure, the businesses had closed like they'd been ordered to, but people still congregated in big groups, the Tit Town was still open and besides the sheer number of people who were out of work, life seemed to continue like normal. We hadn't had a single case here, though I knew the numbers in North Dakota as a whole were rising.

Perhaps if I'd come to the town before the virus, I would be able to have noticed the difference. If I were in Texas, I'd sure be able to tell from what mama and the girls had been sending me.

As soon as I pulled into the driveway, my headlights illuminating the front façade of the house, I knew that something was wrong. My front door was wide open.

I exited the car, not knowing what I should do. I called 911 on my phone, waiting for it to connect as I got closer.

My front door wasn't *open* it was *missing*.

'Please, there's got to be a spare room.'

'We're not taking any reservations,' the only hotel in Grand Yutu told me. 'There's a global pandemic going on if you haven't watched the news.' They hung up on me.

I was standing, still in my jacket and hat that I'd been wearing outside, in the middle of the foyer.

The sheriff and a couple guys had been round to check

the house, but besides the fact that all the doors in my house were missing (not just the outside ones, but *every* door inside my house) and all the plywood had been taken off the windows, they couldn't find anything amiss.

'Kids. A prank,' was all they'd had to say about it.

I might have managed putting the plywood on the windows once, but the hardware store wasn't selling to me anymore, and I had no idea where I could buy some doors with such short notice. The fact stood that I couldn't stay in this house tonight.

I had packed up my stuff and loaded it up in the car. I'd managed to get a staple gun and some tarp from the hardware store with an excessive amount of begging. Apparently, *that* they could sell.

Using the porch light, and then struggling with my phone torch for the rest of the windows, I had spent an hour covering the empty frames, and then the doors. It wasn't like I could go back in there anyway.

After I'd called the hotel, I'd simply sat, idle in the car looking at my options. There weren't many to be honest. Two, I saw. One, was sleeping in this car. Though it was April – it was April in *Grand Yutu.* Which meant it wasn't freezing, but it would still be around that temperature at night even though we were technically in spring now.

The second was asking to crash at someone's place. I knew two people in town. One had rejected my advances to have sex and went from acting like an asshole to a prince at the drop of a hat. So, he was out. Which left Willa.

I waited in the carpark until she'd finished her shift at Tit Town.

I'd left her place at half five when her mama had returned; spent an hour with the police, and another hour tarping up the Manor. Which meant it was only eight when I arrived in the carpark. I had until one in the morning for her to finish. I read the entire time in the backseat of my rental.

Willa had scalded me when she'd seen me waiting there.

'Christ, you idiot! You could have just told mom you needed to crash a mine.'

I'd fallen asleep almost instantly on the couch, only to be woken up by a screaming Kasey who was jumping up and down on the parcel of couch I wasn't laying on.

'I wanna do Anna and Elsa,' she told me as I cracked my eye open. It was six in the morning.

I couldn't sing for crap but with my long blonde hair I'd been relegated to playing Elsa in our play dates. It mostly required us both singing *Let it Go*, battling "marshmallow" who was apparently some big ice monster and then having a sword fight with imaginary Hans. It was a lot better than the princess games I'd played with my mama when I was younger when she'd just wanted me to play "tea-parties" in pretty dresses.

'Urgh, maybe let me wake up a little, Kasey,' I told her, rubbing my eyes.

After breakfast, Kasey practically jumping up and down on her chair with the promise of playing Anna and Elsa, I told Willa I should probably take my stuff out of my car and bring it up here.

I had my suitcase; a box of all the groceries Henry had dropped off, as well as the stuff I'd already gotten before; a box of books from daddy's library that I wanted to keep for myself, along with a box with my old diaries and daddy's journals.

'Wait – before you do… have you asked Dawson yet if you could stay over at his?'

'Why would I do that? You know I prefer your and Kasey's company to that moody giant,' I said, pointing the last bit at Kasey who laughed at the funny voice and face I pulled.

'Yes, but here you have to sleep on the couch with this monster waking you up at the unholy hour in the morning,' Willa said. 'Are you sure you want to be up at this hour every day until you get your place sorted again? She doesn't lose this energy. And Dawson's got a spare room.'

'He has?'

'Yeah…'

'I just figured when he moved back here, he'd moved in with his parents.'

Owning your own place was tricky for even the best of us. Though with the amount of jobs that Henry had, it made sense he'd be able to afford his own place. Rent wasn't exactly astronomical in a place like Grand Yutu.

'He did after his mom passed, but he lived alone for a year when he went to college.'

'He went to college?'

'Yeah, right after he finished his tour. He didn't tell you?'

'We don't talk much,' I admitted.

'I wanna play Anna and Elsa!' Kasey whined. She punctuated it by throwing a *Cheerio* at my head.

'In a minute kiddo,' Willa said. She switched on the TV and gave her the remote.

'So, he lives with his daddy now?'

'Lilac…' Willa looked at me funny. 'Oh my god. You don't know. You don't fucking know.'

'Know what?'

'Dawson's dad died years ago. The year after you and your mom left. In the mining accident.'

'The mining accident,' I said it slowly, as though I was checking I'd heard right.

Willa nodded. 'The one that killed fifteen people and got the mine shut for good.'

*

Willa hadn't pushed for me to take her suggestion up with asking Dawson if I could crash in his spare room… The spare room that he had because both of his parents were dead. One of them in a mining accident.

The hatred the town felt towards daddy now made sense. It was his mine. Though mining accidents happened – there was always a risk – that many miners dying in this day and age would still shake the town. And there'd been no compensation, nothing to help them out as they tried to fix the mine. The strike that had followed had meant the mine shut down for good. And just like the mine had helped boost the towns economy, with it gone, the town had suffered.

Your dad ruined this town. The words were still harsh, but I could understand them now. Everyone needed a scapegoat for their pain. It made sense that daddy – the one who never had to go down there himself but reaped the profits and was the perpetual outsider – would become theirs.

I hated that daddy was their scapegoat, but I couldn't blame them if that were how they wanted to deal with their grief.

If it hadn't been the virus that had killed daddy – if it had been at work, or if there was some way for me to find a person to lay blame on, perhaps that would help me with the pain, rather than the facts just making life seems so insignificant and so *by chance.* Like death could just take you for no reason at all.

Since I was staying over at Willa's place, me becoming the de facto babysitter just made sense.

As soon as Kasey was asleep, either for her midday nap or for the night, I took out daddy's journals from the box and turned towards the year Willa had said the mining accident had happened.

I couldn't believe that daddy had never told us what had happened. The miners were people we'd known, parents of kids I went to school with. Henry's *dad*. I couldn't believe I'd walked around this town for weeks now without knowing, without figuring out why things had gotten so bad.

February 2014

I don't know why I'm still writing in this thing now that Helen's gone. It's turned into a habit I can't stop. I used to write in here after every therapy session and then read through it again so I could re-fresh my mind on what we'd said last time. Get the exact quotes right about what she'd said, what I'd said. I wasn't going to be blindside by Helen or that doctor editing our conversations post-script.

Now, this shit is just somewhere that I can put my thoughts down. You can't fucking talk in this town to one person without the whole place knowing your business.

Helen's been gone seven months now. My lawyers managed to keep most of my money, but she got Lilac. I don't know if that's any comfort. I've never been a good dad. I wasn't cut out for it. Lilac gave me Helen-

What did daddy mean *I* gave him mama? I thought perhaps he'd just got his words muddled, but to say that he was simply writing down his thoughts, daddy was always pretty concise in his journals. Almost as if he read them back since he crossed out mistakes and corrected them at a later date.

-and I always thought that was a means to an end, but it changes you the minute you look into your daughter's eyes and you realise that you helped create THIS. You made that person and you're responsible for them.

I'd never been much of a family man. Growing up in a

trailer and seeing your daddy drink himself to death and your ma skipping town almost as soon as you were born could do that to a person. My new therapist says that's probably where my marriage went wrong. How the fuck could my marriage have gone wrong before I'd even met Helen?

Tonight's session was all about the custody battle. What fucking battle? There'd been no testimonies, no who's-the-better-parent. It was just my lawyers and her lawyers across a table, sliding back and forth that sheet of paper until we'd reached an agreement and we both signed on the dotted line.

How would Lilac feel if she ever found out she was simply parcelled off and divided like one more of my assets? Fucking Dr Lynsey thinks the guilt is what's affecting me. Making me act out or something.

"You're starting to see everything as facts and figures. But you have to realise you have an ethical obligation to your business, to your family, to yourself-" More psycho-analyst bullshit I don't want to listen to.

It pisses me off I'm still sat in one of those cushy offices, still seeing a counsellor – though not a marriage one, now. No marriage sessions for a divorcee.

Jason from work says it was about time. Everyone gets divorced in their forties when they got married young. Most in their thirties. Said I was too long in the tooth anyway to stick out that first marriage for as long as I did. But I'm not Helen.

She's already planning her second marriage to some douchebag her daddy would have approved of. Lilac's bonding with the fucker. She's enjoying her new school, her new life, her new DADDY.

Helen gets it fucking all. Everything her parents wanted for her fifteen years ago. Everything she THINKS she wants. But she doesn't get it. She doesn't understand what she left behind.

She made a mistake, but I was willing to forget all of that. She's always been the one I've wanted since I first set eyes on her. I don't want anyone else. And I won't HAVE anyone else. That fucker might pretend he can fill my shoes, but he doesn't know the half of what it takes to keep a woman like Helen. Pretty soon, she'll get bored of him like she got bored of anyone who wasn't me.

May 2014

Jason scoped out the cabins. He says they're perfect for our corporate meetings. The town's so isolated there's no way any rival company would be able to spy on us there. And I run this town. There's no chance any of this would get back to us.

Rule One: never take a step without checking your lawyer okay-ed it. As long as we get the people who matter to sign NDAs, we've been given the all-fucking-clear. Perhaps there are some perks to having your wife and kid in a different state.

July 2014

Fucking Dawson was making a stink at work today. The unbelievable fucking arrogance of that man to even speak to me after the shit he pulled. I knew it wasn't serious – just some bullshit he's pedalling as an excuse to get in my face, rub it in the fact I'm still paying his wages and had nothing to fire his ass on.

God's fucking gift is what he thinks he is. All the miners love him like he's personally sucking their cock every night. Even threw in that little barb about his wife not being keen on a strip joint in our town – affecting the morality of the whole place. MORALITY. He wants to talk morality.

September 2014

Fuck. Just fuck. WHAT THE SERIOUS FUCK?!

Daddy didn't write anymore entries until almost a year later. From February through to August of 2014 I could read enough between the lines to see where he'd lost interest in Grand Yutu and had started working in earnest on his other business over in Washington.

Jason, his partner in Washington, appeared more and more whereas in all the previous entries he might have only been mentioned once in a couple years.

His bluntness regarding the divorce, about me, hurt enough to make me sob through most of the entries. I'm glad I'd found out now and not back then. My fifteen-year-old self would never have been able to cope.

I knew he was hurting. His love for my mama came across in every entry. I tried to reconcile that these were the thoughts he'd never wanted me to see.

There were many thoughts I'd had in the past about mama and daddy when I'd been hurt and venting and I would never have wanted them to believe that was my only opinion of them – that those thoughts in anger meant more than the sober ones I said to them with a level head and love in my heart. But it didn't make the words hurt less.

I had to read them twice to fully see what had happened – what daddy said when he *didn't* write something, or omitted part of the truth.

Daddy threw himself into his other work, forgetting about the mine. Until later in the year, he never mentioned anything about the town unless it was to do with his *other* business, whereas in the journal I'd been reading from 2012, whenever he'd mentioned work, it was all about the mine.

Dawson – the foreman at the mine, and Henry's dad – had tried to warn him about something, but some old grudge had stopped him from taking it seriously. Had Dawson been partially responsible for the mining accident? Had daddy?

It was hard to know what was true reading an account from his words. Especially since he only seemed to either write after he'd had a therapy session, or when he was feeling overly passionate and needed to vent.

All I knew was that it was September 2014 when everything had gone wrong and my daddy hadn't seen it coming. But from what I'd read, I wasn't sure that daddy was simply the scapegoat the town had needed. Part of me believed there might be the possibility he was actually culpable.

If that was true, then Henry had every reason to hate my family for it.

10

DAWSON

I skated round the rink trying to clear my head. We'd been closed for over a month now and I knew the kids were hurting. If it was winter, we might have stood a chance to make our own rink outside and fuck the rules about gatherings of more than ten people, but we were approaching summer and for once we weren't pleased to see an end to the cold.

The Governor had extended the facilities closures so instead of ending next week, we were having to remain closed until the end of the month. We couldn't even get a definite answer as to whether we'd be open in May.

The *Nokota Horses* had tried to get me to bend the rules, but if we opened, we risked losing the centre altogether, or face jail time. I'd told them if the NHL could hack it, so could they. But it was hardly a consolation.

One of the kids had suggested field hockey, figuring they could at least practise somehow. I'd given it a shot, but it hadn't worked out well.

I'd tried my best to work with what I had. When I'd usually have my classes, I'd meet the kids outside the centre and we'd run laps, then go to one of the fields on the edge of town and do some drills on land. It wasn't hockey, but it worked off some of the energy. Running that many laps and drills for each session was working me almost as hard as I'd had to back in the army. At least I knew I wouldn't be one of those suckers who turned into quarantined couch-potatoes and gained a stone.

Each day I'd set the kids a task on the *WhatsApp* group I had for each of my sessions. Started off with simple things like how many push ups can you do in a minute, but that shit soon got boring so I'd had to start looking up things online that included songs or whatever weird *YouTube* shit they were into these days or videogames.

I was only twenty-five but trying to find out what pre-teens found interesting these days was making me feel *old.* I couldn't imagine having to be a parent. I didn't think I had it in me to be able to relate to kids off the ice. At least the feedback had been positive, so I'd kept up with those daily tasks.

I'd started skating by myself in mornings. I'd been doing some office work one morning and I'd just put on my skates and started doing drills to clear my head. I felt like a selfish prick being on the ice when the others couldn't, but sometimes I just wanted to be selfish damn it.

I'd stepped off the ice when I saw someone standing in the doorway.

'Howdy partner,' Willa said, putting on Lilac's accent. She had on a long blonde wig – something some of the girls wore occasionally when they stripped.

'Willa,' I said.

'I didn't even fool you a little?' she pouted.

'No.' I wiped my head with the towel on the bench and began unlacing my skates. 'What're you doing here?'

'I'm here,' she said, 'to talk about your girl.'

'Don't have a girl.'

'Lilac.'

I'd known who she meant. I just wanted to make it fucking clear that even though Willa acted like there was something going on between me and her, there really wasn't. I'd not seen or spoken to Lilac in the week since I'd called her after Trace and Lucas had pulled that "haunting" shit in front of me.

I'd tried to get Rick to make his dumb cousin see all the legal bullshit he might get pulled in for if he was caught: invasion of privacy and all that. But Rick had waved it off and said that he had Lucas' back. Yeah, like *that* was my problem.

'What about her?'

'She's staying with me.'

'She *is?*'

'Yeah, because one of your friends decided to make her house unliveable. They took off the fucking doors, Dawson. And pulled off the plywood she fucked up her hands putting over the windows. And Hal won't sell her anymore shit to fix it up, so she's had to tarp up the holes and abandon ship.'

Willa crossed her arms, putting on the mom-face that would have a kid quaking in their boots. 'I thought I asked you to handle this fucking town.'

'You did – *I* did,' I said.

I chucked the towel and skates in my duffle bag and slung it over my shoulder.

'Really? You put on your mayor-hat and told them to back the fuck off the cute Southern girl who just wants to pack up her dad's place and get out of here once this pandemic has calmed down?'

'I told them to back off, yeah,' I said.

'She's crying at night – fucking crying on my couch. Kasey crawled into my bed last night and asked me why Lilac's so sad and how she can help. We can't fucking help her anymore than we already are – but *you* can.'

Hearing that Lilac was crying herself to sleep punched me in the gut. I might have been ignoring her, but that didn't mean the feelings that kiss had awoken had gone away. In fact, it was worse, because since my waking brain didn't see her, I'd taken to dreaming about her.

'What do you want me to do this time?' I started locking up the place, Willa following me.

'I think she should stay with you.'

'What?' I choked out.

'You've got a spare room. She's currently breaking her back sleeping on the couch and Kasey's become her alarm clock. Plus, your buddies wouldn't mess with her if she were with you. Sends a stronger message to the town to back off than whatever weak ass warning you gave them the first time.'

'She can't stay with me. If Lucas or Trace found out-'

'What: your shitty friendship with them would get flushed down the toilet? The only thing you have in common with those guys is that you lost someone in the mining accident.

'You might have needed them as a crutch for your anger last summer when your mom passed, but you didn't need them when you lost your dad, and you sure as shit don't need them now. You've just gotten into the habit of hanging round them you can't see what a dumb fucking idea it is.

'People like them are what's keeping this town in the shitter since Montgomery fucked us over. And people like *you* are trying to clean it up. You should be on the opposite sides of the spectrum and instead you're letting your hatred for one family bring you together.'

Willa wasn't telling me anything I didn't already know. It had become all the more obvious since they'd started fucking with Lilac.

I'd wanted to tell them to cut that shit out – to not mess

with her, but I didn't want to hear them have a go at me for planning on doing a whole lot fucking worse to her. I didn't want to hear what they remembered I'd said. I didn't want them to tell me I'd gone soft; that I was falling for Montgomery's heir.

If they thought I was getting close to her again, I knew they'd use that against her. They'd tell her about what we'd planned that summer just to see her break when she realised the boy she'd grown up idolising had wanted to use her as a pawn to get back at her dad and didn't mind fucking her up physically and psychologically to do so.

It made me physically sick in my stomach thinking about Lilac knowing what I'd said that summer with them.

'What would your mom think?' Willa asked me. I knew she couldn't read minds, but part of me was scared I'd somehow said aloud my thoughts and Willa was asking that question in response to them. But she wasn't. Otherwise she would have had a face of pure disgust.

'Lilac was like your family. Your mom loved her like a daughter. What would she say if she knew her son could offer her a roof over her head and was too fucking blinded by hate for a dead man?'

Willa really knew how to hit below the belt.

'Fine. I'll take her,' I said. 'Tell her to get her stuff. She knows her way to my place. I'll see her at six tonight.'

Lilac wasn't at my place at six. Her car was there in the drive, but she wasn't anywhere to be seen.

Me: Where are you?

Lilac: Went for a walk.

It wasn't late, but my block wasn't as safe as it had been back when she'd used to live here. When she was younger, she'd used to walk up and down my street if Helen had dropped her off on weekends without telling my mom beforehand.

Lilac knew when I had practice, but Helen always seemed to forget, or figure dad would just let Lilac in the house if we'd already left for hockey practice. I don't know where dad was in those moments in time, but he was never home to let Lilac in.

We'd get back from practice and see her walking up and down, waiting for us to come, abandoned by her own family – though she'd never seen it that way – and her face would light up when she spotted us.

Mom never had a cell phone, so Lilac had never been able to call ahead and let us know she'd be coming if we were out. I'd not been able to afford one until I got my first job at sixteen, but even if Lilac did text me, I'd never get it since I left my phone in my locker when I was on the ice.

For as good a friend as she was to my mom – or at least pretended to be with all their girl's nights and gossiping and PTA meetings – Helen was a shitty mother to Lilac.

I jogged down the street trying to spot her, but she hadn't stayed local.

Me: Where are you?

She didn't respond, so I hopped in my truck and decided I was going to be that sad fucking loser who drove around searching for her. The neighbourhood wasn't *she-could-get-stabbed* bad, but if she walked a couple blocks over, Trace lived there.

I wouldn't mind testing out that tight Texas pussy.

I didn't want to think about what Trace would do if he was high and he saw Lilac walking right there next to his house.

Fuck. Willa was right. Why the fuck was I still even

friends with those assholes?

I eventually found her a couple blocks in the opposite direction of Trace's house thank god.

'Get in,' I said.

If she was surprised to see me, she didn't show it. She hopped into the truck and put on her seatbelt.

She didn't say anything. Not: what made you offer to let me stay at your place? Or: what made you want to drive around town and find me? Hell, a *hello* wouldn't have gone amiss.

I put some music on from my phone to fill the silence. It was only a seven-minute drive back to my place, but the seconds were dragging exceptionally long as she just *sat* there. Like the last thing she hadn't said to me was that she felt sorry for me for not believing there was an afterlife. Like being this close didn't remind me of how good her body had felt pressed up against mine, or how perfectly her mouth had fit with my own.

I sang to ignore the awkwardness. Since the disjointed voices coming from the Bluetooth speaker on my dash wasn't filling enough of the silence for me.

It was the same truck I'd used to drive her to and from school in. I wondered if she remembered that. How she'd used to put her feet up on the dash in the summer and sing songs at the top of her lungs as I blasted them from the radio which was either silent or ear-bleedingly loud.

The songs playing from my phone were at a reasonable volume now. It cost too much to fix the truck and I kinda liked the nostalgia of its broken ways, so I used the wireless speaker the *Nowak Horses* had bought me for Christmas.

She watched me out of the corner of her eye as I sang. I could see her lips move along to the lyrics. I didn't figure her as someone who knew that small-time Scottish rock band.

'Now I'm losing it all, I'm losing it all. Paved in gold, paid in blood, I gave you control,' I sang.

I went on a few more lines before the chorus kicked in.

'You are the devil. You'll never finish me.'

'I'm the next level', Lilac joined in.

I couldn't help but grin over at her as we sang the rest of the song, turning up the volume from my phone. *Twin Atlantic* played for the rest of the ride home.

Lilac joined me in smiling, her grin almost splitting her face in half, between lyrics. Her voice hadn't improved since she was a kid, but she didn't lack enthusiasm. Her Southern accent putting on that Scottish brogue had me laughing. She hit me on the arm lightly, thinking I was laughing at her awful singing. I mean I was, but not just that.

'You seem in a better mood than the last few times I saw you,' Lilac said when she hopped out of the truck.

'Yeah… you seem in a worse one,' I said. I wasn't in a better mood. I just wasn't being an asshole to her.

'Maybe we're a weighing scale. You go up, I go down.'

'That's a see-saw, Texas.'

I opened the front door and let her in. The food was already simmering in the kitchen. I kept the door open as she took out the boxes from her car and put them in the hallway. I'd take them upstairs to my room later for her.

I wondered if she wasn't asking me what made me offer my house up to her because she was afraid I'd snap at her. But I could only wonder. Unless I asked. But I wasn't going to do that.

Lilac made her way into the kitchen. The smell from the stew permeated the air, making my stomach growl. Lunch had been a long time ago.

'You cook?'

'How else do you eat?' I asked her. 'The slow cooker

is the busy man's friend,' I told her. I'd almost forgot that it was unlikely she ever had to cook herself a meal.

'We usually live off take-out back home,' she told me. 'There's, like, one sister who knows how to cook and she'll only make us a home cooked meal if we pay for her spa days. I mean, it's totally worth it to not have take-out once in a while, but those spa coupons really rack up the dollar,' she laughed.

Lilac was putting on the easy manner, just like I'd heard her put it on when I'd called her up after she'd freaked out about her "haunting". I couldn't get the image Willa had painted for me of her crying to sleep on her couch out of my head. But just like she'd grinned and sang with me in the truck – just like how she'd ignored the shit her parents put her through as a kid – Lilac seemed to bounce back and push down anything negative and just live for *now*. She had one hell of a brave face.

'Sister… you're in a sorority.' It wasn't a question.

'I know, how cliché of me,' Lilac rolled her eyes at me. 'Did you join a frat? When you were at college – Willa said you went before Edie passed.'

'Even if they were keen to have a mature student, pledging seems like the most moronic thing I've ever heard. After six years in the army, I'm not handing my ass to some pathetic white boys with a trust fund.'

'Callum was in a fraternity,' Lilac said.

'Callum… your ex-boyfriend,' I guessed. 'Point proven.'

'What do you mean "point proven"?'

'Whatever kid you *think* was worth fucking is the exact sort I'm not gonna spend my life joined at the hip to in some moronic brotherhood.'

'You *say* it's moronic, but I think a lot of people see being in a sports team the same as a frat.'

'Those people are fucking idiots.'

I got out two bowls and ladled us some food, putting a roll on the plate beside it and passing her over the butter.

'Did you play hockey at college?'

'Some.'

'Were you any good?'

'I was rusty. But going back on the ice was… muscle memory.'

'I haven't skated since I left here,' she admitted. 'This is *so* good.'

I smiled taking a spoonful myself. It wasn't amazing, just an old recipe mom had used to use up all the ingredients left at the end of the week. But add the right seasoning and let it simmer on low for hours, yeah it did tend to taste decent.

'You don't get much ice in Texas, Texas,' I said, referring back to her not skating since she moved back South.

'No, that you don't. I actually missed winter – real winter. Not the hell storms, but snow. Feeling *cold.*

'I know y'all liked to pretend I was some alien, but I grew up here. I felt more alien when I was back in Texas and I had to get used to that *heat.* Like you can dress for snow and put on more layers, but once you're out in the heat you can't actually *do* anything about that. Air-con became my new best friend.'

'Who's your actual best friend?' I found myself asking.

I'd once known everything about Lilac, but now she was a stranger. But I didn't want it to stay that way even though the guilt of my past told me it would be better for her if she was.

'Darci. She's a business major, but her passion's in fashion. She has this idea to create a non-profit that helps people prepare for interviews: clothes, how to talk, how to write a good résumé.

'She's insanely outgoing; has about a thousand extracurriculars going on and has never been on a serious date her entire life. But she always seems to have a thousand boyfriends hanging on.'

'You got a picture?' I asked her.

She pulled out her phone and showed me her lock screen. There was a natural redhead with blue eyes, freckles dotting her nose and a big white floppy hat covering most of her head, hanging off Lilac. Her arms were wrapped around her like she'd jumped up and piggybacked herself onto Lilac. I couldn't see the background, but I had the impression it was on a beach somewhere. Lilac's skin was glowing in the sunlight; her hair blonder than it was now and she was grinning like I hadn't seen since we were kids.

'Spring break last year. We went to Miami – where Darci's from. Did you do anything fun spring break last year?'

'Hockey,' I say.

'Well, that's not changed. Tell me something new about you?'

I'm an orphan, I could have said if I wanted to be an asshole. But I was really trying hard to reign in the asshole act. Didn't make any sense for me to keep it up now my walls were down, and I could no longer hate her for thinking she was exactly like Helen. Plus, I was living with her temporarily.

'You've hit the nail on the head – for the first time,' I joked, at the expense of her awful hammer skills. 'I've not changed at all.'

'Willa calls you the unofficial mayor of Grand Yutu – that seems like a big change from the carefree Henry I used to know.'

I shrugged, grabbing another roll. 'I do the odd jobs around the community.'

'From the way Willa tells it you're singlehandedly

trying to fix this place.'

'It shouldn't need fixing,' I said. I couldn't bite that response back. For once, instead of looking at me infuriatingly cold or unaware when I direct some of that hate for her dad at her, she looked cowed. Almost guilty.

'How bad is it?' Lilac asked me.

Well, this had seriously gotten depressing compared to the light-hearted topic I'd been hoping to go for.

'A lot of people are unemployed. Most of them can't find work, they'd have to travel for it and by the time they'd paid for the gas to get to work and back, there wouldn't be enough to pay rent or for groceries. So they choose not to make the effort at all.

'Those that do work spend every second at their job and when they get home, there's not much to take away the boredom in the winter. We're pretty cut off from the rest of the world here. They can spend a couple hours at Tit Town, or at the bar… but besides fucking, drinking and getting high there's not much else to occupy their mind.

'Tourism is the one boost we get in the summer, though with this pandemic going on, it doesn't look like we'll survive this one.'

I didn't even start on the type of "tourism" this town had to recover from thanks to her dad. With Steve Montgomery dead, this summer might have been the one time we were free from his "business buds".

Lilac stopped eating, putting her spoon down and stood up. She walked over to my side of the table and put her arms around me. It wasn't like when she'd initiated the kiss, this wasn't lust or passion. She was just hugging me.

'What're you doing?'

'Hugging you. You looked like you needed one,' Lilac told me. 'It sucks that all that's on your shoulders.'

She didn't tell me that it didn't *have* to be on my shoulders, or some other platitudes that it would be all okay, she just offered me the only comfort she had to give.

I felt myself melt into her embrace. She smelt of summer, like it couldn't quite leave her skin: coconut and something unnameable, or maybe my dumb ass poor-as-shit-self had simply never had the money or experience to be exposed to it before her.

'You're difficult to hate, Texas,' I mumbled into her hair. I wasn't sure she'd heard me.

'Then stop trying so damn hard.'

11

LILAC

Being back at the Dawson's house was like returning home. More so than going back to the Manor was. Unlike daddy, Henry and – I supposed until last year – Edie had changed the house as they'd grown. But the overall feeling of the place was the same. It was more *alive* than the Manor was.

That's why I convinced myself that it was totally normal for me to practically throw myself at Henry, pressing my body against him like I was clinging to a life raft in the ocean.

When he'd talked about how bad the town had gotten, I'd felt like I could feel the pain and his loneliness in the air.

Just like I'd always thought that daddy had been the saviour of this town, Henry had given up the easy life of being a college student (after years of giving his life to serve his country) to serve this town.

I'd not been able to even really look at him when he'd picked me up earlier. Though I'd accepted his offer to stay, I'd needed a walk to prepare myself. I didn't know how I was going to look him in the eye now that I knew about the mining accident: that my daddy or his could have been responsible. But he'd made it easy. He'd made me forget our parents and just be *us* for a while.

Henry groaned into my ear as I pulled away from the hug. It was a guttural noise, like the moan I could imagine I'd hear with him buried deep inside me.

God, I needed to get my head on straight. I'd had whatever the female version of blue balls was since our kiss. He was trapped in my mind, imprinted on my body and all I wanted to do was be consumed by him.

He stopped me as I tried to pull away from him, dragging his fingers up my arms. I was getting hot in my sweater for the first time since I'd been here. I wanted it off.

Henry's hands reached my neck. My hair was up in a messy bun, leaving the side of my neck bare for him to trace with his fingers. The feel of his fingers against my skin sent a shiver straight down my spine. I could feel the hair on my arms rise as he gave me goose bumps.

He continued to trace his fingers along me, until he got to my lips where he brushed across my bottom lip with the pad of his thumb.

'What are you doing?' I asked as he put his hand to the back of my head.

'*Not* hating you.'

Henry crashed his mouth into mine. Like our first kiss, it seemed to consume me wholly. I could think of nothing other than the pressure of his soft lips against mine, his hands pulling me closer as he deepened our kiss.

My body felt like an inferno. Burning up from the inside, so that I was nothing but a puddle in his arms. I pulled back, taking only a second to pull off my sweater.

I probably should have worried about whether I was giving him the wrong impression – beginning to strip for him, that is – but I didn't care. Let him get that impression. Let him take me all the way. I wanted him, lord how I wanted Henry Dawson.

His hands moved to the skin I'd exposed now that I was only wearing a tank top.

'*Fuck,* you have no idea what you do to me, Lilac.' It was the first time he'd used my real name, not that stupid nickname "Texas".

I loved his hands on me, the way he felt brushing those fingers across the bare skin of my arms, once again going to cup my face as his mouth never left my own.

His hand grazed the underside of my breast and I moaned into his mouth. His body stiffened against mine at my moan.

He slowly lowered the spaghetti strap of my left shoulder, then my bra strap, leaving my shoulder bare. He moved his kisses from my mouth, trailing them down my jaw, to my neck and now bare shoulder. I felt those kisses deep to my core. I wanted them everywhere. I wanted every inch of myself laid bare for him so he could kiss me all over.

I think I might have said it allowed. He pulled away from me.

'Fuck,' he swore. He stood, backing away from me like I'd poured cold water on us. 'I can't do this.'

'What? Why?'

'Why?' he laughed. It was that low chuckle I remember hating hearing the first time. Like he was soulless, devoid of any real humour and that the only thing he could find funny in this life was pain or irony.

'Yes, why? I'm not asking for the world here. Just sex.'

'Just sex,' he shook his head like I was crazy, or he was crazy. I couldn't read his expression.

'Do you not want it? You seem to find me attractive enough.' I looked down pointedly at his pretty obvious erection.

He adjusted himself in his pants.

'That's not it.'

'Then what is it? You kissed me first,' I said.

'If we're going to play that game: you kissed *me* first.'

'Fine, I admit that. But you initiated it this time.'

'I'm not playing the blame-game like we're some ridiculous middle school couple. Me and you aren't happening. End of story. There's nothing more to say.'

'Because you say so? That's the reason I'm getting.'

'Yeah, it is. You can sleep in my room. I'll bring your stuff up for you.'

'No. I can manage,' I said, crossing my arms.

He picked up my sweater from the floor, passing it me. I took it, but still must have had a pretty pissed off look on my face, because he just rolled his eyes at me.

'Don't look at me like that, Texas.'

'Like what?'

'Like I'm the kid who stole your last cookie. I'm not just as sex object to be used. There's a whole man in here with feelings and thoughts. If I don't want to fuck, I don't have to.'

'That's not how I am looking at you. And I'm not going to force you to have sex with me,' I said infuriated.

I left the kitchen, taking up my suitcase, already knowing my way to his room in the small house.

Henry wanted to have sex with me – he wanted it as badly as I did. Whatever chemistry that went on between us was a burning flame and we needed an outlet for that heat.

Darci had joked – only once and only when she'd been really drunk – that a good way to get over grief was sex. It was apparently an amazing coping method. This was before the babies article she sent me. Which made sense considering one led to the other. She'd apologised profusely the morning after; considering my daddy had just died and my boyfriend had broken up with me a few weeks before.

I didn't think that I was using Henry as a sex object to get over losing daddy – but was two months enough time to know whether you were thinking rationally again, or still with a mind addled with grief?

But thirteen-year-old me sure as hell had wanted Henry, and I'd had both parents, both alive and living together back then.

Wanting Henry wasn't something new, formed out of death. It was something old that had been re-awakened in me since returning to where I'd grown up.

And he wanted me, but he was refusing to give in. Stuck in this town, with nothing else to do other than pack up my dead father's house, it looked like I had all the time in the world to figure out the mystery of Henry Dawson and the cock that could – but wouldn't.

Before bed, I read a few more entries from daddy's journals. We'd gotten into 2016 now and the mine had been closed after the strikes that had taken place.

Daddy's new "business idea" for Grand Yutu with Jason took over every page. But mama was starting to appear back into the narrative again, and me. I was seventeen now, going into my senior year. Daddy had started taking an interest, asking what colleges I'd been applying for.

April 2016

Helen messaged to tell me Lilac's planning on going to college somewhere in Texas. She's getting me back involved in Lilac's life because she wants me to pay her tuition. I would have. I was planning on it. Lilac deserves the best education money can buy her – but I'd prefer it if Helen had the decency to just be honest why she's calling after all this time.

I've stopped holding out hope that she's coming back. After the fucking mine – there's no chance. Not with Dawson dead.

Thankfully, Helen putting Grand Yutu in her rear-view mirror and never looking back has worked in my favour. She has no idea what happened two years ago. I don't know if she'd ever let Lilac speak to me again if she knew.

That's not even considering what she would think about this fucked up town now.

Thank god Lilac never asks to visit. I'm surprised sometimes that she never does – not to see Edie who she spent most of her time with when Helen was off in the city. Helen was always so fucking jealous of Lilac's relationship with Edie. It didn't make sense to me. If Helen cared that much, all she had to do was spend TIME with Lilac. It wasn't like Edie did anything special with her.

If the Dawson boy were back, she'd probably visit. But he's still in the army. Has a good few years left. I stayed away in Washington when the funerals took place. I never saw him. He always looked like a bruiser that one. I definitely wanted to avoid him punching my lights out. Though the pain couldn't be any worse than the guilt I already feel.

September 2016

I can feel the town turning on me. This summer Jason went too big. Did too much damage. I hardly spend much time here anymore besides the summers, but I don't even think I'll be able to come back even then next year.

Jason doesn't give a shit. It's not like any of it will pose a problem for business. All the required people signed NDAs and the rest are just small town folk no one would believe over... us.

December 2016

Washington isn't far enough away.

I woke up warm, in only my tank top and panties. I'd fallen asleep easier than I had done ever since getting to Grand Yutu. I could feign ignorance, but I knew it was because I'd gone to sleep with the smell of Henry on my skin, wrapped in his duvet and surrounded by his things.

If there was a physical embodiment of being coddled by all the things you'd loved in your childhood, that was what sleeping in Henry's bed felt like.

By the time I'd dressed and made myself presentable, Henry had already left, though he could have left hours and hours ago. I hadn't heard his truck leave.

There was no note on the side – and part of me was a little disappointed he hadn't thought to tell me where he was going.

I ate my cereal in the silence of the house. Like how I'd imagined daddy all alone in the Manor, my thoughts now drifted to Edie and how it must have been for her after the accident. Without Mr Dawson, she would have been alone, waiting and wondering about Henry. Whether he would leave her, too.

It had always just seemed like me and her those times when she'd babysit, but Mr Dawson had always been pottering around in the background. He'd never seemed to outwardly show that he loved his wife, but he must have done.

Nowadays, when love failed, you didn't stick around. You moved and found someone else, just like my mama had done. If he hadn't loved her, he would have left.

Me: When are you coming back?

I resisted the urge to ask "where'd you go?"

Henry: You're not my keeper.

That's not the response I'd given him last night, but I'd ignored his question, so I couldn't pretend to be high and mighty; hurt at his response.

Me: No, but I have errands to run and I don't want to leave your door open. You didn't give me a key.

Henry: I thought you'd remember where we kept the spare.

I went out into the back garden, pulling up the plant pot with the crack down the middle. Inside there was the spare key. I was surprised they hadn't changed the spot in all those years.

I grabbed my jacket, pocketed the key and walked out of the house.

12

DAWSON

Kissing Lilac the first time had been a mistake, or at least I could argue with myself on that point. But the second time… that was a choice. Fuck, it was a choice that I would make again and again if I could.

The way she'd stared at me with that heat and intensity in her eyes like she could combust if she simply didn't have me there and then was something I'd never experienced with any other woman before.

College had been a wild ride, especially after the few and far between pussy of being on active duty. But even the puck bunnies who'd wanted me had never known me well enough to want *all* of me.

I could just tell when Lilac looked at me that she didn't just want me for my body – no matter what stupid shit I'd actually said to her. She wanted me down to the boy she'd known when she was a kid. And that meant something to me.

But no matter how much we wanted each other – I wasn't that boy anymore. And fucking her wouldn't feel right. Not with Lucas's words playing in my mind. *All access pass.*

I wasn't planning on going through with any of the

dumb shit I'd said in those moments of grief back when mom had died, but I knew that Lucas and Trace still were. And I knew that the whole town was still actively trying to make Lilac feel as unwelcome as possible to kick her out.

I couldn't have sex with her – not knowing all the shit I did and not coming clean to her. But what could I say?

"When my mom died, and I'd realised that your parents hadn't just taken one, but both of my parents from me, I'd planned to have my revenge on your whole fucking family. To do that, we'd joked about kidnapping you, holding you for ransom, making your family believe you were dead. Making them feel the full level of utter despair that every one of us felt that day we found out about the mining accident."

Yeah, as much as I'd fucking hated the thought of Lilac before she'd come back here, I loathed the idea of ever having to come clean and admit that shit to her. "I was drunk" was a good excuse for some dumb shit, but not that.

I didn't want to see her hate me, realise what sort of a sick and twisted fucker I'd become since losing mom, so I'd told her nothing instead.

Lucas: Do you know where bitch princess has moved to?

Trace: Not at the hotel. Someone said she was staying with Willa.

Lucas: She's definitely not back at the mansion.

Lucas and Trace had been blowing up my phone since Lilac had left her dad's place. It'd taken them until yesterday, after Willa had talked to me at the rink, for them to figure she was missing.

As much as they'd loved fucking with her, they said

they probably went a bit too far with taking the doors because now they couldn't watch her on the cam's and know what she was up to.

I hated thinking about them messing with her, but I was glad they no longer had access to watch her without her knowing.

Are you sure you want to fuck me, Texas? I watched you scream when you thought your dad was trying to talk to you from beyond the grave. I know who stole your doors and smashed your windows and know they plan to do a whole lot more until they get what they want and I still haven't told you.

Am I really worth that hug, that admiration I saw in your eyes as the man who looks after a town but can't even admit the horrible things my friends have planned for you...?

I ignored the messages like I had been doing this past week. They wouldn't notice, or if they did, they'd think I was busy – which I was. I still had a thousand jobs going off with this virus fucking up the town.

Viv had made me some weird face mask that was supposed to help stop me from catching the virus, or whatever, but I hadn't put it on, just shoved it in the back of my pocket. A few of the kids showed up for their runs with masks but took them off when it restricted their breathing too much.

I knew I was helping the kids who came to "quarantine-practice" as the kids called it, but my mind couldn't help going to all those ones who didn't have my coaching to occupy their time.

Kids got bored at the best of times here, even when they had high school to occupy their day. I hated to think of what they'd be doing to occupy their time now that nearly the whole town was shut. The adults still had Tit Town.

But what did the kids have?

As long as they were safe, underage sex wouldn't be too bad – maybe a few more pregnancies than usual. But the hard drugs and alcohol… fuck.

It wasn't like Rick had a handle on that shit. And Montgomery had sure made it so that the dealers had a hold on this city before he'd fucked off and died.

I was sweating like a pig even though the weather was averaging seven degrees. Usually coaching didn't take much out of me, since I mostly just had to direct them with the drills – not participate in them myself besides the demonstration. And on the ice, it'd hardly been any trouble at all. But there wasn't a way I could get around the run.

Two miles there, two miles back. Each. Fucking. Session. It was like spending the whole day in perpetual motion. My legs felt like they were going to fall off by the third run (or sixth depending on how you counted it). The kids in the earlier sessions loved taking the piss about how I was old and out of shape. So, I made them run suicides like I would on the ice. That stopped them laughing so much.

'You're a life saver,' Viv told me when she came to pick up Shane and Arnie from "practice". They were red in the face, out of breath and looked like they wouldn't move much for the next hour.

I wasn't doing too well myself. I was propped up against the outside wall of the centre trying to calm my heart rate. If my army buddies could see me now, they'd shit a brick laughing. Perhaps I was out of shape.

Fuck it, though. The *Nokota Horses* were my next and last practice. If they pulled any shit, I was getting Calvin and Graham to carry me back.

'I don't know what I'd do with them if I didn't have you,' Viv said, lingering.

'*Mom,*' Shane whined. 'I need a *drink* and to lie down. Please, let's go.'

Viv gave me a lingering look like she wanted to stay and chat, but her boys pulled her back to the car.

'Maybe you wanna take your truck and drive along side us like a paedo, old man,' Calvin said, appearing in front of me with half of the team after Viv's car pulled away. 'You're not looking too hot.'

'Cheeky fucking shit,' I mumbled under my breath. Not that it was a bad idea.

Arms on our knees, breathing deeply, most of the team were out of breath by the time we finished our work out. I'd pushed them harder on the drills today, and almost ran full-out on the way back. I knew I was taking out my frustration with myself about Lilac on my body and the team, but there wasn't much I could do to change that.

With the kids, I wouldn't push them to breaking point. With these guys I would. They knew their limits and would stop if the really needed to. They needed the challenge. They needed the distraction.

'Where was Miller?' I asked Calvin.

Most of the team had collapsed on the empty parking lot by now, looking up at the sky. The gravel was hard on our backs, and just cold enough to take off the heat from our skin.

He didn't look at me when he answered, just continued breathing hard and looking up at the sky. 'His mom's tweakin' again.'

'Fuck.'

Calvin just nodded. His teammates pretended they weren't listening in to the conversion, but it wasn't like this team kept secrets from each other. I knew they had each other's backs. It's how I trained them.

'Did he say if he's gone to his sister's?' I asked.

'He might've done. But you know…'

'Yeah, I know.'

When his mom got bad, Miller got gone.

'Text me if you hear from him, yeah?' I asked, pulling myself up from the floor.

'Where're you going?'

'To try and track him down.'

The last time he'd disappeared, he'd not been in a good state. He'd been picking fights with the wrong people. He was lucky he'd been able to be patched up by our local doc, instead of having to make the trip to the hospital.

My first stop was always the sister. She worked with Willa at Tit Town and took online college classes. Katie was one of the best dancers there were and got enough tips to own a small house in one of the nicer parts of town.

A lot of Montgomery's friends had given her attention in the past. We all knew that was where most of her savings came from. She might have been one of the only people who was sad that Montgomery was gone, and his summer parties would no longer be taking place. Not because she cared for the guy – but she'd cared about the money.

When you were a dancer, you tended to leave any feelings at the door and do what you had to to get the cash. At least that's what Willa told me. Some girls went as far as they could to get as much as they could. Others had limits. I didn't think Katie Miller was one of those girls who had limits.

The team had used to razz Miller about it until they realised that it got to him – *really* got to him. Mom a drug addict and sister a Montgomery whore – dad god-knows where. What type of person did that make *him?*

Hockey practice was the one place he didn't have to think about his past. He had his team, he had his skates, his stick, and the ice. For an hour and half, that's all there was.

My love of hockey had never been about escape, only

about the sport, but I knew that most kids who came to practice used it as an outlet.

I'd always wanted brothers growing up, but mom had struggled to get pregnant with me, so that had never been an option. Joining the hockey team had given me that brotherhood I missed out on.

Lilac had made fun of it being the same as a frat – perhaps it was kind of, but there was more to it than a bunch of guys living together. When you trained together, played together, lost and won together – striving for something and working as a unit, it bonded you more than any frat could. The army had been the same, only more intense, more serious.

'I'd always wanted a daughter,' I'd heard mom tell Lilac one time as they were sat in front of the TV, painting each other's toenails. She'd been young, probably seven at the time.

'Because boys are smelly and stupid?' Lilac had asked back.

Mom had laughed at her. '*No, because I think Henry would have made a wonderful big brother. Don't you think?'*

'Oh, yes. But he's still stupid.'

'Not smelly?'

'Kinda. But only at the end of the day. He smells fine when he comes out of the shower.'

I'd ended up over-compensating after hearing that conversation and spraying deodorant under my armpits once every hour. Until mom had told me she couldn't afford to keep up with this insane war I had against my under arms. I'd told her I'd overheard what Lilac had said about me.

'*I don't see you cracking open a textbook to study, she also called you stupid.'*

'Lilac always calls me "stupid". She doesn't actually

mean it. She thinks "stupid" is synonymous with male.'

'Synonymous, that's one big word.'

'Told you, I'm not stupid.'

'If you heard us talking about that, you probably heard me say I'd wanted a daughter.' Mom had looked at me worried. '*I want you to know that that doesn't mean I was ever disappointed in having a son. You are the best child a parent could ask for. It's why I'd wanted a thousand Henry's.*

'Unfortunately, God had already given me the best, so he didn't think it was fair for me to have another baby'

'Is that why you like Lilac staying over so much?'

'Do you mind? I know she's been coming by more lately.'

'No,' I'd shaken my head. *'She's cool. For a kid, I mean.'*

'She really looks up to you. You'll watch out for her, won't you? She's far too trusting and only ever likes to think the best of people… a lot of people will seek to use that against her.'

'I'll look after her.'

'You really would have made such a wonderful big brother.'

13

LILAC

I told myself I wasn't being a crazy stalker person. I was simply letting the cards fall where they may. I'd been curious as to what Henry was doing – I wanted to find out more about him – and God had simply placed him in my path. If he caught me, that wouldn't exactly work as an excuse, but it was all I had.

Henry pulled up at a house – just an ordinary one story like the rest on this road. Waiting at the door was a pretty woman. Her hair was black, pulled into a low ponytail. She had no makeup on, but she had a lithe body and from the way her hands pawed at Henry's arm – and he didn't bat them off – I had a feeling he really didn't care if she contoured or not.

You have a boyfriend, Henry had told me when I'd tried to make a move the first time. But he hadn't said anything about him having a girlfriend.

Could be nothing, I told myself. She could simply be a handsy person. The woman pulled him into a kiss, the type that made you blush to witness.

Damn it to hell! Definitely not nothing. I pulled away from the house, driving by as quickly and as inconspicuously as I could.

What a freakin' nightmare. I was the other woman. Or I had been *trying to become* the other woman. Not that I'd be trying anymore.

Henry's resistance now made sense. He wanted me, but he wouldn't have me because he was already taken. Kissing me had already been cheating in my book, but at least he hadn't had sex. You could get over a couple kisses with a stranger, I rationed. But sex was a whole other argument.

From how badly he'd seemed to want me in the kitchen, he must clearly love this other woman a lot. Just not enough to tell me about her.

'How's living with abs-for-days?' Willa teased me as I came into her kitchen.

She was cooking for Kasey who was currently lying on her stomach in front of the TV colouring one of my old colouring books I'd found when we'd been going through my old room.

'Dawson,' she clarified as though I hadn't already known she was talking about Henry. Not that she used his first name. No one in town seemed to refer to him by his given name. It was *weird.* Though it was probably a sports thing. Or a guy thing.

'I tried to have sex with him in the kitchen, but he turned me down because he has a girlfriend,' I whispered so that Kasey wouldn't hear.

'You what – he what?' Willa laughed. 'Christ girl, you two are just one hot-pot mess, aren't ya? Start from the beginning.'

There wasn't much to say, even in the cliff-notes version. Him cooking me dinner, us talking normally for the first time in years, me hugging him, it turning into more, and then him literally laying down the line and saying there was no way we were going to have sex.

'And what was that little bit about him having a girlfriend?'

'I might have stalked him a bit today after I saw him drive away from the centre and seen him meet up with a woman.'

'Dawson doesn't have a girl.'

'Oh, believe me: he has a girl,' I said.

'Oh, ho,' she said, like she was some Santa Claus impersonator or something. 'Believe me, he does not. There's not much that goes on in this town so who's hooking up with who is literally one of the first things that gets spread through the phone tree. Our boy Dawson does not have a girl.'

'Then who was the black-haired woman who kissed him?'

'It's a Wednesday so… who the fuck knows. Dawson doesn't do serious relationships. He might have done at college, but I doubt it. All the single women of this town are crazy for him – most of the married ones, too. Who doesn't want the ex-military, ice-hockey playing super stud who singlehandedly is trying to save this town?'

'Basically, you're telling me she's just the flavour of the day.'

'Basically, yeah.'

I groaned. 'What the hell do I have to do to become the flavour of the freakin' hour?'

'You've got it *bad*,' Willa laughed at me.

'I've been crushing on him since before I knew what sex was. And he's not exactly lost any sex appeal since we've grown up.'

'He was pretty fine during high school,' Willa admits. 'But I wasn't into older men back then.'

'Older boys,' I countered. Henry hadn't been a man back then.

I was starting to think that *maybe* Henry's WUU2 text

really had been sent to me by accident. If mama had given him my phone number asking him to check in on me, he might have simply sent that text to the wrong contact. Or if he was still the player he'd been back in high school, I could have simply been a "send-to-all" casualty.

But what about those kisses – no one kissed with that amount of passion if they didn't *actually* want you, the other part of my brain countered.

'So as it stands, you're basically telling me he'll have sex with anyone in the town whose willing, but won't ever delve into a serious relationship.'

'Pretty much.'

'Everyone but me.'

Willa stopped stirring the sauce in the pan. 'That simply won't do. If my friend wants the D, she'll damn well get the D.'

'Mommy, what's the D?'

What did I say about kids knowing how to pick up on the phrases they were supposed to let slide them by?

'Something undesirable until you're sixteen, kiddo. Hopefully forever for you. I'm hoping you're gay and get to miss out on the horrors of loving men.'

Kasey just crossed her eyes, knowing that her mom was talking English, but not actually understanding a single word. I tried to hold my splutter of laughter but couldn't help it.

Willa pulled out her phone, dialling a number and putting it on speaker phone.

'What are you doing?'

'You want to know why he's not fucking you.' She put her finger to her lips, indicating for me to be quiet.

'What's up?' Henry's voice said from the speaker.

'Dawson – how's living with Lilac?'

'You just calling for a chat?'

'Can friends not call friends for a chat now and then?

Are you in the middle of practice?' We both looked at the clock. It was seven, he might be at practice. Or whatever he was doing with his sessions now that the hockey rink was closed.

'No.'

'Are you busy?'

'No,' Henry sighed.

'Then, yeah, I'm calling for a chat. How's living with Lilac?'

'She stayed the night. We ate. She slept. I slept. In separate beds,' he added hurriedly as though he knew what Willa was going to pounce on. 'You should know how living with her is. She was staying at your place before mine.'

'Yes, but I don't have that raw sexual chemistry like you two do.'

'*Roar!*' Kasey shouted from the living room.

'Should you really be talking about sex in front of your kid?' Henry asked her.

'Are you trying to lecture me on how to raise my kid?' Willa asked, her tone pissed off.

'Fuck, no.'

'Good, because this conversation is *me* lecturing *you* on what you're doing wrong with your sex life.'

Henry chuckled. 'There's nothing wrong with my sex life.'

'Oh really, Dawson. Hook up with anyone lately?'

'Define "lately"?'

'A booty call, in the last day or two?'

'I'd be pretty shit in the sack right about now after pushing myself today at practice.'

'Then you didn't, perchance, happen to get a raven-haired bombshell to help ease out those poor aching muscles for you?' Willa asked.

I hit her on the arm. The last thing I needed was for

Henry to find out I'd been stalking him.

'Katie informed the dancers already?' Henry said, I couldn't tell what he meant from the tone of voice he used. Was he angry? Resigned?

Willa's face scrunched up in confusion. Clearly, she recognised the name.

'What were you doing round at Katie's?'

'Their mom's having an episode again,' he said. 'I was trying to find Miller.'

He wasn't fucking her! Willa mouthed, even though I could hear that in Henry's own words as he was on speaker.

'Did you find him?'

'No, but Calvin called an hour ago and said he has. I told him to make sure Miller stays with him tonight. Get the guys to have some *Fortnite* marathon or whatever shit they're playing these days.'

'Thank fuck he has you and the team looking out for him.'

'Yeah, I know.' Henry was silent for a bit. 'Is Lilac with you today?'

'Why'd you ask?'

'She said she was going out to run some errands.'

'I don't know where she is,' Willa lied.

'Do you think she went back to Hades Mansion?' Henry asked.

'No… but I'm not sure. You could always text her and ask what she's up to.'

'Nah, she doesn't need me to be her keeper. She's a grown woman,' Henry said.

'A very *fine* grown woman,' Willa said.

'It's not gonna happen.'

'What?'

'Me and her.'

'I'm not the one who sent her a nude.'

'I didn't send her a fucking nude.' I could practically hear him rolling his eyes at her.

'I know, very disappointing for both of us.'

'I'm not sending you a dick pic, you thirsty bitch.'

'I'm not asking for one for *myself*.'

'I'm not sending Lilac a dick pic either. Fuck, woman. I thought all you girls complained about how dick pics aren't sexy they're just creepy.'

'Is *that* why you so artfully cropped the image?'

'I can't believe I'm having this fucking conversation with you right now.'

'I know. You should really be having it with Lilac. You want to fuck her.'

'I don't.'

'Oh, please. Lie to the town but don't try and pull the wool over my eyes.'

Henry groaned. 'Lilac's in love with the idea of the boy she used to know. *That's* the guy she wants to fuck. I'm not him.'

'I'm pretty sure you're the same guy, Dawson, unless you were possessed by aliens when you went to Iraq.'

'That's not what I meant.'

'Okay, I'll bite. Now you're much hotter, with better experience, can probably last more than a few pumps before shooting your load…? Sounds like a real disappointment to me.'

'You're acting like I was a shit lay back in the day! I was decent back at seventeen.'

'No guy has ever been "decent" in his teens,' Willa said. 'Not even you Mr abs-for-days.'

Henry didn't reply.

'It's just sex, Dawson,' Willa said.

'She said the same thing.'

'Then what's the big deal?'

'Because it would be sex with *Lilac*.'

'What does that mean?'

Henry made some unintelligible sound that basically said he wasn't going to answer that.

'Do you not find her attractive?' Willa asked him.

I slapped her on the arm. *What was she thinking?!* I felt like we were back in middle school.

'She's gorgeous,' Henry said, sounding reigned.

Willa smiled at me triumphantly. 'Then what's your hold up?' she said.

'We have too much history.'

Willa turned the call off speaker and spoke quickly and quietly for a few more moments before she hung up and turned to me.

'Problem solved: you can get the D.'

'What on earth are you on about?' I asked.

'Simple really: if you were asking for a relationship, you'd be fucked. Having a history means something *then* because relationships are all about the future. But everyone knows sex is all about *now.*

'You wanna fuck. He wants to fuck. All you have to do is convince him it is what it is – just sex, just for now – and you'll get exactly what you want.'

Thirteen-year-old Lilac might have wanted the whole nine yards with Henry Dawson – but I was a grown-ass adult now. And all I wanted was nine inches. And I was damn well going to get it.

14

DAWSON

Willa's questions bugged me more than they should. Clearly Lilac had talked to her about me and what an ass I was being messing her around. Sending her that selfie was becoming the bane of my existence, because I couldn't deny that I'd been the one to initiate the move from friends to something more.

If I hadn't done that, it was likely that Lilac would have kept her old crush on me to herself and had never kissed me. And then I would have never kissed her back. And I wouldn't have blue balls from thinking about her soft skin and how badly I'd wanted to take that black bra off she'd been wearing in that sexy little selfie…

Just as I was pulling into the drive, I got a message from Lilac. There was no text, only an image. It was another selfie. This time, instead of black lacy underwear, she was in a sheer see-through red set. I could see her hard nipples poking through the cups, and her shaved pussy in the barely-there thong.

No "oops, sent this to the wrong person" message followed. Clearly, Lilac was upping her game. As if it wasn't impossible for me to push her away already – she'd now thrown down this gauntlet. Looks like blue balls was going to become a permanent state of existence for me.

'Lilac?' I called into the house. Her car had been parked outside next to mine. She didn't answer me.

I made my way upstairs. Mom used to call me down for dinner, but I'd always had my headphones on and had never been able to hear to answer her. Lilac might be the same.

I poked my head into my old room. It looked tidy, the bed made, and her stuff piled up neatly in the corner of the room. The only thing out of place was the red underwear I'd seen her wear in the pic only a moment ago was on the floor.

'Lilac?' I called again.

I came into the room fully, but she wasn't there. The room smelt of her sex; the scent strong in the air, like she'd been touching herself in here – or fucking.

I went into the master bedroom that I'd slept in last night since she'd taken my room, but she wasn't there either. I called her name again.

Where was she? I checked the message she'd sent me again. She'd taken the picture in my bedroom. The bedroom with the underwear now on the floor and with Lilac nowhere to be seen, even though her car was parked out front.

I called her phone. If she was just teasing me, surely she'd come out now that I'd followed her trail and found her underwear. Why wasn't she answering when I called her name?

Lilac didn't pick up.

All access pass.

I wouldn't mind testing out that tight Texas pussy.

Lucas and Trace's words spat out at me from the darkest parts of my mind, running the worst scenarios. What if they'd found out that she was staying here? Tracked her from town and followed her here. She might have taken that picture willingly, but what if *they'd* sent it to me from her phone. After they'd taken her?

I clenched my fists tight. This was all my fucking fault. I should have put a stop to this. I should have told them to cut it out after they'd broken into her house the first night. I certainly shouldn't have just *sat* there whilst they'd messed with her house and watched as she ran around the Manor scared. Anything they did to her was on me.

How could I have been so dumb to befriend those assholes in the first place? I knew that when I'd originally come back to Grand Yutu I'd been in a dark place. And I'd spent this past year trying to make the best of a bad situation.

Trace and Lucas had been my outlet – my selfish bit of darkness that I kept separate from the poster-boy image of the man trying to fix a broken town.

Along the way, I'd probably stopped needing them as a crutch for my darkness and instead had continued to hang out with them out of habit. Feeding off their hate and fuelling it with my own.

As mom had always said: if you lie with dogs, you can expect to get fleas. That hatred and darkness were the fleas I'd caught and never seemed to drop until I'd stopped hanging out with them and started seeing things more clearly. Started seeing Lilac again more clearly.

I texted Willa. Lilac had not been over at hers an hour ago when Willa had rung me, but that didn't mean she hadn't stopped by now. I waited for the response, but knew that was a long shot – after all, Lilac's car was parked out front. But perhaps she'd gone for a walk and she was just not replying to *my* messages. I could get Willa to call her too and see if she picked up.

Willa text back and said that Lilac wasn't replying. I tried Lilac's phone one more time, but she still didn't pick up. I paced around the top floor of the house.

I tried her phone another two more times before I called Lucas.

'Do you have Lilac?'

'What the fuck are you talking about, mate?'

'Lilac. She's missing. Have you taken her?'

'Yeah, I know she's fucking missing. We were the ones who told *you* that, shit-for-brains,' Lucas laughed.

'Tell me now if you're lying or I swear to fucking god I will rip your dick off and feed it you.'

'Woah, man, no need to get graphic. We wouldn't screw you over like that. When we're ready to pull the trigger, you'll be the first to know.'

'There's not going to *be* any fucking trigger pulling. You've taken it far enough with her. Montgomery's dead. Karma got him before we did, and it ends with him. You've scared her enough. She's not going to be coming back after this.'

'Are you going soft on her? She have some sort of magic cunt that made you forget she's what's wrong with the world?'

I hung up. If Lucas didn't have her, it was possible, though unlikely, that Trace might have taken her. I should have called him first, since he lived closer and would have easier access, but Lucas was more of the brains of the operation, Trace just tended to go along with whatever Lucas said.

I'd almost hit dial when Lilac appeared in front of me. She was wearing a different lingerie set. This one a dark blue colour – my favourite shade.

I smiled as soon as I saw her. Thank fuck. She was here. She was safe. And god, she looked like heaven. It took a moment for me to realise that Lilac's face looked anything but happy to see me.

'What the hell was that about?' her voice was trying to be strong, but there was a quiver in it. Like she was fighting back tears. 'Who were you on the phone to?'

'Where were you? I called your name – you didn't answer,' I said.

'Who were you on the phone to?' she asked again, this time more slowly.

I played back my conversation with Lucas in my head, quickly. I didn't know how I could lie out of that one. There was probably a way, but I'd been lying to her since the moment she'd come back. I didn't have it in me to keep pretending. Part of her would already be pulling together pieces of what I'd said and drawing her own conclusions.

The last thing I'd wanted to do was explain to her the truth – but here was the moment it had to happen. Thinking Lucas had taken her made me realise how much I'd let slip simply because I was scared for her to hate me. Right now, her hatred was preferable to her being in danger because she was ignorant.

'I couldn't find you, so I thought that you'd been taken.'

'What do you mean "taken"?'

'Kidnapped,' I clarified.

'That's not a logical conclusion to jump to, Henry,' she said. She crossed her arms. It was probably to make her feel more covered, but instead, it just pushed her tits together. My cock needed to seriously learn to read the room right now; this was not the time.

'It is when you know what I know.'

'What's that supposed to mean?'

I rubbed my temples, taking a deep breath. Here went… everything.

'The person I was on the phone to was one of the guys who've been messing with you, the ones who broke into your house.'

'You *know* who broke in?'

I nodded.

'How long?' I didn't answer her. 'You've always

known?' she guessed. I nodded once more.

Lilac backed away into my old room and opened up her suitcase. She grabbed the first piece of clothing she could find and pulled it over. The layers kept on piling themselves, one on top of the other. As though she was trying to shield herself from whatever I was going to say.

'Explain. Now.'

Once she was dressed, she resumed the crossed arm position.

'Six years ago, there was a mining accident in town – one that killed fifteen people. My dad had warned yours that the structure needed reinforcing, that the load baring frames weren't as strong as they should be. But your dad ignored the reports. He was spending all his time over in Washington and started letting things slip with the mine.

'A lot of the miners were talking about striking until he took their warning seriously. But your dad scared them with some lawyer talk that meant if they so much as hinted about not showing up to work they'd be out on their ass and have to pay the company reparations for lost work.

'When the part of the mine that collapsed was found to be the same one my dad had warned yours about, everyone had figured it was a pretty cut and dry case of negligence on your dad's behalf. Fifteen people had died. There were forms and emails and everything that said those miners hadn't thought it was safe to work and their boss had forced them to anyway. The fifteen's families – my mom included – took your dad to court.

'All they'd wanted was justice. Instead, him and his company lawyers tore them the fuck apart. I don't know how they hid the evidence or got it thrown out of court because I was only on leave for the funeral; I wasn't there for the months of litigation that followed.'

I'd been so clueless. I gritted my teeth and forced myself not to think about how much I'd ignored what was happening at home back then.

'An "independent" company was called in to do an investigation into the miners' testimonies and the state of the mine, but they found no evidence of negligence on your dad's behalf and nothing wrong with the mine – it was just some freak accident. No one could have seen its collapse.

'They tried to contest the ruling. And that was when your dad slapped every family with a lawsuit of his own: slander of the company name… I don't remember the details exactly of the whole list your dad piled up against the town, but every one of them was a load of bullshit.

'He took them for every last cent. Mom lost most of dad's life insurance to the original lawsuit, but she almost lost the house after that second stunt your dad pulled. Over half of the other families *did* lose their homes; the rest had to mortgage their house.'

Lilac's eyes were glassy with tears. She'd been enraged the first time I'd accused her dad of ruining this town, but she wasn't now. Her expression was entirely accepting.

Part of me knew that she wasn't crying for her dad – the loss of that hero paternal figure she'd always looked up to. Those unshed tears were for the families who had been damaged by his greed and neglect. For my dad and the other fourteen miners who'd lost their lives.

'That doesn't-' she cleared her throat, no doubt the tears making it hard for her to speak. 'That doesn't explain to me who was on the phone and how you knew about them and didn't tell me.'

'I'm getting there,' I said, sighing. I wanted her to know the full story. To know *why* I'd been so filled with hatred and grief. That my plans for revenge wasn't something that had just happened on a whim. Fuck. I was trying to justify it in some way, however sick of me that was.

'During the second lawsuit, most of the miners quit. Afterwards, the company who'd investigated the incident might have said that there was no foul play or neglect involved, but the damage from the collapse meant the mine wasn't going to work at the capacity your dad needed it to towards the profit margin he'd set.

'Your dad dismissed the rest who hadn't quit and closed down the mine for good. But he wasn't nearly finished with the town.

'The summer after the mine was shut down, your dad rented out all Elm Cabins.'

The cabins were the one tourist hotspot. Halfway up Miner's Mount, a ten-minute drive from the town at the base, twenty cabins created a private "village" that Montgomery had installed with the profits after five years of opening the mine.

From there was enough of an incline that in winter you could get a decent naturally-occurring ski slope – though hardly anyone knew about Grand Yutu enough to consider it a great location for a ski resort.

'Since no one had to get into the mine anymore, your dad hired some of the guys in town to bulldoze the old mine entrance and grounds and expand the "village" to create some white collar retreat for his work buddies from Washington. The Ash Cabins were larger than Elm. These big luxury buildings that looked like they cost as much as your McMansion.

'Word around town spread that he was trying to boost tourism: make up for the damage he'd done to the town, perhaps. But even those who tried to think the best of him were soon proven wrong as soon as those associates of his started arriving in town.'

I hated to think about this moment in time where the town I'd loved had turned into some unrecognisable cesspit. The guilt that I'd been overseas and completely unaware still punched me in the gut anytime I recalled what I'd missed and what my mom had to cope with alone.

Lilac waited for me to go on.

'It was called a "company retreat": team building exercises for the new employees your dad's business in Washington were hiring. I don't know how other companies welcome their employees, but I doubt they usual include party favours as the general start-up package.'

'Party favours?' Lilac asked.

'At first it was just drugs.' I laughed, though there was no humour in the sound. *Just* drugs – as though that didn't to this day wreck our town and people's lives like Miller's mom.

'Then your dad bought out one of the bars in town and opened the strip club. High from the drugs they'd taken in the cabins, those new employees would go into town and spend thousands a night on dancers and booze. That was bad enough, but it didn't stop there. Those bastards didn't want to just *look* anymore. And what those new employees wanted; management was there to provide.

'They made their very own escort service here in Grand Yutu. If the dancers wanted a little bit more cash, all they had to do was give management a nod, a wink-wink or whatever the fucking signal is they had, and their body became part of the deal. It didn't seem like the dancers had much of a choice with how your dad was running things.

'Rick tried to put a stop to it, but these guys had lawyers and connections the devil himself would be envious of. Your dad had gotten away with murder – involuntary manslaughter, however you wanted to label it. What was a charge of prostitution on top of that?

'The next summer was more of the same, only bigger. More drugs, wilder parties. A new batch of employees.

'Your dad banked on the town being so isolated for his retreats to keep running smoothly. It worked in his favour being able to control the local police. But he didn't count on the small-town network figuring out that his "retreat" had a hidden agenda beyond giving his employees the *Wolf of Wallstreet* experience.

'From the contractors your dad hired to build the new cabins, the town found out that they'd installed each building with state of art surveillance.

'It was like those fraternity group hazing things: only on a massive scale. You got videos of your fellow brothers in a compromising situation and if you ever needed that bit of leverage over them – you had it.

'How do you get the perfect employee who would risk doing anything for your company? Guarantee they never leave to a rival, taking your trade secrets and clients with them? You make sure that if they weren't willing to put their neck on the line for you, you had the power to destroy them for good.

'None of the employees had a clue what was really going on.'

I sat down on the bed. Lilac stayed standing. She was soaking everything in. I could see her mind absorbing everything I told her, feel the cogs in her brain moving; the data on her dad being re-written with every word I said.

'2016 was when the town took the biggest hit. I don't know what the fuck was in the water when they hired that batch of employees, but they must have dragged the barrel for the scum of the earth.

'Nothing was good enough, big enough, bad enough. They weren't content with the party favours provided for them. They called in their own dealers. They propositioned dancers who'd set their limits, and the serving girls. They even moved on to the girls who didn't even work at Tit Town.'

That year, Montgomery's employees didn't just stick to the cabins and the strip club. They saw the whole town as their playground. In the day, they'd spend their time sleeping and doing fuck knows what in the cabin – then as soon as it got dark, they'd head down to town.

'They'd smash up local business windows, piss out on the street. One of them even took a dump on the high school steps. Some of the dancers said the men roughed them up. A few people had said they'd seen the men during the day chat up a few of the high schoolers who were on summer break.

'That year had been breaking point. The town started investigating what the contractors had told them and learnt about your dad's blackmail scheme. Rick managed to use it to blackmail your dad into taking his "retreats" elsewhere.

'Rick didn't have any hard evidence, and your dad had made sure to cover his back with NDAs and whatever other legal shit his lawyers had drawn up to protect him. But Rick had enough. Your dad didn't come back to town after that. He kept the Manor, but he lived over in Washington.

'The damage had already been done to the town, though. The accumulation of the mine shutting down and all those people losing their jobs, to the drugs his summer parties brought in… he ruined a lot of people and they had no way to get out.'

I clenched my fists hard against my thighs. Now we got to the part I'd never be forgiven for.

'When I finished my tour in 2018, I'd barely spent any time back at home before I moved out to college. Mom kept the worst of it from me, though I probably could have found out myself if I'd bothered to stick around long enough.'

I shook my head at my past self's selfishness.

'What I hadn't realised was that mom wasn't coping as well as she'd been pretending to for me. If I'd had known how badly things had gotten in town, maybe I would have been clued in. But that shouldn't have mattered… dad was gone. And I'd been away for years. I should have known that would affect her.

'I was on my way back home after my first year of college when I'd found out about her accident. I came home and learnt about the shit with the mines: the closure, the lawsuits; Tit Town opening and your dad's "parties". But none of that compared to when I found the note she'd left for me.'

My throat felt tight. I could feel the tears in my eyes prickle against my eyelids as I closed them, trying to compose myself.

She'd left the note my old gym duffle bag: the one I'd taken to hockey practice during high school. I'd taken my skates with me to college, but none of my old *Nokota Horses* jerseys or my old shoulder pads which no longer fit since I'd been away.

To others, it might have seemed weird that that's where she'd left her note, but it wasn't to me. Mom had always left me notes in my gym bag, so I'd find them when I was getting changed before a big game. One last motivational message from my mom: talking to me where she couldn't follow. This had been nothing like that.

It had been a long letter, two A4 sides with mom's writing smudged by the fall of her tears that had wet the ink as it dried upon the page. There were many things she'd said. But there was one particular part that I couldn't stop reading; that wouldn't stop replaying in my mind.

'I never intended to hurt anyone with this secret. It was my exact intention to STOP the hurt that I kept it. I could never do it to Lilac. You understand. You must. You were her first and fiercest protector.

'So, I kept Helen's secret. And it festered and infected this town. It was what drove Montgomery mad, I have no doubt in my mind. What led him to become careless with his mine; what soured his soul and corrupted the family

man we'd all known into that soulless creature who ate up every good thing and polluted this town like a pestilence.'

'My mom kept a secret for yours. She never said what it was, but it was enough to make her go mad with guilt; enough to break your parent's marriage apart.

'My mom was convinced it was that secret that ruined this town. Her parting words in the letter she'd left me made me believe her "accident" had been her way of finding a permanent solution to run from the guilt.'

Lilac moved – like she was going to hug me. I put my hand up to stop her. I wouldn't accept her comfort. I didn't deserve it. And she would hate me more than she already would if I let her give it to me.

'I couldn't hate her. I could never hate my mom. Not for keeping a secret for a friend, or even for killing herself and leaving me behind. She was everything to me. So, I chose to hate your parents instead.

'Your dad's negligence had killed mine and your mom's secret had also taken my mom from me. Mom would rather take it to the grave than hurt you and your mom – even though you'd both abandoned her to live in a town where your dad was destroying every last thing my mom had loved about living here.

'I started drinking and fell in with some of the guys who'd lost family in the mining accident. Lucas and Trace – the guys who broke into your place – they both lost their dads in the collapse. Lucas also lost his brother.

'When the mine shut down a lot of people tried to go back into farming, but your dad had bought the land and wasn't willing to sell it back. Wheat-Locke Farm hired as many hands as they could, however it still left a lot of people unemployed.

'This town's resilient but not everyone manages. Lucas and Trace are part of the town who haven't adapted. Running your dad out of town pacified that bunch for a while, but your dad got away with murder and made *them* pay for it.

'I felt a lot of hate back then. I was in a really dark place. That's when I started talking with the guys about how we'd really make Montgomery pay. In Washington he seemed untouchable, but everyone has a weakness. Your dad's was you.'

My mind was set on telling her every part of the truth now. I'd gotten this far. But my body was sick. My palms were sweating, and my stomach felt like it had a boulder inside. I'd used to get the same feeling when I was about to hit the ice before a game; only now there wasn't excitement just pure dread.

'Mom's worry for my life was the worst she'd felt her whole life – and if I could make Montgomery feel a shred of that pain, then I would. The plan I kept coming back to was kidnapping you and holding you for ransom. We even considered making him think we'd killed you. That even after he'd paid us, he'd not get you back. Just so that he'd know what it would feel like to lose his money and the one person he loved most in this world.'

Lilac stood frozen. I waited for her to say something, but she didn't. Then, she moved. She grabbed something from her purse and dodged me – I'd stood as soon as she'd moved – and ran down the stairs.

I followed, speaking quickly as she tried to get away.

'I don't think I would have ever gone through with it. Thinking about hurting them through you was the best way I had at coping with mom's death.

'I didn't even think of you as a person when I came up with the plan. It was years since I'd seen you. I thought since you'd never tried to contact me or mom you didn't care. I thought you were probably just like your parents.

'I forgot who you were, Lilac. I'd been away from home for so long and was clouded by grief.'

She didn't answer me. She didn't look at me. She just tore open her car door and got in.

'I never searched you out. I forgot about the plan after I stopped drinking and started to clean myself up!'

Lilac sped away so fast, she left the mark of burning rubber on the pavement.

I couldn't tell if the smell in the air was from the tires, or the burning pit left in my chest where my heart should have been.

15

LILAC

There were too many thoughts spinning round my head as I replayed every word Henry had said to me. A thousand points that made my heart bleed. For the town, for Edie, for everyone who had lost something because of daddy.

But I couldn't think about any of that now. All I could think was that I wanted to get away. I had nothing in the car with me, all of my stuff was still at Henry's house. But there wasn't anywhere I was going *to.* Mama required a flight, daddy was dead. I just knew that I didn't want to stay here. Not in this town where everyone hated me. Where everyone wanted me gone. And rightly so. Why would they want a reminder of the man who had destroyed this town?

I knew I shouldn't be driving like this, not when there were tears obscuring my vision and my hands shook on the wheel. I couldn't keep a steady grip.

The roads, which were already pretty damn empty considering how cut off from the rest of the world Grand Yutu was, seemed emptier now. Perhaps even though North Dakota didn't have a stay-at-home order people were still trying to keep to their houses? Or perhaps it was simply because of the darkness of the night.

Between Miner's Mount and the flat plains of the farmland leading towards Route 83, as soon as you left the town limits, the lights faded out into nothing and all you had to go on were the full-beams of your car.

I hadn't gotten to the edge of town yet, but the streetlamps were pretty sparse, and those that did exist were generally smashed out. Most probably damaged by daddy's summer business associates.

My phone began to ring. It was shoved in my back pocket, so I had to move awkwardly to get it out. It was Willa.

Lord. I could have gone to her. I had one friend in the town at least… unless. No. She must have known about Henry and his friends' vendetta against my family. She'd warned me to get out of town the first time we'd seen each other at the bar. She knew the town had run daddy out of Grand Yutu and would want to do the same to me.

Me: Did you know about their plan to kidnap me?

I sent the text as I drove.

Willa: WTF?

Me: Don't play dumb if you did. Henry admitted everything. His twisted way of getting revenge on my parents for how they "killed" his.

Willa didn't respond, she just tried ringing again. I ignored her. When her call stopped, Henry's started.

No freakin' way! That asshole did not get to call me. He'd had his say. He needed to shut the hell up for, like, forever.

I was reaching the town limits.

All this time, I'd thought daddy'd actually saved this

town. I'd believed my daddy was the good guy. I'd wanted to follow in his footsteps and learn how to improve the lives of small-town people with simple but effective change. Instead, daddy had been this town's ruination.

It wasn't like he ever denied it in his journals either. He never said he was innocent. He even mentioned ignoring Henry's dad's warning. He'd mentioned the NDAs he'd gotten his employees to sign and how Jason had "gone too far" or something along those lines…

Lord, would that help? Having in his own words that he had been in the wrong? Those families still deserved justice for losing their loved ones. They deserved for the world to know that the accusation of slander had been false and that they'd had every right to try and seek justice from the man and company who had wronged them.

With daddy dead, I had inherited everything. I could give them whatever money back daddy had taken from them. It'd probably take time: I'd need to know exactly how much had been taken and from who. I would pay them back with interest or whatever I could to make things right. Henry had said they'd lost their *houses…*

The tears were falling down my cheeks now in a steady stream. I'd been able to hold them off whilst Henry had told me his tale, because I hadn't the right to feel empathy for all that they had lost when it had been *my* daddy who had taken it from them. But there was no one to see my cry now.

I fumbled with my phone, trying to find Lisa's number. As daddy's PA, she'd know. She would have all the records from that time. Unless that whole GDPR thing stopped her from being able to share those records with me and then I'd have to find some other way of finding out who needed to have their money returned to them. If she didn't know, then she'd know someone who could help me.

I was so intent with composing a text to her, that I hadn't realised I'd not looked at the road for a while. Until in front of me all I saw were the blinding headlights of a truck and I swerved, then all there was, was darkness.

I came to a minute or so later. My airbag had deployed, and I felt like death. My head and nose *hurt* like I'd been punched in the face. I fought to push the airbag away from my face, then unbuckled my seatbelt.

A moment later my car door was yanked open.

'Are you okay?' Henry's voice was calming to my scrambled mind.

'Yes.'

'Good,' he paused for a moment whilst I climbed out of the car. I had veered off the road and drove into a ditch, hitting a tree, though not very hard. 'Because what the *fuck* were you thinking? Do you have any idea how dangerous it is to drive with a messed-up head? Are you trying to punish me by making me relive my mom's fucking death or what?'

I forgot that I was mad at him. I forgot that less than thirty minutes ago he'd admitted to me that he'd once planned my kidnapping. All I could feel was a hollow guilt deep inside me.

'I'm sorry. I was texting-'

Henry swore, seeing red. He grabbed me by the arm – not hard, but enough to make me wince a little – and dragged me to the passenger side of his truck.

'Get in.'

'I'm not going anywhere with you.' I could call a tow-truck myself. Not that I knew the number. But I could *Google* it.

The last thing I wanted was to go straight back into Henry's company. I needed *space* from him. I needed time to process that whilst I'd been feeling as though I was getting my old friend back, he'd been keeping the secrets of the men who had been tormenting me and breaking into my home.

'You're getting in my car and you're going to go home and sleep this off.'

'Sleep *what* off? Being immensely disappointed – hurt, angry. You can pick any synonym of those and it would be right. You *hurt* me, Henry-'

'That doesn't give you the right to put yourself in danger. Your life isn't just something to be wasted… I'm not fucking explaining this to you.'

Henry shoved me into the seat, locking the truck door behind me. I tried the handle, but I couldn't get out. It was an ancient model and could only be opened from the outside with the broken lock. People had always assumed that Henry was some old-fashioned gentleman when he let me out of his truck to get to school – but that was literally the only way I was able to exit the car.

Henry climbed into his driver's seat, but he didn't start the car right away. He pulled out his phone.

'Hey, Roy, sorry to call you so late. I'm on the road out of town,' he gave the specifics of where we were, 'and I've got a tow request. A small rental, driven off the road into the ditch. The front's pretty banged up.'

Roy on the other end said a couple things. Henry nodded along.

'Thanks, I'll call you tomorrow,' he hung up, and started the engine.

'You can drop me off back home,' I said. I was planning on finding some late-night bus or taxi. I wasn't actually going to stay alone at the Manor where Henry's friends could easily take advantage of me what with the no doors and windows.

'Not happening. You're not staying alone or running off in the middle of the night.'

'Finally gain a conscience now that you've come clean?' I asked. He certainly didn't have a problem with his friends messing with me before.

'When I was scared as shit something had happened to you and I finally realised what a big fucking ass I was being, yeah.'

I didn't expect him to admit it.

'Did Willa know about your plan to kidnap me?' I asked.

'No,' he said.

'Then I'll stay with Willa.'

I pulled out my phone and called her up. She picked up on the first ring.

'What the fuck is going on?' she whispered into the phone. Loud pulsing music played in the background. I forgot that she'd be working at Tit Town.

'I need to stay at your place.'

'Henry called me and said he was tailing your car because you'd sped off like a crazy person and were likely to hurt yourself.'

I didn't like that he had been right. 'I crashed my car.'

'*Fuck.*'

'I need somewhere to stay,' I said.

'Where are you right now?'

'In Henry's car. He picked me up and won't let me go.'

'Put me on speaker,' she said. I did.

'Henry, don't let her fucking go anywhere,' Willa told him.

'Willa-!' I started.

'You're not running off, crazy pants. Jesus, girl. You crashed your car. Don't you think the best course of action is to head straight to bed and sleep it off.'

'You're telling me I should stay with the man who planned to kidnap me with his buddies.'

Willa made a sound that I couldn't read. Perhaps

disbelief that Henry would do something like that.

Henry finally spoke up. 'I talked about it. I never had a solid plan.'

'That you never got down to the logistics is supposed to make it all better?' I looked away from him, directing my attention on my phone as though I could see Willa's face and was talking to her rather than some disembodied voice. 'I'm *loving* the idea of staying here, Willa. I feel really freakin' safe in the company of a man who doesn't fully pre-meditate his crimes beforehand but allows for that air of spontaneity.'

'You're pissed I didn't dot the I's and cross the T's in my plan?' Henry asked.

'No, that's- That's not what I was fucking saying!' I swore. Henry almost swerved the car. Willa let out a gasp. I never swore. Never.

'Dawson. Try not to be dickshit right now, would you? She was just in an accident.'

'How much did you know, Willa?' I asked, my anger flaring now. I wasn't going to just take Henry's word for it. I wanted to hear from her that I had at least one real friend here.

'Everyone knows the fifteen's families want revenge for what happened to them. Lucas and Trace have always been the ones the most vocal about it – and Lucas the most dangerous because he's family to the sheriff.

'I told you to get out of town because I knew everyone would treat you like shit because you were Montgomery's daughter. It wasn't like I thought you were in danger from *Henry.* I wouldn't have tried to get you two together if I thought that.'

'I'm not a danger,' Henry said. I glared at him. 'Fuck, Lilac, I'm not! If I hadn't come clean and was still plotting with those guys, *then* I'd be a danger. But I haven't even *thought* about that shit since Christmas.

'How can I be a danger to you if you know exactly the sorry shit I said in my past and that I'm *sorry.*'

He gripped the steering wheel so hard I thought he was going to pull it off.

'You're sorry you got caught. I don't know if I can believe that you're sorry you planned what you did.' Not when he'd spent so long detailing how he was justified in seeking out revenge for what daddy had done to this town and his parents.

'I got caught because I was scared those guys had followed through on the shit I'd said when I was drunk. And I was out of my mind with worry, trying to think of where they could have taken you and how I could get you back and make sure you were safe.'

'You can say this all now, but it's just words.'

'And it was just fucking words back then, too! Your dad died of a virus that's killing off thousands. A dad you only saw once a year and was a pretty all-around shitty person. You sort through your grief by boxing up his house and giving away every last one of his possessions.

'My *mom* died. The only family I had left, and she left a suicide note telling me that with me moving on from this town, she didn't see any reason to keep living in this hell where she was all so fucking alone.

'I wanted a reason not to blame myself for leaving for the army and then going straight to college when I got back instead of spending time with her and taking care of her. Blaming your family seemed like a pretty logical step to get out of my self-loathing and when I was drunk, I said some dumb shit to make myself feel better.

'You'll notice that I never went out and tried to kidnap you from your precious life where you had no fucking clue what your dad had done to destroy this town. Because it was just *words*. It was just shit I said to make myself feel better.'

His words carried a vague sense of déjà vu with them and I realised it was a reiteration of what he'd been saying to me as I'd run out of the house to my car.

'If it was just words, then why did you have to come clean like you were ridding yourself of some dark secret?'

'Because I was! You thought I was this great guy who spends his life looking after the town, and I didn't want you to look at me like you are now, knowing that I fucking *hated* you for no reason just because of who your parents were when you goddamn know how much you used to mean to me growing up. We were like family.'

Henry's chest rose and fell erratically. He was breathing hard like he'd run a mile. I could see the pain in his eyes, the worry on his forehead that hadn't left since he'd pulled me from the car.

'Lucas and Trace you should worry about,' Willa said. I'd almost forgotten that she was on the phone with us. 'Those guys spend more time high or drunk than most of the worst addicts in this town. But Dawson's not like that, Lilac.'

'I don't need you fighting my battles for me,' Henry told her.

'Screw you, dickshit. I'm still pissed as fuck. I just don't want Lilac doing something stupid like calling the police on your ass and accusing you of attempted abduction or whatever – if that's even a felony.'

'He still knew who was messing with me. He still knew what was going on at daddy's house and didn't say anything.'

'Yeah, neither did half the town. If he'd told you who it was – what would you have done? Gone to the sheriff? Who would have laughed you off and probably handed you to Lucas rather than him bring in his own cousin.'

Whatever quick conversation she'd had with Henry seemed to fill her in a lot on what he'd admitted to me –

either that, or she had been lying about not knowing Henry's side.

'Your town is corrupt.'

'Yeah, we fucking know it. We live here and will have to for the rest of our lives. As soon as this pandemic's over, you'll be back to your normal life and forget all about us,' Willa said. 'Don't deny it. You might call once in a while or send a friendly text, remember the family you helped out giving away your dad's old furniture: your good deed for the trip. But in the end, you're going to leave and we're going to stay. I don't believe you're responsible for the shit that your dad did – but you're sure as hell not one of us, are you?'

Willa hung up.

I stared at my phone. At what point did she become angry at *me.*

'She's just being dramatic cos she's pissed you got yourself into an accident and thought she was in on the whole kidnapping thing. She shows worry in a weird way.'

'I'm not speaking to you.'

'That's fine. Where here, anyway.'

Henry pulled up into his drive. He got out of the car and opened the truck door for me. I tried to judge if I could make a run for it or not, but Henry seemed to guess what was on my mind and he steered me into the house, locking the door behind me.'

'I'm not staying here.'

'You've got nowhere else to go,' Henry said, simply.

'I can go to Willa's.' Even though she'd hung up on me and told me I should stay here…

'Lucas and Trace figured you're hiding out there – so, no, you can't because you won't be safe there. And the hotel is shut, and your dad's place doesn't have any fucking doors or windows and if you set foot in that house they'll know because they can use the security system your dad had set up.'

I tried not to flinch at the thought of them using my daddy's own security to spy on me. I probably didn't manage it.

'What's the big deal now? I've been in this town for nearly two months – most of my time alone in the house. Why would they suddenly try something worse now I'm staying with Willa?'

'Because before they thought I was still on their side and didn't call them threatening to beat the living shit out of them if they'd hurt you. They don't do well when pushed into a tight corner and I don't like to think about them acting rashly and doing something to you they haven't thought through. The other stuff was like pranks. But if they get desperate – thinking that you're slipping through their fingers, they might pull something darker.'

'I don't want to stay here.'

'I didn't' want you in this town at all, but we can't all live happy sunshine lives where we always get what we want.'

Henry looked exhausted. He ran his fingers through his hair, then rubbed his eyes. 'Come on,' he said.

'What?'

'You're going to bed. It's late. You crashed your car. Your adrenaline will drop pretty soon, and you'll be exhausted.'

I *really* didn't want to stay here, but he was right that my options were pretty limited.

Honestly, after being in a car accident and finding out Henry's secret, mama could go screw herself. I'd stay the night, but after that, I was calling someone to take me to the airport and I was going home.

I'd already finished packing away most of daddy's stuff. His clothes were in boxes ready to be sent to Darci, and the books were all sorted to be sent to the library. The art and sculptures around the place could be put up for sale – as could the rest of it. I was done staying in this town. I'd get Lisa to sort out the rest. I didn't owe my daddy anything anymore to go through all his personal belongings.

Henry led me to his bedroom. 'You're going to stay here, alright? No more running off and hurting yourself.'

'Yes.'

Henry sighed. 'I really wish I could trust you not to put yourself in danger.'

'What do you mean?'

He went into his chest of draws and pulled out a tie.

'What are you doing?'

'I know this doesn't exactly bode well for that whole: it was only words. But I'm going to tie you to the bed. This is not some part of a kidnapping ploy.'

'I swear to god I'm going to freakin' scream if you try and tie me up.'

'It's just so I can make sure you don't run in the middle of the night. I can't trust you not to make a break for it again.'

'Whatever you want to tell yourself, but I'll be damned if I'm letting you tie me up.'

'It's not really like you can stop me, Texas,' Henry sighed.

'Oh, don't try and pull that "I'm sorry I have to do this" act. My daddy might be dead, but you still hate my mama for abandoning yours. If you think I don't believe you would ransom me to her you've got another thing coming.'

Henry moved quickly, making me forget that he'd had years of army training. I tried to scream, but he had shoved one of the ties he'd been holding in my mouth. I tried to spit it out, but by the time I did, he'd knotted my hands up with the other tie and had looped the one in my mouth around my head and tied that as well.

'I really didn't want to have to gag you, but I can't have

you waking the neighbours. Mrs Peters struggles to sleep as it is with her arthritis and her having to call the sheriff would make me hiding you here from the Olsons a big waste of time.'

'I hate you,' I spat through the gag. It was muffled and he couldn't hear the words, but he must have read what he said through my eyes.

'Yeah, I fucking hate myself right now, too.'

He finished off by tying my bound arms to the bed with a tie that I recognised Edie picking out for him for his sixteenth birthday.

If only you could see what your son turned out like now, I wanted to tell her.

16

DAWSON

I'd left Lilac in my room, going downstairs to call Roy again to see if he'd managed to find her rental okay. I checked in on Willa, too. She'd been about to start her shift when Lilac had run out on me.

I'd had the briefest of conversations with her – summarising the shit she already knew most of and coming clean to her about the stuff she didn't. Unlike Lilac, I'd been using voice commands to take phone calls in my car – not texting like a fucking moron.

For fucks' sake, she could have killed herself by texting whilst driving. How many fucking afterschool specials had we sat through in high school telling us how dumb that shit was? Lilac wasn't dumb – far from it, so how could she have put her life in danger so fucking recklessly?

An hour had passed when I went to check on Lilac. I cracked open the door. She was still awake tied to my bed. I'd had some fantasies before that night of a woman tied up in there, but this sure as hell wasn't the circumstances. None of the women would have ever held a candle to Lilac, either.

If there was any chance she'd forgive me for what I'd once thought about doing back when my mom had died,

I'd shot through that with this stunt. But I'd had to make sure she was safe, and I didn't trust her not to put herself in more danger. Perhaps the gag was a little too far, though.

'I'm sorry,' I said to her as I took the gag from the mouth.

As soon as her mouth was free, she didn't scream and shout at me like I thought she would. Instead she took a huge bite out of my hand. It cut through the skin in some places and hurt like fuck.

'Ow.'

'You bastard! You absolute crazy, deluded-' she continued her rant as I unknotted the one that tied her to the bedpost and climbed into bed with her. She leapt up trying to get away, but I pulled her back down.

I'd hoped she'd be asleep when I got back upstairs, then this part would have been a lot easier.

'What the hell are you doing?'

'I'm going to sleep, but I still can't risk you running off in the night.'

'You're not sleeping *here* with me.'

'I am,' I said. Though I doubted I'd very much be doing any sleeping.

She ranted some more, tossed and turned, but eventually, she settled down and I felt her breathing even out. I didn't sleep a wink.

Instead I just watched her, thinking about what could have happened if she hadn't been so lucky swerving out of the way of that truck. If I hadn't been the one to find her first, and instead Rick had, and had called Lucas up and they'd taken advantage of her in her weak state and tried to follow through with one of their plans to get back the money they were owed from the Montgomerys.

I thought about the night I'd been told about mom's accident. Seeing what her car had looked like afterwards. How for those few minutes before I'd been able to reach her, I hadn't known whether I'd lost Lilac, too, just when I'd finally gotten her back.

I was an asshole and a bastard and every bad word she wanting to call me. But I was still *here* and I would damn well make sure she was, too. I wouldn't let Lucas and Trace hurt her in any way. I knew they still wanted revenge, just as the rest of the fifteen's families still wanted justice, but they couldn't have Lilac to get it.

When the sun rose up, I accepted that I wasn't going to be able to sleep. Though my mind was warring with the worry and self-loathing, my body still responded to being pressed up against her. It didn't understand that I'd lost the right to react to her that way the second she'd found me talking to Lucas on the phone. Fuck, if I was honest, I'd never had that right since I'd said all that crazy shit a year ago in the first place.

Lilac's stuff was still piled up in the corner of the room. A couple boxes filled with stuff from her dad's house, along with her suitcase she'd brought with her. A few books poking out from the top of the box caught my eye. I pulled one out. It was pink, the same colour her childhood bedroom walls had been – though of course I only knew that now I'd helped moved all her furniture to Willa's place. Back then, she'd only even been round to our house, we'd never been invited round to the McMansion.

I flicked through the first pages, seeing the young scribbles and realised this must have been Lilac's diary from back when she lived here.

May 2012

Today started out exactly like any other day. Woke up, got dressed, walked Kitty around the block and then waited for Henry to pick me up outside the Manor. His truck pulled up three minutes early, like usual, and I hopped in.

School was normal – except Wyatt wasn't at my locker.

I asked Charlotte about it in homeroom since they live on the same street. She said that he must have been running late, but she didn't quite meet my eyes.

At lunch, I sat with the girls until Elijah came over and handed me a note. 'I'm sorry, L,' he said when he passed it me.

Like, what did THAT mean, was my first thought.

I opened the note and I could literally feel every girls' eyes on me.

Willa is so damn impatient I swear to god she practically snatched the note out of my hand to read it before me. She's ALWAYS like this. I shouldn't be surprised. She always eats all her popcorn before the film starts. Reads the LAST page of a book before she's even finished the first chapter for class. Does she not GET that some things are just WORTH savouring and waiting for?

I mean, this totally wasn't one of those cases. This was a read-it-as-fast-as-your-eyes-can-move cases, but STILL!

The note was written by Wyatt. I could tell the minute I opened it because I'd been reading his handwriting for, like, four years now since we'd always shared the same English class and he always let me borrow his notes.

"Unfortunately, things aren't going to work out between us. I can't be your boyfriend anymore. I'm sorry. Better luck next time, champ".

'The serious fuck?!' Willa had said when she read it.

Hadley echoed Willa's statement.

'Champ?' I think I'd said.

The better luck next time was a kind sentiment, I supposed – but what sort of luck did I need? That next year, when I was a freshman, I'd find someone who didn't dump me by a freakin' NOTE? Or that I'd find someone who liked me enough not to dump me at all? Like how could I have BETTER luck when I didn't know what I'd done wrong THIS time?

'If you want me to kick him in the balls, I'll totally kick him in the balls,' Hadley said. 'Or get Willa to do it. Or we could BOTH do it.'

I was starting to feel a bit sick, but I managed to tell my friends that I most definitely did not want Wyatt to be kicked in the balls. Mama said that violence was never the answer and you certainly never showed an ounce of hatred or anger towards someone you loved because it would damage that relationship forever. You could never take back words or actions.

I mean, I guessed the whole "love" thing had never really happened with Wyatt. We'd only been dating a few weeks. And there was no relationship to damage since he'd ended it with a note. But I still didn't want my friends to beat him up.

'I think I'm going to go talk to him,' I'd told them. He wasn't in the cafeteria, so I knew he'd probably be out on the front field with the rest of his friends.

'Do you want backup?'

'No, I'm fine.'

Elijah and his friends did that awkward, slap-look-who's-here-slap on Wyatt's arm when I walked over to them.

'Hi, Wyatt. Can I talk to you for a second?' I'd asked. I one hundred percent didn't let any of my sadness show in my tone.

Like, I couldn't be overcome by emotion right now because I didn't know WHY this had happened. He'd never said specifically there was anything WRONG with me. He might just feel like we needed to go in different directions.

His mama had managed to get him into some summer camp in another state and he might be thinking that he'd meet a girl there and it wouldn't be fair of him to string me along. That was nothing to do with ME. That was simply him being a nice guy and letting me go before things got messy.

Like with Ava and Lincoln when they'd said they'd see other people last spring break but then Ava hadn't realised that Lincoln had meant they'd CONTINUE to see other people when we got back to school and he hadn't TOLD her that, so he was, like, dating half the year whilst Ava thought they'd gone back to being exclusive. He'd totally made out with at least seven people. I even think he'd touched some other girls BOOB! Before he'd even made it to second base with AVA- HIS GIRLFRIEND! And they'd been going out for TWO months!!!

(I know I shouldn't gossip, but it's not gossip if it's written down because I'm not spreading it to anyone. And Hadley already told half the school anyway, so even if anyone DID find out from me, they probably already knew anyhow, or would know EVENTUALLY).

Wyatt seriously didn't look like he wanted to talk. He'd probably sent the note to avoid all this awkward conversation. I told him I knew as much.

'Look, I know y'all want to get back to your lunch, but you can't think this was a nice way to break up with someone. I've been your girlfriend for almost a month, which is pretty darn serious, and I think this is something that we need to talk about face-to-face.'

Wyatt was my first kiss. My first boyfriend. He'd dated Jessica DeLaney and the girl with the yellow headband (I don't remember her name but she was in my maths class last year) for almost a month each so it didn't seem like this thing would be as big a deal to him as it was to me. That was probably totally presumptuous since ALL relationships were important. But all I meant was that he was my FIRST and I was his THIRD.

'I just don't think we should go out anymore.'

'Yes. I understand that from the note. I was wondering if you could tell me why.'

'What?'

'Tell me why. You said that it wasn't going to work out, but I'd like to know if I did something wrong. Because if I'd somehow did something to upset you, I'd like the chance to apologise.'

Mama always said you had to face sadness with a reasonable and rational head. Put yourself in their shoes. Think from their perspective. Don't assume you know best and that you're more hurt than the person you're approaching. When someone hurts you, there's always a reason and a lot of people who lash out and hurt others are in a lot more pain than you can imagine.

'You're a grater face,' Wyatt said. He turned bright red when he said it.

'I'm what?'

'Your braces feel like they're cutting open my mouth every time we kiss. I can't do it anymore. I feel like if I made out with you one more time, I'll lose my lips and tongue and be hideously scarred for life. You're not worth it.'

His friends had chuckled. I think my hand had flown up to my mouth and I'd tried to cover my braces. 'Oh. I'm sorry,' I might have managed to say before I fled back into the school.

Henry had totally known that something was up when he waited for me in the parking lot. I couldn't even sing along when he put the radio on. I was forever keeping this mouth shut around boys until I got my braces off. Which wasn't for another TWO years.

'Okay, Lilac, spill. What are you thinking?'

'Nothing,' I'd mumbled.

I WAS NOT admitting to Henry what happened. He was the HOTTEST senior there was. NO. The hottest PERSON there was in all of Grand Yutu. I was NOT going to tell him that my only boyfriend had broken up with me because my kisses physically did him damage.

I thought they'd been perfectly fine. He kissed me hello at my locker in the morning and we'd made out like THREE whole times. If it was so bad – why'd he do it the other two times, you know? Or at least if he'd done it the first time because that's what boyfriends did and then realised he didn't like it, perhaps the second time was to see if it would get better? But the THIRD time? Why then?

'If you don't tell me, I'll have to ask around what happened at school.'

He was LYING. There was no way a guy like him would be seen sniffing around for info. Though he'd probably just get someone in his class who had a sibling in my year to tell him what had gone on.

Like the time he'd found out stupid Cora Thompson had cheated off my pop quiz and I'D gotten detention because SHE said I was the one who had copied from her. And then he'd found out from Cora's sister who was in the year below him and was one of the girls who was ALWAYS watching hockey practice hoping she'd be able to get with one of the players. And he'd asked Cora's sister for a favour and she'd just DONE what he asked because when Henry Dawson asked you to do something, they did it. Cora's sister had told her parents exactly what she'd done, and she got grounded for a week.

'Don't think I won't.' Henry was very protective of me. Edie said that's what big brothers did – but I did NOT want Henry to be my big brother. You did not have thoughts about making out with your brother unless you were completely deranged.

But there would be no more fantasises about making out with Henry because I was a GRATER FACE! And I would irreparably damage his perfect face if he kissed me and then the rest of the female population would MURDER me for my grievous act against all womankind.

I supposed it would be less embarrassing for me to tell him what happened with Wyatt than him asking about it at school. At least then I could keep most of the details to myself.

'Wyatt dumped me.'

'Oh,' he'd said. He didn't say anything for the rest of the ride, and I didn't pay much attention until I realised he'd not taken me home, instead he'd driven me to his place.

'Mama's home at seven today,' I said. Her and Edie were out on one of their gal-pal trips to the city, but since I'd only be home alone for a few hours it meant I was fine to stay over at the Manor.

'Come on,' he had just said, grabbing my backpack.

When we'd got to the kitchen, he pulled out a tub of ice cream and instead of putting some into a bowl he just handed me the whole thing and a spoon.

'What's this?'

'I've dated enough girls to know that this is part of the breakup ritual.' Henry then pulled out a bowl of puppy chow his mama had made a couple nights ago, grabbing a handful and shoving that chocolatey-peanuty goodness in his mouth.

He texted on his phone whilst I scooped a few mouthfuls of ice cream.

'Which idiotic romance are you feeling?' he asked when he'd finished on his phone. 'Aubree says the best breakup films to watch are Legally Blonde, Notebook and John Tucker Must Die.

'I'm voting for the last one since it has "death" in the title and might gain me a little bit more man-cred back if dad comes home and finds me binge watching your girl-films with you on the couch.'

I hadn't cried yet, but knowing that Henry had just text his girlfriend about my breakup so he knew what films would be best for me to watch made my start crying uncontrollably. I don't know why. It was the most embarrassing thing that happened – more than being called grater face by my ex-boyfriend in front of all of his friends.

'Hey, hey. It's okay. She wouldn't put a horror on that list, I already told her you won't watch-'

I'd just cried harder. He'd scooped me up into a hug like when I was younger. We didn't hug much since I'd started middle school.

'That boy is a fucking idiot for dumping you,' he said. 'You're too good for him. And he knows it. He just wanted to be the one to leave before you left him.'

I sobbed into his t-shirt. Henry was a saint. Literally the best guy there ever was. Wyatt would never have been able to live up to him even if we'd dated for years.

We'd ended up watching Notebook, which had been fine at the start, but utterly heart breaking at the end when I'd ended up crying all over again.

'I'm never going to find someone who loves me like that,' I sobbed.

I was being dramatic. I knew that. I wouldn't be in braces forever. And I was only thirteen. But what I wanted to say was that MY Noah was sitting in front of me and had NO CLUE he was my Noah and instead he was going to find an Allie who wasn't me and would give her the best life. Noah's didn't just grow on trees. They were special and Henry was the most special person I ever knew. There'd never be another one like him and because I knew him now, it meant no other boy in the whole world would ever live up to him.

It would have been easy to get on with my life if I'd never experienced Henry's love because then I wouldn't have the absence of it to compare it to. But I'd known him since I was five. I'd known him longer than I'd NOT known him. And I loved him, and I knew he loved me – just not in the way that I wanted him to love me.

'Sure you will. You're a thousand times better than Allie.'

'I'm not. She's gorgeous and talented.'

'And mouthy and annoying,' Henry rolled his eyes. 'You're gonna be a knock-out when you're older,' Henry told me. 'And you'll find something you love doing and be the best at it. Just not darts. You need to give up on that.'

'I might find LOVE, but it won't be like how it is with Allie and Noah,' I said.

'How do you know? Fuck, I haven't even found love yet and I'm a dinosaur compared to you,' he joked, poking me in the ribs.

Then I said the most embarrassing and honest thing I had ever said to Henry in my whole freakin' life.

'If I could choose to spend forever with someone, I'd choose you.'

Henry had just smiled at me. 'You, too. You're family. I'm not going anywhere. You'll always have me.'

That hadn't been how I meant it at all. But I forgot that because Henry pulled me closer, kissing me softly on my forehead. It wasn't the type of kiss I wanted from him. Not the sort I fantasised of at all but it meant more to me than any one of Wyatt's kisses.

I looked over to where Lilac lay, unconscious, tied up on my bed. Fuck. I was a monster. I really was.

I placed the diary back in the box and went downstairs, planning on making breakfast. I flipped a couple pancakes, checking to see if I had any strawberries and bananas – since that was what Lilac used to like when she was younger with them.

I remembered that moment: seeing her heartbroken and watching her cry and wanting nothing more than to beat the shit out of that snot-nosed punk who'd hurt her. I'd known she'd had a crush on me, but I'd figured in that moment in time she hadn't been mentioning *that.* Lilac liked to pretend to my face that she never saw me as anything other than her big brother – so her coming out with that "forever" comment didn't seem like she was saying she'd want to be Allie to my Noah.

Thirteen-year-old kids didn't really know what "love" was. At least not the romantic kind. I thought she'd been on about *real* love, more real than the sort that flared with lust and faded over time. She had been my family. And I did love her. I still loved her. And I'd fucked everything up.

I'd finished and plated up and went back upstairs. I cracked open my bedroom door. That's when I saw that the bed was empty, and the ties had been discarded on the floor.

'Fuck!' I swore.

I checked the room, did a quick sweep of the house, but she was gone. I rushed out of the house, trying to see if I could spot her.

The sane thing to do in her situation would be to run down the street and get help from someone living on the block – but I might have been missing from her life for eight years, but I knew my Lilac had never gone for the sane option. She'd always been daring.

The *in*sane option would be to try and escape through the woods off the back of my house. It was easy to lose someone there, but it was also seriously easy to get lost, too.

'Lilac you fucking nutter!' I shouted as I delved into the undergrowth. I hadn't even put shoes on.

Fuck, this was a stupid idea. But I couldn't let her hurt herself which she was most likely going to do. It took me twenty minutes and calling on some basic training that had been ingrained into me from the army, but I managed to track her down.

'You escaped! Congrats! And your plan is now…?' I asked her as soon as I spotted her.

Lilac whipped around. Her expression was a mix of annoyance and amazement that I'd been able to find her – or perhaps been able to find her so soon?

'I'm getting the hell out of this town.'

'That's a good sentiment and all, but you're really not.'

'You wanted me gone, well, I'm gone. Someone else can pack up the house. I'm finished here. I've had enough psychotic men to last me a lifetime.'

'When I said I'd protect you, I meant it. But I didn't just mean from Lucas and Trace. I meant from your own insufferable stubbornness. The death tolls are still rising. If you try travelling now, you're exposing yourself to god-knows how many infected people.'

'I'm not staying.'

'Yes. You are.'

I grabbed her by the wrist, but she dug her heels in. My feet were freezing, and I'd probably cut the shit out of them. I didn't have time for this.

Guessing her weight and bracing myself against the load, I swung her up and over my shoulder, grabbing the back of her legs with one hand and bracing her back with the other. Thank fuck I bench pressed her weight regularly or this would have really fucked my body over. More so than the quarantine "training sessions" already were.

'Put me down, you oaf!'

'When we get back inside, sure.'

More curses, more name calling. When she saw my house, she started hitting me really hard on my ass and back. If the bite was any indication, Lilac was definitely not pulling any of her punches. She wanted me to *hurt.*

Mrs Peters ended up seeing me as I walked back into

the house.

'I remember those days,' she said to herself. Fuck knows what Mr Peters got up to back in the day.

Lilac tried to shout at her that I was kidnapping her and holding her against her will, but the woman was ninety-odd and I mowed her lawn in the summer and drove her to church every Sunday since her husband died. She probably thought that Lilac was the senile one.

'Breakfast will be cold,' I said, locking the door behind me.

She slumped in the seat, but still cut into her pancakes. She was stubborn and dumb sometimes, but she also knew when she was beaten. And it wasn't like not eating would hurt *me*. We'd not even gotten to have dinner last night since we'd had the blow-out instead. She must have been starved. I knew I was, and I'd already eaten about ten pancakes whilst I was making hers.

'I just want to go home,' she sounded defeated.

'And I just want to keep you safe.'

'You can't just choose to be the hero in my story after you spent years planning on being the villain.'

I'd never spent *years* planning on hurting her. I'd spent two – three months tops – before I'd told myself to put those plans in the back of my mind and do something productive to help this town rather than waste my efforts on things that would never really happen.

'Life's not a story, though, is it, Texas? And I'm not deluded enough to think that I'm a hero.'

'Good – because you're not. Not in my books.'

'I'm not a villain either. Life doesn't work like that. It's not black and white.'

'So, I was just the murky shade of grey you decided to work with?'

'I've always thought Lilac's a kind of grey,' I joked to her.

'No. You don't get to do that.'

'Do what?'

'That smile, that look. Like you're charming and that everything's fine because you look like some model from a freakin' catalogue and I know how well you can kiss.'

It was the first insight I'd gotten since coming clean that she was still as attracted to me as I was to her.

'Do *this?*' I asked, smiling.

It was a cheap shot, the smile I knew worked since most of the puck bunnies had fallen for it in college when they'd been hanging around the team and had overlooked the guy who mostly sat on the bench.

She threw her fork at me. It hit me in the chest. Hand, feet, back, ass, and now chest. There were currently less and less zones this girl hadn't got a hit on in the last several hours.

'You tied me up – and you're keeping me here against my will. I'm not just going to forget those things because you smile at me, Henry.'

I winced.

'What?'

Since I'd been honest with her about everything, I didn't see a point with stopping now. 'You're the only one who calls me Henry.'

'What are you on about?'

'Everyone else calls me Dawson. I go by Dawson. Mom was the only other person who called me Henry. I think you only ever did because you only hung out with mom. Even when you started school and you heard that everyone called me Dawson, you still kept on calling me Henry. Like I was yours or something.'

Lilac's cheeks blushed red.

'What?'

'When everyone else called you that and I didn't – even the girls you used to hang around with never used your first name… it sort of… felt that way. Like I had a piece of you they didn't.' It was the first time she'd spoken without hatred or anger in her tone. I'd forgotten how much I missed her normal voice.

I moved unconsciously towards her. I didn't realise until we were both standing a foot apart. 'You did have a part of me. We were like family.'

'Until you left,' Lilac said.

'I'm sorry it took your dad dying for you to come back,' I said.

'You're not sorry you wanted to use me in your revenge plot?'

'You know I am. I told you I am.'

'I *was* your family… do you still feel that way?'

'Yes.'

'That's why you want to protect me now?'

How stupid would it be for me to tell her that it had been easy to forget how much she had meant when I'd left. That it was easier for my mind to block out the girl in blonde pigtails who used to follow me around like a shadow and I'd protected all throughout middle school from bullies who wanted to use her dad's successes against her, or boys who were only after one thing.

But now that she was here in front of me, all of those memories had come back. That her simply being here and being Lilac had helped break down every one of those walls I'd put up that came with any fond memories I'd had of the Montgomerys.

'Yes.'

'Is that why you wouldn't sleep with me? Because it would have been like sleeping with your sister?'

'No,' I growled.

'Then why?'

'Because you didn't deserve for me to take advantage of you when I was still lying to you,' I told her honestly.

'You deserved better than that.'

'You're not lying to me anymore. What's your excuse now?'

17

LILAC

I could see the confusion written all over Henry's expression. Hell, my own brain was screaming at me. This was the same man I'd fled from twice in less than seven hours. He had not only planned on kidnapping me in the past, but last night he'd actually gone through with it – though for different reasons.

But as I'd tried to fall asleep last night, after the anger had worn down and I'd exhausted all the swear words I could call him, I'd had enough time to think more about what he'd told me.

I still thought he was sick for thinking up the plan to kidnap me in the first place. I didn't think it was right that he'd kept from me the identity of the people breaking into my house. Or that he had known about the software that could be used to spy on me. But I also didn't hate him with every fibre of my being.

Having slept on it, my first thought had still been to leave. I wanted out of this town and that hadn't changed. If it wasn't for the pandemic, I might have tried again. But the death toll and positive coronavirus cases were still rising. Now that I was sitting, the adrenaline ebbing, Henry's words started to make me see a little bit more sense than: run first, consequences later.

It was the age-old problem of the devil-you-knew. Here, I knew the threat, and I had Henry (potentially) to protect me from it. Out there I had absolutely no control as to whether I would contract the virus and pass it on to others if I travelled back home. In a choice of a battle against humans out for revenge, and a pandemic killing thousands in the US by the week – I knew which one I stood a better chance at fighting.

It might have been a trick to keep me here – after all, if I did test positive for the coronavirus after making my way back to Texas, there was no certainty that I would die like daddy. But as much as I couldn't *trust* Henry, I still knew when he was lying.

I'd known from the first phone call we'd shared that something was wrong. And I'd known that he was keeping *something* from me, and that asshole attitude he had towards me wasn't right. Now that he'd told me the full truth – I could see where the omissions and sly digs had come from.

Henry wasn't lying when he told me he wanted to keep me safe. Neither was he when he said, 'you didn't deserve for me to take advantage of you when I was still lying to you.'

He wouldn't have sex with me whilst he was still keeping secrets. It hadn't been that he had a girlfriend, or that I wasn't attractive enough. Or that what my daddy had done to him and this town was too much for him to get over. It was that *he* didn't feel right putting me in a vulnerable position when he'd not been honest with me.

I didn't know whether it was the adrenaline from the run, the sugar high from the pancakes or simply the fact that I had wanted this man from the moment he'd sent me that topless selfie – but no matter everything that I'd found out these past few days… I still wanted him.

God, I wanted to have sex with that man.

'You're not lying to me anymore. What's your excuse now?'

Before he could respond, I pulled my top over my head. I was still wearing the sexy underwear I'd bought new for him – one of the "errands" I'd run – back when I'd been trying to seduce him before everything had gone so wrong.

'Lilac,' he said my name like it was stuck in his throat, like it pained him. His eyes flittered over my chest, to the swell of my breasts and down my bare stomach, then held my gaze.

'You had an accident yesterday. You've not had much sleep and last night was… a lot.'

'I already know every reason not to.'

I slipped my shoes from my feet and dropped my sweatpants.

'But there's one good reason we *should.*'

'What's that?' he asked, his eyes were staring hard into mine like he was trying to actively hold my gaze so not to be tempted to drop his eyes to… anywhere else.

'Because I want it – and you owe me.'

I wouldn't back down. Not about this. Not after I'd wanted him for so long. I couldn't trust him – not with a lot of things. But I now knew what Darci meant about angry sex. How your body could still be so freakin' turned on for a guy even though your heart couldn't make up its mind whether it wanted to rip apart or burst with love.

Henry still looked hesitant. Like it was tearing him apart to do the right thing.

'It's just sex,' I reminded him.

I unclasped my bra. I slipped out of the straps and let the cups fall down to the floor. Henry moaned; his eyes unable to leave my chest now.

'Just this once,' he said, so quiet like he was telling himself more than me. A promise I didn't want him to keep, but would allow him to make anyway.

Before I could move, Henry rushed me. One second, we were standing a few feet apart, the next his body was pressed against my own. My ass pressed up against the kitchen counter, but only for a moment before I felt his huge hands grab it, pulling me towards him.

He kissed me, hard and deep. Like I was oxygen and he was starved of it. I pulled my hands up to his face until I wound my fingers though his hair: just long enough that I could pull. I kept him close, afraid that he'd break away from our kiss like he had done before and say this was a mistake.

I didn't freakin' care if this was a mistake. I wanted him. I wanted him inside me. My body craved him and after he'd bound me with his ties against my will to his bed, (like I was playing some part of *Fifty Shades* with him!) I was damn well getting a release.

'Lilac, tell me what you want me to do to you.' He stopped kissing enough to speak, but I wouldn't let him move his head away, not with how hard my fingers tugged on his hair.

He kissed me again, his tongue flicking against my own. The more he kissed me, the wetter I could feel my panties get. I had never been this turned on just by kissing before. But it was like my body was experiencing *years* of pent up sexual tension.

Henry moved his hands up my waist, to the underside of my breast until he skimmed my nipple. I gasped at the feather-light contact and he chuckled under his breath. He moved across again, touching the tip of my other nipple as it pebbled under the light pressure. Then, when I wasn't expecting it, when I thought he was moving his hands lower, he pinched it *hard.*

I squeaked, the sharp pain disappearing in a second, but the shock had been enough for me to lose my grip on his hair. He used that advantage to grab my wrists, pinning my hands above my head, using the cabinets fixed to the wall behind me to brace myself.

He kissed me across my neck. The feel of his tongue as he lightly nibbled on my flesh, along with the warm feel of his breath had my body breaking out in goose bumps. His stubble scratched me as he moved and the sensation of that purely masculine feel across my skin had my knees going weak.

Had I ever had *sex* before? Had Callum truly been any good if simply kissing my neck could do so much for me – more than the times Callum had attempted to use his mouth to do *other* things.

Henry had barely touched second base and already I was ready for him. Ready to beg. Ready to do whatever he asked.

With his one free hand he moved back to my breasts. Barely teasing at the nipple, he had me whimpering under his touch.

'I won't do anything you don't want me to do. I have to know you really want this. That you're sure.'

Lord, I wanted this. I wanted him.

'I do. I want this – you,' I whispered.

'You want *this?*' he asked, pinching my hard nipple lightly, then pulling it away.

'Yes.'

'What else do you want?' he asked. He kissed me once more, but only briefly.

His hand had stilled on my ribcage, just below my left breast, not quite touching but tantalisingly close. I realised he was waiting: waiting for me to tell him what I wanted.

But how did I put into words what I wanted him to do to me? I'd never been good at dirty talk. Me and Callum had never spoken much during sex. How did I *phrase* it; the places that needed Henry's touch?

'I want your mouth on me,' I said.

Henry kissed my neck once more, sucking slightly, enough to leave a mark. 'My mouth is on you,' he teased.

I could feel him smile against my skin. He pulled away, his blue eyes flashing with mischief. That sexy smirk he'd always worn for all those other girls I'd seen him with growing up was now for *me.*

'Down there,' I said.

'You want me to lick that perfect pussy of yours?' Clearly dirty talk wasn't a problem for Mr Experienced.

'Yes,' I said.

He moved his hand to the waistband of my panties. 'These will have to come off,' he said.

'Okay.'

Henry fell to his knees in front of me, dropping my hands.

'Keep your hands on the cabinet,' he told me. 'If I do something you *don't* like, put your hands on me and I'll stop.' He looked up at me through those thick lashes any girl would be envious of having. 'Or tell me – if you can manage to speak that is.'

He hooked his thumbs around the edges of my panties on my hips and slowly pulled them down towards my feet. As he did, he kissed along my hipbone, then down to my inner thigh.

Henry grabbed my leg, positioning my calf so it rested on his shoulder. He hovered over my sex, his head not quite in the right place to reach where I so desperately wanted his mouth.

He trailed his fingers back along my leg, first the one hooked over his shoulder, then the one that was keeping me balanced on the floor. Then, when my attention was focused on feeling his hands on me, Henry bent his head down and swiped a lick down my pussy.

'Fuck, you're so wet for me.'

Henry's tongue was firm against my lips, licking then entering me slightly. He teased, alternating between giving my pussy attention to giving my inner thighs, stomach, and hips butterfly kisses. Whenever I felt him near my clit, my hips pushed towards him, trying to force the contact, but that's when he'd pull back up his head and change to kisses. We both knew he was driving me wild.

'Is there something you want?' Henry said, looking up at me.

He placed one hand on my ass, placing the other so it was *just* touching my pussy – though not adding any pressure or movement that would give me pleasure.

'Yes,' I half whispered; half moaned.

'Tell me what you want, Lilac.'

I gulped. His finger twitched slightly – so, so close to my clit. 'I want you on my clit,' I said.

Henry grinned. His thumb brushed over my swollen clitoris. I felt my sex tighten, the feeling reverberating inside me. 'Then you'll probably need to get in a more comfortable position.'

Using my ass to lift me, Henry pulled me up and sat me on the countertop; in the corner so my body was bracketed by the cabinets, his body locking me firmly in place. He was still on his knees, his face now positioned directly in front of my pussy.

'Perfect height, see,' he said, before he went down on me.

I couldn't put into words what he did to me. The sensation of his tongue on my clit and pussy was an intense swell of emotion. I could feel the pressure within me build.

My hands braced themselves on the counter, keeping me upright. I was glad for the corner position he'd put me in because without the walls steadying me, I thought I would faint from the feeling.

Henry's hand held my hip, whilst his other disappeared

between us, under my leg until I felt his finger thrust inside me. His finger within me, hitting that perfect spot, as his tongue worked my clit made my vision darken and all I could feel or think was *Henry, Henry, Henry.*

'Yes,' I said, my voice a hoarse whisper. 'Oh, god. Don't stop.'

Henry listened, continuing to bring me to my peak. His finger pumped inside me at the exact tempo I needed until my climax hit me with wave after wave of pure pleasure. I could feel my inner walls tightening around his fingers as I shuddered under him and he slowed his tempo to match my fading orgasm.

Henry licked his lips. 'Do you still want to fuck?' he asked me. As though I would stop there.

'Yes,' I said, though how I was able to form words I couldn't quite figure out.

Henry returned to his feet, pulling off the black t-shirt he'd been wearing with one hand. He left me for a moment, returning with a gold foil packet and threw it on the side just next to me as he unbuttoned his jeans.

I could already see the swell of his hard cock before his pants had dropped to the ground.

'Is this what you want?' Henry asked again.

He stepped towards me, and out of his jeans. His tight black boxers strained against the size of him.

I nodded. He stepped closer, between my legs. His cock resting on my pussy, one layer of fabric separating us. My clit was still sensitive from my orgasm, and I tried not to squirm under the light pressure of his hot member.

'If you don't want this, Lilac, we don't have to go through with it. At any time, you can tell me to stop and I won't mind.'

I couldn't resist. I grabbed his cock through the boxers, surprising myself at how thick and hard he was. I held as he twitched in my hand, wanting to be free. He groaned, biting his bottom lip. Hard.

'You wouldn't mind?' I teased.

'I would *understand,*' he re-phrased.

'Why do you keep trying to persuade me to not go through with this?'

'I want you to be comfortable with me,' he admitted. 'I don't want you to think you made a mistake afterwards. I want you to know every step of the way you had a choice: and you chose me.'

'I do, Henry,' I said, bringing his face towards me. 'I choose you to *fuck me.*'

At my words, Henry slipped out of his boxers, tearing the foil packet, and sliding the condom over his shaft. I barely had a moment to witness the famous "Dawson-D" as it had been dubbed back in high school before he had plunged inside me.

For all his care about making sure I'd wanted this, Henry didn't meander around. Already soaked, my body accepted him willingly. Balls-deep, Henry filled me in one thrust, almost pulling me from the countertop so my ass was hanging in the air, only his cock and my hands bracing myself on the surface keeping me upright.

'*Fuck,*' he said once he was fully seated within me.

Henry stretched me out in the most delicious way. Though I hadn't had much of a chance to admire, I already knew he was much bigger than Callum – or any vibrator I'd ever had in the past. Longer, wider, bigger, better – he was just *more.* He was everything.

Henry pulled out, almost fully, before slamming back into me. He groaned once more, grabbing one ass cheek, holding my hip as I wrapped my legs around him to make it easier for him to get a better purchase.

'Tell me how you want it, baby,' he said.

'I want you deep,' I told him. 'And I want you to fuck me *hard.*'

I wanted to be taken. I'd had enough mediocre, long-term relationship, a quickie before bed sex. I'd had sex with the nice guy who didn't say things like "fuck" or that he wanted to eat out my perfect pussy. I didn't want the polite, Southern charmer. I wanted the brooding, dark, dangerous man. I wanted the side of Henry that had been kept from me as a child: the side I hadn't been ready for until now.

My crude language seemed to drive him wild, his cute "Texas" corrupted under his hands.

Henry did as I'd ordered, pounding me deep. I had to brace myself harder as his cock pistoned in and out of me. I wanted to reach out and touch the hard muscle of his abs, claw at his perfectly sculpted back, but I couldn't move my hands for fear of falling completely from the side.

I settled for bringing my mouth towards the hard bicep of the arm from the hand that gripped my hip and bit down.

'No biting, wild cat,' he told me, gripping me tighter with the hand I'd already bitten earlier today. 'Unless you want me to stop?'

I groaned, but he soon fucked that complaint right out of me. I could feel a second climax building.

'You're so fucking perfect,' Henry said. 'So. Fucking. Wet,' he said between thrusts.

He must have felt me begin to reach the crescendo of my orgasm as he moved his thumb, flicking it over my clit to push me over the edge.

'Fuck, *Lilac,'* he said. 'I'm going to come.' He said it like both a warning and a question, like he was asking permission from me.

'Yes,' I told him, 'yes.'

Henry came with his whole body, his hands gripping me so hard I felt like they would leave bruises on my thighs where he pulled me to him so his full length was deep inside me as he came.

He didn't leave as he finished, instead he pulled me closer to him, so our chests touched. His heart beat fast and erratically inside his chest, against my soft breasts; my sensitive nipples brushing against his hard pecs. He kissed the top of my head, lightly.

I doubted he remembered, but the first time he'd ever kissed me – before the pandemic and us becoming reacquainted – had been right there on my forehead. In this very house.

I smiled; my body finally satiated. Our lives – this world – might have gotten screwed up since then, but I allowed myself this one moment where everything seemed just *right.*

18

DAWSON

It felt like some stupid cheesy saying you'd find in a *Hallmark* film but being with Lilac just felt right.

After we'd fucked and had a shower together (I'd used the excuse I needed to keep an eye on her, but really I just wanted to prolong the time I had with her naked), we'd both gotten dressed and I'd called Calvin whilst Lilac set up her laptop on the coffee table.

She had a few lectures today. I hadn't realised that she'd still been doing her online classes between packing up her dad's house and babysitting Kasey. She'd be going into her final year this fall – if colleges opened up again. I didn't even know where she'd gotten into. What she'd decided to major in. But I'd been trying so hard *not* to know her and anything about her, it made sense that I wasn't informed about everything that had been going on with her – even when she was living in the same town as me.

'Hey, man. Is Miller still around at your place?' I asked after he'd picked up the phone.

'Yeah, most of the boys, too.'

'They eating you out of house and home yet?'

Calvin chuckled. 'Almost. Mom nearly had a heart

attack when she saw that Graham had gotten into the caramel rolls she'd made for Laney's birthday on Sunday.'

'Fuck,' I couldn't help but laugh. 'Tell her I'll leave some cash behind the register at *Billie's* and she can pick up some extra stuff to make up for it,' I told him.

'Will do.' Calvin paused for a second. 'You just callin' to check on Miller?'

'Nah – partly, but I've got a favour to ask you guys.'

'What is it, coach?'

I'd meant what I said about protecting Lilac, which entailed not letting her out of my sight. She wasn't going back to her dad's house and Willa agreed she should stay with me.

I couldn't bear the thought of leaving her alone in my house. It wasn't that I ever thought Lucas or Trace would be dumb enough to turn up here and take her – if they ever suspected she was with me. It was that I still didn't trust her not to run if she was left alone.

We might have fucked, but I wasn't so deluded I believed sex resolved all the history between us.

As much as I wanted to be able to watch her every second of the day – I had a whole town to think of, not just her. I had responsibilities. And with the lockdown, my job was more important than ever.

'I can't come to practice today,' I told him.

'Your old man legs finally gave out!' Calvin laughed. He'd used enough volume and I heard enough chuckles that I knew he'd been saying it for the effect of his teammates listening in the room.

'Something like that,' I said. 'I've got three sessions this afternoon that I can't cancel on. I was hoping you and the *Horses* would do me a favour and take over?'

'You mean like coach, coach?'

'Yeah. Run the same route we take, only at a slower pace and run a few of the drills with the kids. You can split the three shifts between you or do them all as a team. Could you manage that?'

If the rink was still open, I would have just taken her with me and made her sit in the seats or stand with the moms. But I couldn't expect her to go on the workout regimen I currently had going on.

I'd been so worn out from yesterday's training (and staying up all night with no sleep, probably) I'd hardly been able to stand as I'd fucked Lilac. Not that I was going to let something so insignificant as the inability to *stand* stop me from fucking that girl.

'Sure, coach. No problem.'

'I'm gonna text the parents to let them know to expect you.'

Since it wasn't a formal training session and they were no longer paying for their lessons, it wasn't like me putting the *Nokota Horses* in my place was fucking with some child-protection shit or hiring minors to work for me. It was more a volunteer-work thing. Most of the kids would probably love training with the high school team since they all wanted to be them when they grew up.

'You're not going to work?' Lilac asked me when Calvin'd hung up.

She'd still been on her college website, staring so intently at the screen that I was surprised she'd listened to my conversation.

'Until I've talked to Lucas and Trace, I don't want to let you out of my sight.'

Now that Lilac knew everything, there was nothing stopping me warning them off Lilac for good. Thinking she'd been taken by them was a massive wake up call. I couldn't live with myself if they finally took the next step from just scaring her.

Handling Rick might be a problem. He covered for Lucas because he was family, but he also had a vendetta against the Montgomerys. Lilac's dad had killed both Lucas's dad and older brother when he'd not bothered to listen to the miners' warnings. And after all Montgomery had pulled with his summer blow-outs, turning this town into a sex and drug haven where the sheriff could do shit to stop it… yeah, Rick didn't mind fucking with Lilac at all.

I didn't have a plan to handle it, but I would.

'I'm under house arrest?'

'The whole world's practically under house arrest, Texas. Think of it as practicing some well-reasoned self-isolation.'

Lilac had looked like she was going to grumble, but then a wicked smile played on her lips.

'I'll agree,' she said. 'As long as I get conjugal visits.'

She wanted to go *again?* My cock twitched in response. Yeah, it was up for it. But I knew better than to let a horny Lilac get away with more than she could handle.

Last night her world had been tipped upside down and the two male heroes of her life (okay, hero might be stretching it a bit far for me, but I'd been someone she'd looked up to as a kid) had become "villains" as she'd characterized us.

'Nice try, wild cat,' I said, using the nickname that had appeared to me as she'd bitten me for the second time in as many days during sex. 'But that was a onetime deal because I owed you for last night's "kidnapping".'

She pouted, but shrugged her shoulders like she'd only been kidding, returning to her lecture.

Fuck me if my whole body didn't sag in disappointment that she'd let it go so easily.

The rest of the day, I'd tried tracking down Lucas and Trace. First, I just messaged them asking to talk tonight, but they didn't respond. I hadn't expected them to. They might spend most of their time high, but their brains weren't totally melted. Lucas knew that last call had meant my priorities had changed – and if I wasn't with them, I was against them. Simple as that.

I then called Carolyn asking if I could videocall with Rick. He'd scheduled a time to talk to me. Carolyn hadn't been too pleased that I hadn't given her any information about what I was wanting to chat to the sheriff about.

I wasn't looking forward to that conversation, but it had to happen.

Whilst I waited for Rick to get back to me, I scrolled through the *WhatsApp* chats to see how the kids had taken the *Nokota Horses* training sessions.

Calvin had set the kids the task to do at home. Some "level up" challenge he said he thought would be "funny af". Already a couple of kids from the earlier sessions had sent in their responses.

My favourite was Arnie and Shane jumping over varying heights of toilet rolls since it ended with Viv screaming that she wasn't going to be able to return them since they'd opened all the packets. At least now I knew who the TP hoarder of the town was in case we ever ran out.

'What are you chuckling to yourself about?' Lilac asked me, peering over my shoulder.

She had on a knitted burgundy jumper that slipped off the side of her shoulder, and some black leggings that perfectly hugged her ass. I actively thought about anything but her naked body, which was imprinted in my mind. It was difficult. Though she'd used my shower gel and shampoo, she still had that soft scent of coconuts.

'A few of the kids from my class on this… app,' I finished lamely.

She watched the video as it replayed. 'You don't have *TikTok?*' she asked me.

'You *do?*'

Lilac passed me over her own phone. She logged into her account using her *Twitter* sign in.

A video feed pulled up first, but she swapped to her profile where I saw a gallery filled with past-Lilacs and a girl I recognised as Darci from her lock screen.

I clicked on a random video. A song I didn't recognise played in the background whilst the video remained blurred. After a few seconds, the video focused and zoomed in onto her eye. From the detail her camera picked up, I could see each individual fleck of gold in her iris.

I clicked on another. This one was her and Darci. A dance song played whilst Lilac and Darci posed in different positions, their top changing in colour as each beat of the song changed until at the last moment it swapped to slow motion as they both flipped back their hair and winked at the camera. They were hot, sure, but I couldn't see why they'd do it. Unless the purpose was simply to look hot?

'What's the point of this?'

Lilac just rolled her eyes at me. 'There's not a *point.* It's just fun.'

I shook my head. I watched several more videos of her. They were only short, so it didn't take long, but each one made me see more of the Lilac I'd missed out on whilst we'd both been outside Grand Yutu.

I didn't hate her for the ordinary life she'd lived whilst I'd been in the army, or this town had been suffering because of her dad. Not like Lucas and Trace would. Not like I'd done when she'd first come to town.

Instead, I realised how ridiculous all that hatred I'd directed towards her had been. Lilac wasn't malicious. She hadn't played a part in what had happened to this town. Lilac wasn't like Helen – and had seemed genuinely shocked and upset to learn about her parents' part in my parents' deaths. She had been unaware, sure, but how had

I been able to justify my hate for her when I'd been completely unaware of what was going on with my mom, too?

My phone began to ring, and I saw Rick's name on the caller ID. 'I've gotta take this,' I said, passing her phone back.

Lilac just nodded as I left the room.

The conversation didn't last long and none of it was what I wanted to hear. At one point I raised my voice so much I'd ended up having to go outside. I didn't want Lilac to overhear me.

Rick told me he had no idea where Lucas and Trace were, but they were free men and he wasn't going to restrict them just because "Montgomery's princess was a little uncomfortable". I told him I didn't want Lucas messing with her anymore and he'd basically told me to go fuck myself.

I'd even warned him that the shit his cousin was planning didn't stop at breaking a few windows and directing his own *Paranormal Activity*. That we'd planned abduction, blackmail – a whole bunch of shit, and that it was likely that they'd still try and go through with it.

Rick pointed out that Montgomery was dead: there was no one to blackmail anymore. But that didn't mean shit and we both knew it. Lilac had inherited her dad's money. Lucas might still plan on going through with the abduction part if just to threaten her to transfer the money directly. And it wasn't like Lucas and Trace had ever seemed put off at the idea of being alone with her in a dark room.

Without Rick on my side, and with the town still freezing her out, it didn't bode well for me being able to stop Lucas and Trace unless I physically watched her day and night. I'd already missed todays sessions; would the *Horses* be able to cover for me until I found Lucas myself?

Lucas had Trace and a couple buddies around town, but

he wasn't exactly US forces. He barely had any muscle though he was a fast fucker and you could never be sure whether he was packing or not. Tracking him down and putting the fear of god in him man-to-man might be the only way I'd put him off his Lilac plans since the regular law wasn't going to cut it here.

Lilac knocked on the kitchen window, motioning to the cup of coffee she'd made me and was leaving on the side for me. She smiled. Like a few hours ago she hadn't been screaming and kicking me as I slung her over my shoulder – and I had the bruises to prove it.

Fuck. I was being selfish keeping her here. I could pretend that she was safer where I could keep an eye on her, and she didn't have to travel and risk exposure. But she would be far safer back in Texas with her mom. There was *possibly* a risk she could contract corona going home – but Lucas and Trace were a certainty. They *would* come looking for her.

Why have you been fighting so hard to keep her here? I asked myself.

I paced whilst I thought about the answer to that million-dollar question. Take me back a month and I couldn't wait for her to leave – take Lucas' broken window warning and never come back.

But now that there were no more secrets between us, or ridiculous misplaced hatred, it was that "never come back" that haunted me. As soon as Lilac left Grand Yutu, she'd never return. Without her dad here, there'd be no reason for her to make the trip to a town that despised her, and I'd never see her again.

Before the wall that had separated my memories of our childhood together, that hadn't meant anything to me. But now I remembered everything – and it *hurt* to think about what I would be losing this time. Just like it had hurt so much leaving when I was eighteen that I'd had to close off the part of my mind that Lilac and everything I loved about Grand Yutu belonged to.

If Lilac left now, it would be like losing the last part of my family. I wanted her to stay. I wanted to get to know this adult-Lilac who was both exactly the same sweet girl I'd loved and this new sexy woman I couldn't help but dream of.

But Lilac couldn't stay here. For one, she didn't belong. Lilac was a big city Southern girl who was born to live in the sun. She had college to get back to. A life. Friends. Family. Grand Yutu was the middle of butt-fuck nowhere.

The only reason she was staying was because I was selfishly forcing her to. Mom's note came back to me.

I thought that the worst day of my life was when you told me you'd decided to enlist. I couldn't understand how you wanted out of this town that loved you so badly that much that you would risk the life I'd prayed so hard to bring into this world.

Your dad was the one who convinced me you were doing the right thing and that I shouldn't be selfish. I had chosen my life here. And it was up to you to choose what you wanted to do with yourself.

Just like mom had to let me go and make my own choice, I had to take my dad's advice and let Lilac live her own life and make her own choices.

'I think you should go back to your mom's in Texas,' I told her as I came back into the house.

She was sat on the couch in the living room with her coffee, looking through… old newspaper articles? I couldn't quite see her laptop screen from where I was.

I let the words leave my mouth before I thought about them. If I thought, then I'd convince myself not to say them and to keep her around.

'What?'

Lilac's eyebrows met in the middle as she screwed up

her face. It was easy to see her emotions play across her expression. It wasn't like it took an expert to figure she'd be confused by my total 180.

I'd tied her to the bed last night to stop her from running off, and I'd tracked her down when she'd escaped this morning. Now I was telling her she should leave? That made complete sense.

'You're safer in Texas than here. For you to be safe here, I'd have to watch you 24/7 to make sure that Lucas doesn't try anything. He wouldn't with me around, but Rick's not exactly warning him off the idea and he'd take the opportunity to get to you as soon as it arises.'

'You *literally* told me I'm not going anywhere-' Lilac started.

'I didn't want you driving off in the middle of the night when you were upset or running off in town where Lucas could get to you. You didn't even take your *stuff* with you either time you attempted your little escape. This wouldn't be you running off this time.

'It'd be me driving you to the airport and you getting on a plane and going home like a normal person. I'll even give you one of the masks a mom of a kid I coach made me,' I said, smiling. I was trying to make light of the idea like it wasn't killing me to think about her going.

You don't mean it. You want her to stay. I told my brain to fuck right off.

'I'll need to call my mom,' Lilac said.

I nodded my head, picking up the coffee and taking a tentative sip. She made it exactly how I used to like it when I was eighteen. One sugar and a splash of milk. I'd started taking it black when I got into my twenties. I didn't even know how she took hers. Lilac had thought coffee was disgusting at thirteen and the only hot drink she'd ever had was hot chocolate.

If she stayed, you'd get to know how she takes her

coffee. You'd get to know a whole lot more, too.

Lilac called her mom, going through the pleasantries.

I tried to keep my face neutral as I heard Helen's voice on the other end of the line. The hate I felt for my mom's ex-best friend hadn't gone away. When she'd called me asking to check on Lilac, I'd punched the wall next to the landline. I was handling hearing her a little better now – if only for the sake of her daughter.

Lilac didn't mention what was going on in town. From the way that she spoke, it was becoming clearer and clearer that Lilac hadn't mentioned *anything* to her mom. Not the break in, the "haunting", the towns' people refusing her custom.

If Lucas really had gotten to her last night instead of just some mix-up, Lilac's disappearance would have come completely out of nowhere for Helen. Outside of Grand Yutu, no one would know what happened to her. And since the Montgomery name made her the most hated person in the town, anyone coming looking wouldn't have been given any shred of help to discover her.

Lilac mm-hmmed as her mom told her about the schools remaining closed for the rest of the year; the new executive order that had just been unveiled, outlining the plans to re-open the state and the new safety procedures they were putting in place to make sure that it didn't contribute to a spike in coronavirus cases.

'Sweetie, I still think you're safer where you are,' Helen told her. 'I haven't seen *any* corona cases in Grand Yutu, but Texas is still pretty high in the figures.'

'Mama, they're not going to have figures for Grand Yutu. It's hardly on the map. North Dakota as a whole is practically as bad as Texas.'

'Lilac, don't exaggerate now,' Helen told her. 'And we both know that Grand Yutu is in a bubble, not Dakota.'

'I've finished packing up daddy's house-' Lilac started.

Her mom interrupted her. More prattle about how she was safe inside the bubble; that she could use this time as a break from the world. Use this isolation to catch up with reading or – I couldn't even help the laugh that escaped when Helen mentioned catching up with *me* as something Lilac could do. Reminding Lilac how much she used to love spending time with me.

Lilac hung up the phone.

'I guess I'm stuck here,' Lilac said.

She didn't sound angry. Or upset. Her tone sounded… certain. Not resigned, but almost pleased.

'You didn't tell your mom what's been going on,' I said.

'There's a *pandemic* "going on",' Lilac said. 'Phil has enough stress as it is calming mama down now…' Lilac just shook her head at me. 'It's not as if she could help if she knew. It makes no difference to her.'

Lilac's words reminded me of mom and how she'd tried to protect me from the truth, too.

'Besides, I can do more good here.'

'What are you on about, Texas?'

'I can't leave in good conscience knowing how much *wrong* daddy has done to this town. Everyone here might not want me sticking around, but I want to try and fix what he did. They hold me responsible – you held me responsible – for daddy's actions. Shouldn't I try and fix that?'

'I might never have gone through with the shit I planned last year, but Lucas isn't like me, Lilac. He doesn't have our history stopping him from enacting any of those fucked up revenge fantasies.'

'Because they haven't gotten justice for their families!'

I forgot how infuriating that "walk in their shoes" shit Lilac always pulled. That girl clearly hadn't grown out of her empathic nature. Only it hadn't been in the face of abduction and blackmail back when she'd been a kid and had been dealing with bitchy girls at school.

'I've already contacted Lisa – daddy's PA – and she says she might be able to help me get the families' money back. But she's not got all the information and says it would be easier for me to find all the stuff she needs if I stayed in town.'

I could see the determined set of Lilac's jaw. She wasn't going to back down from this. Not now that she had a plan to help.

It had never crossed my mind that Lilac finding out about what her dad had done to Grand Yutu would make her want to *do* something about it.

Lilac's mom had told her to stay here. And she had a plan. There was no way I was going to be able to convince her to leave (*not that you want her to go,* that little voice reminded me).

If Lilac was staying, that meant it would become my job to look after her whilst she sought out justice for the fifteen's families. I couldn't let Lucas and Trace get to her. Not when I'd been the one to put her on their radar in the first place. For however long that was, I was going to stick to her like glue. Before she left me and this town for good.

19

LILAC

My graduation was set for a couple of weeks with zero pomp or circumstance. Like taking a videocall from your friend after a night out, I would join in the livestream and I would end the call a graduate.

When I'd told daddy I planned on graduating in three years instead of four he'd told me it was ambitious, but could be done, and he wouldn't expect any less from his daughter. I'd always been fairly smart at school. College had come more natural to me than other students. I'd thought that the sooner I could get out of education, the sooner I could start living in the real world and making a difference.

Daddy had never had a college education. Not like mama. He'd made his millions with a high school diploma, a keen sense of business and a whole lot of luck. I didn't have that same aptitude for business so part of me graduating early had been trying to prove that I was good in other areas. That I was as smart as him.

Now, he wasn't here to see it – and I'd crammed a four-year education down to three for nothing. For neither a man who was worth it, nor a ceremony that would do my endless hours of anxiety, stress, panic, and sleepless nights justice.

Class of 2020. There would never be a person in the world who didn't know what that meant. The year the world turned upside down. It was par for the course for Generation Z at this point. I'd started pre-school the year of 9/11. My senior year when Trump was elected. And now my final moments of "adolescence", before I stepped out into the wide world, had welcomed me with a pandemic and a failing economy.

Darci was planning on dressing up for the occasion, as were most of the seniors from my sorority. Their parents were throwing them a house party, though it would only be them attending with lockdown measures still in place. Of those graduating, there was only me and Georgia who didn't feel like joining the preparations for the twisted joke that was the end to a $90,000 education.

There would be no walk across the stage, no pictures on the lawn. Just the guest speaker for our virtual commencement ceremony on our various devices, miles away from the college we had never even properly said goodbye to.

Georgia was the one sorority sister from our house who didn't come from a well-off family. Her mama, whenever she'd spoken about her, had reminded me of Edie before Mr Lawson had started making a living wage with the mine.

Georgia, having moved back home, had to share her room with her two sisters who were still at high school. She hadn't been employed long enough to file for unemployment, and she'd once again become a "dependent". She said it was like being seventeen again, only her sisters were her "age" now.

Her summer internship programme had been cancelled and whilst I'd been clearing out daddy's house, she'd been searching for job after job with no success.

Georgia reminded me that it wasn't simply people like those in Grand Yutu who were suffering now. Most graduates made up a large portion of the retail and service sector after leaving college – but where was leisure and hospitality now? And what happened with all those kids with the schools shut, like Georgia's sisters?

Willa said Henry started his job coaching as an attempt to keep the kids off the street now that the rec centre and cinema had shut down and there weren't many places for kids to hangout after school. Only so many were interested in the gym or ice hockey, but it had been better than the nothing available to them before. Still, he had struggled to keep kids off the streets when the athletics centre had been open on extended hours – now that it was shut along with most of the businesses in this small town…

Mama told me my empathy was both a blessing and a curse. The ability to put myself in the shoes of other people and feel their suffering as my own meant I was in the unique position to be able to look at this world with unselfish eyes.

But *empathy* didn't help people. In itself it could be a selfish thing, taking upon that pain for yourself, when the hardships were one you could walk away from. And that is where the "curse" came in. Because I found it difficult to walk away when I saw suffering. I wanted to be the one to fix things.

I couldn't help Georgia. I couldn't solve this pandemic and all the crises that came with it. Instead, I focused all my attentions on something that I could help: cleaning up the mess daddy had left behind.

'Are you helping Dawson with the centre's finances or something?' Willa asked as she walked in through the front door, Kasey not far behind on her heels screaming: *Into the Unknown!*

I'd given Willa one of daddy's smart-TVs and loaded it with a *Netflix* and *Disney+* package for Kasey. Willa had told me she'd since been watching *Frozen 2* on repeat. As the cinema had been shut when it came out last year, she'd not had a chance to watch it.

'No, this is all the paperwork left behind from Edie's lawsuit against Montgomery Mines and the details I could get from the other families.'

She knew briefly that I wanted to help out the families daddy had sued, but we'd not really spoken much about it. Mostly, she'd just demanded details about me not only attempting to run from Dawson again, but that I'd slept with him, too in the short amount of time that she'd not been speaking to me.

24 hours of Willa silence to punish me for believing she'd known about the kidnapping plot. And then – back to normal. As though she'd never been cross at all. I'd forgotten how weird she could be sometimes.

Willa was concerned I was having a break down or that the car accident I'd been in had given me concussion. Or that Henry had a magic penis since I'd gone from crashing my car on a wild getaway to settling in to stay for as long as it took to get justice for the fifteen and their families.

'This is a lot of shit,' Willa said, briefly picking up a few sheets, sifting through them before returning them to the kitchen table I was working at.

'I know. I think I'm probably going to have to hire Lisa to help me sort through everything.'

'Lisa being…?'

'Daddy's PA.'

'Do you think that's a good idea?' Willa asked me.

'What do you mean?'

'You're trying to help, aren't you? This Lisa chick worked for your dad who basically bent these people over a table and fucked them in the ass.'

I winced. But it was true.

Lisa hadn't sounded surprised when I told her about the lawsuits from Grand Yutu and the fifteen's families. She *had* seemed shocked that I was planning on giving them the money back. Until she recalled that I wasn't daddy and money wasn't everything to me like honesty and basic human decency was.

'Sorry, but you know what I mean. Not to continue the crude imagery or anything, but his PA would have basically been the one to hand him the lube. Do you really think she'll be much help in cleaning up the mess left behind? She was loyal to him and still works for the company.'

'A company I, apparently, inherited – if that's what this list means at least.'

Daddy's will reading hadn't been as comprehensive as it could have been considering the rushed job we'd had sorting things out in the midst of the coronavirus outbreak. I'd gotten the bare details that I'd inherited his fortune and a large collection of properties and land daddy had owned. But I'd been mostly told that the properties themselves, if businesses, were self-sufficient with on-site managers and staff that didn't require my input – unless I saw a need to change direction in the future.

Daddy's shares in his business in Washington had been given to me, also. At the time, a lot of his business partners had offered to buy me out of the company. I'd hesitantly accepted knowing absolutely nothing about his business. Knowing that his partners would run things better than I ever could, I'd believed I could use the money I got from his shares and donate it to a coronavirus charity rather than just having the money sit in my bank account, accumulating interest I didn't need.

Now I knew exactly the type of men that "business" hired, I was glad to be apart from it, even if part of me wondered whether I would have been able to change the culture of the company if I'd remained hold of daddy's portion of the company.

But his businesses here in North Dakota had solely been in daddy's name. There had been no one vying for their complete ownership. From Montgomery Mines, to the Whistling Crest Resort (the cabins on Miner's Mount both the Elm and Ash "villages") and a few other small-town businesses. I didn't know much about the other businesses – either the location or what they sold/provided, like the Blue Night Club) since they'd all been purchased the years after I'd moved to Texas.

'Shit. You own the cabins?'

'And the mine and a bunch of other properties.'

'But the mine's shut down.'

'But daddy still owned the land. It's why he was able to expand his "resort". Lisa said there was planning for it to expand further before… well, I assume before the town ran him out.'

Willa's face, though heavily made-up, seemed to dim slightly, as though she were thinking about what it would have been like if daddy and his business friends hadn't left the town but had instead come back and claimed more of Grand Yutu for its own.

'Mommy! Here's how we need to do things,' Kasey said, with her hands on her hips. She'd been entertaining herself up until this point, watching something on her *iPad* her meemaw had gotten her for Christmas. Now that the episode was finished her entire attention was on us.

'You be Honeymaren, Lilac is Elsa and I'm Anna. Where's Dawson?' Kasey suddenly frowned as though she realised there was a flaw in her plan.

'He's upstairs.'

'Good.'

'He's not coaching?' Willa asked.

'No. He's taken another day off. He won't leave the house since Lucas and Trace are missing.'

'He won't leave the *house?*'

'Why do you think I asked you to come here rather than meet you at your place?' I asked. 'I'm not allowed out of his sight.'

'I don't see him around *now,'* she said.

'He left literally as he saw your mama drop you and Kasey off to give me "privacy".' I groaned in frustration.

The younger me had been used to Henry's protective nature. I might have grown up as his shadow, but he'd grown up thinking of himself as my armour.

It was as though since he'd opened up to me about everything, he'd taken back on that old role. Which not only meant going back to thinking of me as his little sister (which is not at all creepy and screwed up after we'd had mind blowing sex yesterday) but resuming his old role. Only now he had something he *literally* had to protect me from.

Part of me wondered whether his worry about Trace and Lucas was disproportionate. I'd been freaked out, angry, scared, confused – you name it, when Henry admitted to his plan to hold me for ransom. But the more time I had to calm down, the more I saw it from his perspective. And I knew as much as he'd plotted those things, he was right that he'd never actively sought me out to put the plans into motion. It had simply been his dark and twisted way of coping.

Wasn't that the same for Lucas and Trace? Hadn't they *all* fantasised about doing things they never could just to dream of a world where they could mete out justice of their own?

Then again, Henry had only shown his anger towards me when I came to town through his bitter treatment of me and snide comments. His friends had turned into dark vigilantes. They'd broken into my house, spied on me through daddy's surveillance system and toyed with me: making me believe that I was being haunted by my dead father.

Henry was convinced that was all a preamble to a larger plan. He didn't believe they would stop until they had justice for their families and the money that was rightfully theirs.

With them currently missing, Henry believed that meant they were biding their time until they could follow through with whatever plan they had – not wanting Henry to catch them before they'd had a chance.

Reluctantly, I'd agreed to his house-arrest. I didn't want to admit to him that I felt safer now I was no longer alone, isolated in the Manor where the silence and loneliness had been oppressive, always making me believe that there was someone out there watching me. Waiting. Which there had been.

'Dawson!' Willa cried from the kitchen. 'Get your sexy butt down here.'

Henry appeared a moment later. He was in grey sweatpants and his old high school hockey jersey. He'd filled out a lot since then, so it was tighter on his chest and biceps, as if he was already wearing his shoulder pads under there.

'What's up?'

'You're not coaching.'

'The centre's closed,' he said. He opened the fridge and poured himself some orange juice. 'Juice, Cee?'

Kasey nodded up and down vigorously.

'A *quarter* of a cup,' Willa said. Kacey got seriously hyper from juice. 'What about your training sessions?'

'The *Horses* are running them for me this week.'

'This *week?*' Willa raised an eyebrow. 'You're focusing on your other jobs about town then?'

'No.'

'What, pray tell, are you doing with all your spare time?' She had on that strict schoolmarm voice which was freaky coming from a woman in tight pleather leggings, six-inch heels and a ripped grey top which showed her black bra through the holes.

'Babysitting,' Henry said.

'Woo!' Kasey said, thinking the "baby" he was sitting was her. 'Oh, Kristoff, you're perfect!' she leapt up and he caught her in a practised move, with one arm keeping the glass he'd just poured steady.

'Now you see my urgency with this,' I told her, gesturing to the stack of papers. 'The sooner I can get through all this and give the families justice, the sooner Henry can get off guard duty.'

'How simple will that be?'

'Not as simple as I hoped, but not impossible.' I'd only been working on it for a day, after all.

'The town's not going to be any more sympathetic to our girl if they realise she's the reason you've quit coaching and are no longer in "office",' she said, referring to Henry's un-official status as Grand Yutu's mayor.

'We're in lockdown,' Henry said.

He was still holding Kasey up in the air who was using his shoulders as a little runway for her Olaf toy, bopping him on the head with his carrot nose. When she'd put down her *iPad*, she'd exchanged it for Olaf from the backpack Willa carried round with her of "Kasey supplies".

'And I'm working from home.'

His phone buzzed a couple times in his pocket as if to prove him right. He'd claimed the coffee table as his "office", plugging in his ancient laptop and notepad.

I'd originally been working there, but when he'd seen this morning how many boxes of paperwork I was working through (the papers Edie had saved from the lawsuits) as well as using my *iPad*, *Mac* and phone to communicate with Lisa and search through the online files she'd been able to send me, he'd offered me the kitchen table.

Lisa was working from home like Henry claimed to be doing. She was already, technically, still working for me in the capacity of handing the selling of daddy's apartment in Washington – and I'd added the Manor to that list, telling her I'd boxed and labelled where the contents needed to be sent to. Getting her to work for me in helping me sort through the crockpot of legal jargon had been as simple as asking and sending her another monthly paycheque.

Since the lawsuits had officially been closed, all I was looking to do was find the correct figures of what the families had paid in legal fees for the two lawsuits; the sum they'd requested as compensation from the suit for company negligence; and the amounts daddy had taken from them in the second suit.

Once I had those figures, I planned on giving them a lump sum of the total owed to them. Or a monthly payment plan if that was better – I didn't know how tax would affect that. I was going to hire an impartial advisor when I'd finally got the figures and see how best to proceed.

I was focusing all my efforts in fixing *that* issue first with the hopes that once the families had been given justice, Lucas and Trace would have no reason to come after me anymore. Then I'd focus on the rest of the mine's employees and what they'd lost when daddy had shut down.

'Lilac doesn't need guarding when she's with me,' Willa said. 'You don't have to "work from home",' she put on Henry's low voice, 'right now.'

'I feel better knowing she's close by,' Henry said. Then he quickly added, 'it's easier to make sure she's safe that way. And that you and Kacey aren't in any danger of being caught in the crosshairs.'

'Fucks' sake,' Willa said, throwing her hands up in the air. 'Can't you just find Lucas already and tell him to cut the shit? She's gonna give him his fucking money back. All he has to do is sit on his ass and wait for the cheque.'

I already knew that Henry had been working on doing just that. Yesterday, whatever call he'd been taking about finding Lucas hadn't gone well. He'd not had much luck today, either. I knew part of him wanted to go out there and find Lucas himself, but that would mean leaving me and he was adamant he wasn't letting me out of his sight until I finished my work here and left town.

His presence made me feel the urgency more than the threat of Lucas did. A need to hurry sorting things out for the fifteen's families so Henry's life could get back to normal once I'd left town.

A small fraction of myself had been glad when Willa had arrived, and Henry had gone upstairs because it had meant I no longer felt his pressing gaze.

Even after everything he'd admitted to me about using me to blackmail daddy, his presence drew me in. I wanted to spend more time with him. Talk to him. Be like how we used to – but with the added bonus of being grown up now. Not that that was what he was wanting me to think, I knew.

Henry wanted me gone. It's why he'd practically thrown me on a plane back to Texas. He was only tolerating me now because mama had told me to stay here and I was working on helping out the people of the town he loved so much. But as soon as this job was done, he'd send me on my way.

'Justice isn't as simple as giving them money,' Henry said, scrubbing his hand over his stubble-scruff in frustration. 'Outside Grand Yutu, Montgomery is still seen as the hero who saved this town and a great boss who did everything and anything for his employees.

'Most of the families would accept the money as what

was already due to them. It's what Lilac *should* be doing with that money since it's theirs already, taken from them unfairly. That doesn't make Montgomery pay for what he did. It just rights a different wrong altogether.'

'The fucker's dead,' Willa said. 'He'll be paying in hell.'

I think I must have let out a squeak or some sort of sound as both Henry and Willa turned towards me.

'Sorry,' Willa apologised for the second time.

I nodded. 'No, I know what daddy did was wrong and you and the town have every reason to hate him. It's just… he's still my daddy. It's difficult to… hate him and hear him be spoken about like…' I trailed off.

I'd read from his own words in his journals the exact sort of man he was when there was no audience. He'd loved me, I knew that. And he'd loved mama. But the ability to love and show you cared for a few people didn't make you an overall good person. My daddy had done a lot of bad in this world, more so than good.

'If you're saying Lucas isn't going to stop coming after her until he's gotten true "justice" then that means she's never going to be safe here,' Willa said. 'You're not just going to be working from home for the next week, but until she leaves Grand Yutu for good.'

'Then I guess I better get back to work,' I said.

*

As I worked on getting the money back to the miners' families, I continued to read daddy's journals. Henry's words about daddy's legacy and image played on my mind.

The families had been taken to court for slander of Montgomery Mines and daddy's good name. There were newspaper articles from all the way over in Washington, not only in North Dakota, which dragged the miners through the mud – laying the blame of the collapse on *them.* Saying that the families had been more concerned with making a dime and suing daddy than grieving for their loved ones. I could understand – especially with what daddy had done to the town *after* these lawsuits – why simply getting money back wasn't enough.

I hoped that perhaps I would be able to use daddy's journals to clear the families' names. Montgomery Mines was mine now, and daddy's shares had been sold in his Washington company so I didn't fear much backlash from people concerned that daddy's true reputation coming out might damage their business.

If I managed to use direct quotes from daddy's journals, as well as testimonies from the families about what had truly happened here and sold them to the media – would that be enough "justice"? For the world to know daddy's mistakes and that innocent men had died for them.

I felt sick each time I thought about it. It was hard for me to reconcile my daddy with the man this town spoke about and the entries in his journal.

Thinking of Edie made me push through. She had lost everything staying loyal to my family. She had rather kill herself over the guilt over whatever secret she had been keeping for mama than hurt me. No amount of pain inflicted upon myself in helping this town she loved so much could ever repay the loyalty and love Edie had shown me throughout my whole life.

On the fourth day staying over at Henry's house, I'd found the note Edie had left him. It was still in his bedroom, kept in the draw by his bedside table.

I cried as I read the last words she'd left for her son. Henry had told me she was depressed; he'd found anti-depressants when he'd been clearing out the master bedroom after her death. But she didn't *sound* depressed throughout most of the letter. How did one *sound* depressed, anyway?

Edie started out the letter nostalgic – remembering coming to the town to the first time, Henry's birth and watching him grow up. Then there had been a decided shift in the middle of the note. Her pen had changed, as though she'd stopped writing and come back to the note later on.

Her writing was more hurried in the second portion – trying to get the feeling out onto the page. Some words seemed shaky, like her hand hadn't been steady when she wrote it. I could almost see the frantic, desperate sadness that filled her just by looking at the words on the page, if not by her words.

"Helen's secret".

"I could never do it to Lilac."

The words shouted out at me more than anything else. I couldn't imagine anything that mama wanted hidden from me so badly that her best friend believed it was the reason daddy had left this town in ruins – and would rather die than confess.

People with depression didn't often see things the way they were. Black and white and hyperbolic thinking were routine symptoms. Seeing things as either good or bad – and taking a bad event out of proportion, feeling like the end of the world, rather than being able to separate those feelings rationally from the facts.

Perhaps in the end what had seemed like a small secret had then *amounted* to something that seemed worse. Yet, the town *had* been ruined. Mama *had* left daddy behind. And Edie's husband and fourteen other men had died.

Was I just trying to downplay whatever this "secret" was so I could be left with one parent who wasn't the cause of so much pain?

I'd asked Henry if he had any idea what mama's secret was, but all he'd had to go on was the same letter. He'd never considered calling mama up to ask her.

Since he'd gotten over his dark period, Henry had preferred to simply ignore the existence of any of the Montgomerys. Pretending we were simply a nightmare this town had dreamt up and couldn't hurt them as long as we weren't thought about.

I didn't have any such compunctions about it. I couldn't find anything in daddy's journal to do with mama's "secret" – but I could have missed hints towards it as I had no idea what it was. That left the simplest option: calling mama and asking her.

I saved it for a day when Kasey was coming over. When I babysat, Henry would play with Kasey with me between working online until it got to her naptime. Then, I'd put her to bed upstairs and come down once she'd fallen asleep.

I pretended to be hassled this morning, waking up late and not having time for a shower so that when Kasey *did* fall asleep, I could tell Henry I was going to wash up. He would stay downstairs and I would have a chance to call mama in private.

Mama hadn't expected the call. I had the shower on to block out the noise of the call if Henry happened to come upstairs. She'd asked what the noise was originally, until I'd played it off as the sound of the rain hitting the windows.

'I've been spending more time with Henry,' I said, edging my way into the conversation.

I could hear mama's smile in her voice as she said, 'you always did love that boy.'

I ignored it. Our parents had both known about my obsessive little crush. It was likely that Henry had, too, though I would have been mortified at the time to know he had.

'Henry told me that before Edie died, she mentioned a secret you'd made her keep. One that broke yours and daddy's marriage.' I didn't mention how Edie believed that it was also what changed daddy and ruined this town.

'You know I never speak about our divorce with you, Lilac,' mama said.

'Yes. Because I was a child at the time, and I wasn't old enough to understand why marriages fell apart, only that my parents didn't love each other anymore. But I'm not a child. And I'm not asking for myself anymore.

'I want to know what this secret was that Edie still felt guilty about keeping it for you years after we'd left. And why she thought that keeping it would protect *me.*'

Mama let out a small sound, as though she'd been about to speak, but her voice had hitched last minute, and the words had choked in her throat.

'You were her best friend for years mama, but you never kept in contact after we moved to Texas. Why is that? *Why?*'

Mama's voice was quiet and sullen when she answered, 'it was what she wanted.'

'What?'

Mama cleared her throat. 'It was what Edie thought was best. After… everything that went on, she couldn't look at me anymore, let alone speak to me. When I took you to Texas, it was with the promise that I'd never come back. Her only regret was that she couldn't see you anymore.'

'Why, mama?'

Mama let out an audible sigh.

'Your daddy and I were never meant to get married. When we met, I was already engaged to a boy your granddaddy had picked out for me. His family owned the second largest ranch to ours, and he came from old money. When I'd finished college, the plan was that I'd come home and marry Jacob.

'Your daddy was the complete opposite to Jacob. But there was a confidence about him that drew me to him. Whilst I was away in college, I fell pregnant with you. We married in secret, knowing your granddaddy would never approve. He didn't. He told me until I divorced my husband, I couldn't come back home or speak to any of my family.

'Daddy never expected Steve to amount to much. Your daddy used to say that he'd be rolling in his grave knowing that my husband earned more than daddy and Jacob's little ranch combined.

'We stayed in Texas until you were five until your daddy found the coal in Miner's Mount. He made his first million in Grand Yutu, but there was never enough to satisfy your daddy. He always felt he had to *prove* that he was worth more than Jacob and my daddy. But it was never good enough. Money didn't buy the old family name or the history.

'The first few years were good. Until they weren't anymore. Your daddy had put all his efforts into Montgomery Mines and Grand Yutu but had mostly forgotten about the businesses he'd been running beforehand. He didn't just want to succeed at *one* thing. He had to have it all. But he was one man. He didn't have time for everything. I was the one who fell through the cracks.

'I was lonely. In the middle of nowhere. I'd not spoken to my family for years. No one in town ever warmed up to me – besides Edie. They knew I didn't belong here. I could hardly step out of the house in autumn it was so cold – impossible in the winter. And we lived in a bubble – so cut off from everywhere.

'I started driving into the city just to feel like I was connected to civilisation in some way.'

Mama paused. I could hear the clink of ice cubes as she took a drink.

'The more distant your daddy got, the more I started to dream about what it would have been like to marry Jacob. We'd been high school sweethearts. I had loved him. Just not with the same passion as your daddy… With your daddy gone, that passion left, too.

'And then there was you. You were so in love with the Dawson boy. My little girl who had all her life ahead of her. With first kisses and the possibility of a husband that didn't love his businesses more than you.

'I didn't know at what point I'd become one more acquisition: one more trophy to prove that he was as good as any old-money chump. Perhaps I'd always been part of that symbol. But I didn't start to feel it until we started therapy and digging into your daddy's inferiority and history.

'I'd suggested therapy hoping it would make your daddy see that I was *lonely*. That I wanted to move back to Texas and have more than just a life trapped inside the bubble. But he didn't care what I wanted… how I *felt.*

'Your daddy was fine as long as everything *appeared* to be working on the outside. He hated couple's therapy because it was going into the mechanics of the relationship: looking under the hood rather than just admiring the paintjob.'

Mama's mechanical terms reminded me of Phil who had a series of classical cars. It made sense his phrases would come into her way of speaking about this time. No doubt she'd spoken about the failings of her first marriage with her new husband and how best to avoid the disappointment of another divorce.

I'd read daddy's own thoughts on therapy. He *had* hated it. But he'd really tried. He wanted the marriage to work. He had wanted mama to be happy with him.

'The year Henry left for service was when the car broke down, as it were. Edie was home more often, less distracted by hockey practice. That's how we were caught.'

'You were… caught.'

Mama's voice sounded strained, like she was trying not

to cry. 'I'd been having an affair with Mike.'

Mama let out a cry. I held my breath, unable to speak.

'Edie found out and she was so upset. Lord, she had every right to be. I didn't know what I was thinking, only that I wanted to be loved and be looked at like Henry looked at you. I wanted to be noticed. Mike noticed me.'

'He was Edie's *husband*,' I said.

I felt sick. Daddy's words from his journal came back to me.

MORALITY. He wants to talk morality. Daddy had been talking about Mike Dawson.

'I know, Lilac, I know. It was only supposed to be a one-time thing, but hockey practice gave us the perfect time to see each other. Both our children and partners were busy… I shouldn't have continued the affair. I know that. But I needed *something* up here.'

'You shouldn't have *started* the affair,' I said, bitterly. My own thoughts turned to how I'd briefly assumed I had become the other woman when I'd kissed Henry. How I'd forced myself on him and he kept trying to push me away. Could a lack of loyalty and faithfulness be genetic?

Mama didn't respond to my statement. Instead, she continued with her story.

'Edie wanted me to come clean to Steve. Mike promised he'd stop seeing me. He was all she had now with Henry gone and he couldn't leave her. But Edie didn't think it was right that Steve was still in the dark. Edie'd had the choice to stay with Mike once she'd found out, but your daddy didn't. We were going to counselling together and he was trying hard to mend the broken pieces of our marriage. Edie couldn't stand the thought that I'd been secretly breaking them further behind his back.

'I was selfish and scared. Not about Steve finding out. For once, it seemed as though I'd found my way out of my marriage and the bubble.

'I think perhaps I'd subconsciously continued the affair and become more reckless in hopes Steve would find out and we'd have to divorce.

'The thing I couldn't bear was you finding out. I didn't want you to know. You were such a beautifully compassionate child; it's what I love most about you. But I couldn't see you taking my side in this. You loved your daddy with your whole heart back then. He was your hero: the man who saved the time warp.

'I couldn't imagine a world where me and your daddy divorced, and he got to keep you. You were fourteen, you would tell the courts who you wanted to live with. Your daddy had the means to provide you with a good life. He was an upstanding citizen. I was the adulterer who her own daughter would turn her back on.

'I told Edie she couldn't tell anyone about the affair – that I'd come clean to Steve, but if anyone found out what had gone on then he would cut you off for good. He'd leave us both penniless. Edie knew how much he loved you. That no matter what I'd done, he'd never hurt you.

'She wouldn't believe me at first, until I told her about Jacob: how I'd been engaged before your daddy and if he found out that I'd been unfaithful, he might wonder whether you were even his. A paternity test would prove that you were Steve's, but I made Edie believe it might not. Steve might still look after you, even if you weren't his, but there was always the chance he'd disown you as a bastard.

'That was more than Edie could abide. It was the thought of hurting you that made her keep the secret. If you found out your daddy wasn't really yours – and we were forced to leave the only life you'd ever known – it would have destroyed you. Edie had always been sensitive about losing a parent. She'd lost her mama to cancer when she was seven. She couldn't do that to you.

'She swore she'd keep it a secret, but that I couldn't stay here with you. I needed to go back to Texas where I belonged, and make sure Steve never found out what I'd done. If I kept you away from Grand Yutu, you might never have to know and would be safe from my mistakes.

'I came clean to Steve about the affair and I told him I wanted a divorce and to take you with me. He fought me at first, but he had his businesses to run. He weighed up the cost of battling me and what it would do to his businesses and chose them over me. Like always.'

Daddy wrote a lot about mama in his first journals, since they were based on their counselling sessions. But he'd never spoken about her like she painted him out to now.

She made a mistake, but I was willing to forget all of that. She's always been the one I've wanted since I first set eyes on her. I don't want anyone else.

He'd known about her affair. But he loved her more than her mistake. He'd gone to counselling because he'd wanted to make it work. Daddy might have screwed up with this town: but he had tried hard not to screw up with her.

Pretty soon, she'll get bored of him like she got bored of anyone who wasn't me.

He'd always thought she'd come back. That she'd chosen him once and that she just needed time away. He hadn't chosen his businesses over her – over us – he'd given her the space he thought she'd needed.

Neither of my parents had any idea what had been going on in the mind of the other.

'I left Texas with you and I never looked back.'

'You never *came* back,' I half whispered. I think my words were left drowned out by the sound of the shower.

Mama never came back to fill in the missing pieces of daddy's picture of the perfect life. And instead, he'd filled that time with more work – more money schemes to prove himself to the woman who married Jacob 2.0.

And Edie had been left with a broken marriage she kept up, so daddy never caught on to the secret that wasn't even a secret at all. But a lie.

Henry had been right. My parents really were responsible for the deaths of his. And no matter how much I tried to give them justice; it wouldn't bring either of them back.

MAY

20

DAWSON

With businesses allowed to open again, the town began to slowly return to normal. There were still guidelines that we had to follow: six feet apart at all times, hand sanitiser practically placed around every square inch of the place, and signs encouraging people to wear masks. But it was better than the complete lockdown we'd had before.

It would be impossible to start up training again with the six feet apart rules, but for once I didn't mind bending them a little. As long as the centre *looked* like it was following all the rules and protocol, I figured we'd be fine.

It wasn't as if any of the moms or kids would report us. And I'd made sure to have a conversation with each of the parents beforehand and anyone not comfortable with it, didn't have to turn up to practice.

I'd divided my classes into smaller groups of only six kids, trying to minimise the amount of people on the ice at any one time. When they were running drills, it was easy to keep them at a distance, staggering them on the ice. It was harder when we got into the play as they needed to get in each other's faces, but it wasn't as if they were in contact for long periods of time. And we'd had no trouble with the training sessions outside the centre, so this didn't seem too much of a stretch.

No one who had a cold or fever was allowed to attend practice, or anyone who had family displaying symptoms. We hadn't had anyone in Grand Yutu test positive for coronavirus, but it was still good to be cautious. For once, the isolation of this little town was finally working in our favour.

The equipment was sanitised after every session and the kids had to follow the guidelines around the centre and try to keep a distance on the ice. They were so fucking happy to be back they probably would have showered in rubbing alcohol just to be allowed to put their skates back on.

Able to coach on the rink again made things easier with Lilac, too. She didn't have to be cooped up in the house, feeling like she was holding me back from my other responsibilities.

I still felt like there was a long way for us to go before I'd gained enough of her trust back to even ask for forgiveness for what I'd once planned – but after the first time we'd had sex, Lilac never brought it up.

Instead, she'd been working these past couple weeks in making things up to *me* and the families who had lost everything thanks to her dad.

She hadn't been able to find much information on the families from her dad's old PA, but I'd given her the names of the miners who had died in the accident along with the names of their families; where they'd used to live back then, where they lived now.

She was hoping to contact them eventually and personally apologise for what her father had done and make amends – but with the town still wanting to run her out of Grand Yutu and Lucas still on a warpath, I'd told her it wasn't the right time. Though I felt fucking guilty as shit since I was potentially lengthening the amount of time those families would be without the money they desperately needed at a time like this.

Lilac told me she wasn't going to give up until she'd payed back every cent owed to them and then some. Lilac had never expected to inherit her dad's money – and she'd told me how sick she felt that for months she'd had the money of all those poor families, and she hadn't even known.

The old me might have been bitter. Hated her for how little money meant to her as a Montgomery that she could have millions and a few extra thousand from each family had meant absolutely nothing to her. But that had all changed now I was no longer looking through hatred-tinted-goggles.

Lilac watched from the same seats the moms took up whilst their kids practiced on the ice. Posters on the walls told spectators to find seats six feet apart. It wasn't a big arena. We had about two hundred seats per side, fifty behind the goals. It left enough room for the moms to spread out – not that they did.

The limited seating made it easier for me to spot if anyone came in through the entrance and keep an eye on Lilac. The gym was in a separate part of the centre and that was the area I was most worried about. Trace and Lucas' friends would likely turn up there, rather than the rink.

Since they'd gone underground, I had been wary of keeping Lilac's whereabouts as secret as possible. The less they knew about where she was staying and how she was spending her time, the better. I wasn't stupid enough to think that they'd give up their vendetta.

When Montgomery had been alive, they'd drowned their loathing and pain in alcohol and drugs knowing no matter how many revenge fantasies they dreamed up, Montgomery was untouchable.

But Lilac was an easy target. Someone they could make

pay for everything that had been done to them. Lilac might have her dad's money, but she didn't have his influence or connections. She was just a young college student, isolated in a town that hated her. *That* they could work with.

Since Lucas and Trace were mostly on the fringes of the town, I didn't worry that the moms would tell them personally that they'd spotted Lilac here. But as Lucas was an Olson, it meant the news would likely get back to him through Rick. The moms loved to gossip about any woman they saw with me, and the sheriffs department tended to be the centre for gossip thanks to the receptionist, Carolyn.

As I skated round, once the kids were set doing drills, I'd check on Lilac. Each time I looked she was either messing around on her phone texting her sorority sisters, reading from her *Kindle*, or watching the kids practice.

Seeing her there in the stands reminded me of when I'd been the one having lessons on the ice and she'd been waiting with my mom for me to finish.

'Who's the lady mom's talking to?' Arnie asked me.

We were doing some one on one work and I'd paired myself with Arnie. He was a quick kid, and agile on the ice unlike most of the other guys in his class, including his older brother. When he got into high school, he'd make the team for sure.

I looked over to where Arnie was gesturing to. Fuck. Viv talking to Lilac wouldn't be good news. Viv had a jealous streak which I'd happened to find out the hard way the first time we'd had sex sometime last year. Didn't help that for most of her kids, I was the only male role model they had. It was difficult to set a girl straight when her babies constantly saw me as their father-figure.

'Lilac.'

'Is she your girl?' Arnie asked.

I hit the puck towards him. It almost sailed past him, but he swooped to catch it.

'No.'

'Do you *want* her to be your girl?' he waggled his eyebrows, skating back in figures of eight.

'Go be a pain in the ass to Andrews, kid,' I told him, calling up Jones who'd been partnered with Andrews.

When practice finished, Viv made sure to come and talk to me, touching me on the arm, on the shoulder. It was like a dog pissing on its territory.

It shouldn't have annoyed me. Lilac wasn't mine. I wasn't hers. We'd had sex once, and even though everything about it had me re-playing each minor detail in my mind – it was just sex. Just like she'd said it would be.

Whatever attraction she'd felt, she'd simply wanted to get it out of her system: probably tick me off her list since I'd been on it for over a decade.

In the time she'd been at my place, there were the odd occasions I thought she was flirting with me, but I could have just been imagining it. That girl could be washing the dishes and I'd think she was coming on to me she was that attractive.

But she'd been nothing more than a friend. Not exactly how we'd used to be as kids, but easy and simple. Like her and Willa. It was more than I deserved. I'd fucked her over in the past and she wouldn't get past that. And after corona cleared up, she'd leave this town and never look back: Willa was right about that.

'Another flavour of the month?' Lilac asked me as I leaned over the barrier to where she was sat.

'Huh?'

She knocked her head back, gesturing to Viv.

'Urgh, yeah, kind of.'

'None of those kids are yours, are they?'

'No,' I spluttered. 'I'm no one's dad.'

'Had to ask,' she said, like me fathering a kid could just be one of the many secrets I'd kept from her.

I knew she was still getting over the lie her mom had told. I thought knowing Helen's secret would help me get over mom's death more, but instead it had just flared up the anger I'd buried inside. I'd managed to keep it from Lilac, but I pitied Lucas and Trace if they tried something now. I needed someone to vent my frustration and anger out to.

My next class wasn't going to show for another twenty minutes. I hopped off the ice and walked over to the lockers we kept the rental skates in. I pulled out a pair her size and threw them down by her feet. They hit the rubber matting, hard.

'Do you think you still remember how to skate?' I asked her.

Lilac looked down at the skates, then back up at me. A smirk lifted right to her eyes. She took off her trainers, pulling on the skates. She didn't really have the right socks, so they would no doubt rub a little, but she would only be in them for a few minutes so the damage shouldn't be too bad.

She awkwardly stood up, wobbling a bit whilst her body got used to resting on the thin blades. I held her hands as she made her way over to the ice. Moving from solid ground to ice had never been a problem for me – I couldn't remember back to a time I'd recognised the difference. But Lilac struggled. If I hadn't been holding onto her arms, she would have fallen flat on her ass.

'Damn,' she said, looking up at me, her eyes wide.

'I've got you,' I said.

'I know,' she said back.

I held her hands, dragging her slightly forward. 'Do you remember the basics? Feet pointing the direction you want to go, don't lean too far forwards or back. Try and keep your feet shoulder width apart.'

Lilac nodded, absorbing the information. She'd never

committed to proper lessons, either in figure skating or hockey. She'd only joined me occasionally after class.

Coach Logan, who'd worked at the centre back then, had given her a few lessons her dad had paid for, but she'd never really shown any interest beyond it being one place she couldn't follow me. She hadn't like being told "no" as much as she did now and so had demanded that she learn to follow me on the ice.

I let go of her hands. She stayed on her feet, so that was something. But she didn't move.

'Remember to keep your knees bent,' I told her.

She exaggeratedly bent her knees, keeping her eyes on me the whole time.

'Push off using your right foot,' I directed. She did, wobbly, but she was moving. 'Push to the side, not back.'

Eventually, she started to get back into the rhythm of things and I held her hand, giving her a bit more speed. I let go at one point, literally skating circles around her.

'You're showing off,' she accused me.

'Yes,' I smiled.

'Stop it, you're distracting me,' but she was laughing as she said it.

I made my circles around her wider, but faster.

'Urgh, you're making me dizzy,' she said. I could see that she was getting wobbly again, so I grabbed her arms stopping her from falling. Immediately she became more stable on her feet – and grabbed me back, pulling herself closer to me.

'Gotchya,' she winked.

'Did you just trick me, Texas?' I asked.

She held tight on my arms. 'Maybe.'

'Tut-tut,' I said, but I didn't let her go.

We were close now, her looking up at me with those big brown eyes.

'Can I tell you a secret?' she asked me.

'Sure.'

'Whenever I watched you skate after a big game, I always wished you'd invite me onto the ice with you and you'd kiss me in front of everyone. That's how I wanted my first kiss to happen. In front of the whole crowd, with you just winning the game.'

Instead, it had been with that punk Wyatt and he'd had the fucking gall to break up with her because of her braces. I'd kissed girls with braces. If you liked the girl, it wasn't that big of a deal. He'd been an asshole… I also shouldn't know any of that since I'd only found out from her diary. But I wasn't fucking admitting to reading her teenage self's thoughts.

'That's a pretty damn dramatic first kiss,' I said.

'I was a dramatic kid. Do you not remember all the school plays I used to try out for? Or how obsessed I was with cheesy romances with all those big romantic gestures?'

'I remember,' I said. She'd gotten her love of eighties rom-coms from my mom, after all. They'd always put one on when Steve and Helen dropped her off for one of their "date nights".

Though I'd told myself us fucking had been a one-time thing and believed that Lilac no longer wanted me the way I wanted her, she gave me that *look.* The one you just know means a girl is waiting for you to kiss them. When I didn't right away, she licked her bottom lip, all whilst looking me in the eyes.

I dare you, her eyes said. *Kiss me like you should have back then.*

I'd never been able to resist a dare. I bridged the gap between us, lifting her slightly off the ice, making sure she was stable as she leaned into me and I leaned down to envelop her face in my hands.

She felt perfect here. On the ice with me, her body

pressed up against my own. She was warm and soft. Summer wrapped up in a person.

I was winter, I knew that: everything about me was cold and hard. I'd weathered the storms. But somehow, I still craved her. Even if we were never meant to be.

If I hadn't been so focused on the kiss, I might have even been stupid enough to compare myself to that dumb snowman in the film Kasey was always watching who was in love with summer, not knowing how badly getting close to the sun would destroy him.

'Coach! Save it for the bedroom!' one of the guys called from the edge of the ice.

It was McAdams, a guy in his sophomore year, who I'd caught making out with his girlfriend in the locker rooms of the gym. I'd probably said the exact same thing to him then and the shame had engrained it into his mind: enough so that I knew that little asshole was enjoying this moment a shit ton right now.

I flipped him off, pulling Lilac back to the edge of the ice. Hoots of laughter followed as the rest of the high school team filed in through the door.

Lilac pulled off her skates whilst the other guys warmed up on the ice.

'So, who's you?' she asked me, looking out over the barrier. She was stood next to me: me on the ice, her on solid ground.

'What do you mean?'

'After you graduated, all anyone could ask when they held try-outs for the *Nokota Horses* was "who's this year's Dawson"?'

I chuckled. I supposed there always was that *one* kid who showed a little bit more potential on the ice – like they belonged more in skates than they did in shoes on the hard ground.

'That one there, Calvin,' I said pointing him out.

He was an amazing D-man. The puck barely made it into the zone before he'd manoeuvre it back out right under the eyes of the opposing team's forward; like they'd never known what hit them.

I watched as she followed Calvin's path on the ice, like she'd used to watch me when she couldn't follow. Her eyes eventually stopped and rested on mine.

'Shouldn't you be coaching, *coach?*' Lilac teased me.

I shook my head at her, and skated to the centre of the ice, getting the boys to line up for me.

The kiss, like it had the first time, clouded my mind, consuming all my thoughts with Lilac. It was worse now, knowing her eyes were on me – not just having her haunt me in my mind.

There were enough under-breath comments about the coach's "girlfriend" that I had them skating suicides for the last twenty minutes of practice. Lilac just laughed when Calvin came up to the plexiglass, breathing hard, and said something to her.

'What'd he say to you?' I asked her.

'Nothing,' she smiled, wickedly. 'Your team's just pleased you're getting lucky after practice. Calvin wanted to offer me some protection since you're probably all out with all those hockey moms.' Lilac twisted a strand of blonde hair between her fingers.

'But I don't have any extra-smalls coach, so you're out of luck.'

'You cheeky fucking-!'

'Don't worry, honey,' Lilac said, pulling out a *Trojan Magnum* from her jacket pocket. 'We're covered.'

Calvin hooted with laugher, the rest of the team joining in. This fucking girl.

'And what are you doing with that?' I asked her.

'Like your team said: you're getting lucky after practice.'

*

Lilac removed her top as soon as I shut the front door to the house.

'Lilac-' I said hesitantly.

'What?' she pulled herself closer to me, grabbing the front of my jersey.

'I thought this was a one-time thing.'

'That was before.'

'Before what?'

'Before your previous flavour pissed me off,' she said. I thought back, trying to understand what she was saying.

'Viv? You're jealous of Viv?' I pried her fingers away from my top, holding each hand in my fists.

'I'm not the little girl who has to sit on the side-lines and watch the older, sexier women get to have the man *I* want. I'm old enough to take what I want.'

She was definitely not that little girl anymore. And fuck if I didn't like jealous and confident Lilac.

'You just happened to be carrying a *Magnum* around in case you got jealous?'

'Willa said it pays to be prepared and she guessed your size,' she told me. 'Thank god she was right, hmm?'

Lilac tried to pull her hands from mine, but I tightened my grip on her wrists. 'You want to stake your claim?' I asked her, pushing her up against the closed door. I transferred both wrists into one hand, using the other one to trace the line of the tops of her pants where it met her hot bronze skin. She'd liked it before when I'd taken control.

'Yes.'

'So once because I owed you, once to make me yours?' I nuzzled my nose into her neck, watching as she reacted to me, physically shivering as my breath touched her delicate skin.

'Fucking me won't make me yours,' I said.

'I'm not asking for forever,' Lilac said. 'I'm just asking for right now.'

You once asked for forever, I wanted to tell her. *And I would do anything to be able to turn back the clock and give it you.*

I didn't say anything. Instead, I let go of her wrists and picked her up. She wrapped her legs around my waist, thrusting her core into my hard erection.

'I can do that,' I told her.

Lilac moaned as I brought my mouth to hers, carrying her upstairs to the bedroom.

I should have realised that something would have to give. If I believed in a higher power, I would have said that God was punishing me for failing his test.

No, I couldn't just protect Lilac and be the friend she needed me to be. Instead, I'd had to give into temptation and possess *all* of her.

I hadn't been able to keep my promise as a kid. And I hadn't been able to keep my promise as an adult. Once hadn't been enough. Now I was paying for it.

Calvin: Hey, coach. This is going to seem pretty out-there, but I figured it was better safe than sorry, you know.

Calvin: Howard's dad was at Side Street and he heard someone talking about going up to Miner's Mount, getting some supplies to go spelunking or some shit it sounded like. With these social distancing rules, we thought maybe they'd gone a bit stir crazy. Tryna get a thrill outta something.

Side Street was a bar closer to the edges of town than the one Willa worked at. It had almost closed down a few times, and it hadn't survived well after Montgomery's summer parties.

Calvin: Mentioned it to Rick but instead of saying he'd check in on it he mumbled something about your girl Lilac. Seemed strange as shit since she didn't look like the dare-devil type. But she's from outta town and might not know the caves up there connect into the mines and it ain't safe. Why a LOCAL would risk it I've no fucking clue.

Calvin: Wanted to give you a heads up. What with Rick mentioning your girl and all. Sorry if it's wasting your time, coach.

On the face of things, it might not have seemed like much. But the words I'd spoken *months* ago filtered back from the dark recesses of my mind.

Ironic if the bastard lost his girl the same way we lost ours. Hide her deep in the mines where he never fucking went. He wouldn't think to look for her there. Then we give him the coordinates and he has to go fish her out. Montgomery should know what it feels like to be under that earth.

It had to be Lucas. Calvin was right that no local would go exploring in those mines – or be that vocal about it. Also why else would Rick not look into it, unless it was part of Lucas' plan for Lilac?

I looked over at Lilac's sleeping body, peaceful, completely unaware that shit was hitting the fan around us.

She'd fallen asleep after sex, her head resting on my shoulder. I'd told myself it was the last time – that it didn't mean anything more than fucking. But I'd still stayed beside her whilst she slept. Because I was a selfish asshole and wanted to give myself every second I could have with her before she left.

And now I knew Lucas' plan. Of course that fucker would pick the mines. Of course he'd remember the worst shit I'd said.

I couldn't tell what his plan was now: not blackmail since Montgomery was dead. But Lucas had been pleased enough scaring Lilac. Taking her into the mines would definitely give her a fright.

But Lucas wasn't going to go through with his plan. There was no way I was letting Lilac out of my sight far enough for him to get his hands on her. And if by some twisted, fucked up fate he did manage to take her, at least I now knew his destination. And that sorry bastard would pay if he ever laid a finger on my girl.

21

LILAC

Something was wrong again. I could tell just by the way that Henry was acting around me. It wasn't like he was pushing me away exactly, more that he was extra careful around me.

Sleeping with him a second time had been a mistake – especially if this was what I got for being such a stupid, horny woman. Viv taunting me about "having" Henry had made me see red. I should have been above it. But I wasn't.

I knew she was feeling insecure, like she was losing a man she'd seen herself being with, the new daddy to her babies. But all I'd seen was one more girl taking away my Henry. Having what *I* couldn't.

It didn't help that Viv had been the popular cheerleader-type in high school. Rumours had gone around school that *she* was the one who'd taken Dawson's virginity. I'd known it wasn't true. Or at least I'd hoped. Especially when she'd ended up getting pregnant and my tiny pre-teen self had been terrified it was Henry's and I'd lost him forever. I couldn't compete with a baby-mama.

'Lord, Lilac, pull yourself together. You're not in competition with those other women. Henry is not a prize to be won. You're simply the latest flavour of the month before he moves on.'

'I mean, *I*'d call him a prize,' Willa said, popping up behind me and surprising the living day lights out of me.

'Hell, Willa! I nearly peed myself!'

'Why are you in here mumbling to yourself like a crazy person? Thank fuck our state's not having to go by those stay-at-home orders or our town would turn into a bunch of crazies talking to themselves, like you.'

'Not self-isolating,' I said under a mumbled breath. 'I'm under house arrest, remember?'

Willa sat down with me. 'Photo albums?'

I nodded. Spread out all across the floor of the master bedroom, where Henry slept, were all of Edie's old family albums. From the first year of her marriage to Mr Dawson all the way up to Henry's eighteenth. After that, the pictures had stopped.

I was taking a break from the miners' case. In the midst of all the paperwork Edie had accumulated from the two lawsuits, there'd been a screwed-up corner of a letter in her own handwriting. "Lilac", "you" and "have" were the only words that I could make out. I'd wondered what this letter had once been. Something left to me, like the note she'd left for Henry? Or simply notes on the case. But why my name?

I'd spent weeks in this house, surrounded by memories from my childhood. I had Henry here with me now. But I still missed Edie. That's when I'd decided to look through the albums. Remember her as she had been, before she'd become lost in the sea of depression and had written herself out of life.

'Edie,' I said, hoping that would explain enough to Willa.

She sat down next to me and took a look at the page I had open. It was when I was seven. I'd lost my front teeth and was hiding my smile from the camera – though Henry had had no trouble teasing me. In the picture he'd smeared chocolate cake over his front two teeth, so it looked like they were "missing", and he was grinning without a care in the world.

'Sexy,' Willa laughed. She was being sarcastic, but even back then I'd found him *so* attractive. Even when he was being goofy and poking fun at me.

Kasey screamed, giggling with glee downstairs. 'Faster! Faster Kristoff!'

'Dawson's getting more than he bargained for saying he'd let me come up and get you,' Willa said. 'You can't leave my girl alone with a person for a second before she has them wrapped around their finger.'

'Just like her mama then,' I said, playfully nudging her.

Henry came up the stairs a moment later, Kasey riding his back. He held Olaf in one hand whilst Kasey all but strangled his neck holding on. He plonked her down as soon as he got to the doorway.

'O*hhh*,' Kasey said. She seemed mesmerised by the collection of photographs on the floor. 'A puppy!'

'Kitty,' I said.

Kasey looked at me like my hair had turned green. Dawson chuckled.

'It *is* a puppy, Cee. Lilac just named her dog "Kitty" – because she's completely normal that way.'

Willa mouthed "fuck off" to him behind her daughter's back and he just laughed to himself, backing away, his arms up in surrender.

'I wanted a cat,' I told Kasey, 'but my mama was afraid it would run off and freeze in the winter. So daddy had gotten me a puppy for my birthday instead.'

'I want a puppy.'

'Not happening, kiddo,' Willa told her.

Kasey set her jaw, and stamped her tiny little foot. 'Fine!' she ran from the room screaming, '*Dawson!*'

'He's not going to buy you a puppy either!' Willa shouted after her. '*Lilac*, huh? Not "Texas"?' Willa asked me when she was gone.

I rolled my eyes. 'That was for Kasey's benefit, not mine. He still calls me Texas.'

'But he never called you Lilac before.'

He had, during sex. But I wasn't going to say that. Nor was I going to pretend that it meant anything now. Even if a small part of me hoped it did.

The small portion of normality that we'd manage to carve out for ourselves in the midst of this pandemic and Henry's devotion to protecting me from his old friends crumbled on a seemingly ordinary day.

The weather was finally warming, and the town had stopped actively trying to sabotage my stay here. I was mostly ignored, but accepted by the hockey players and – begrudgingly – their moms thanks to Henry's sway.

Willa would come over with Kasey every other day and I'd babysit until seven when Willa's mama came to pick her up after her shift at the clinic.

I was making progress with the miners' lawsuits and Henry and I had worked out a rhythm working and living together. Being able to sit in the stands and watch him on the ice made things easier for him now he wasn't having to shirk *all* his responsibilities to the town, but he was still pretty much working from home every moment he wasn't coaching.

'Lilac, fuck woman. You're going to saw your hands off.'

'I am not,' I told him.

'You're using a bread knife to cut up sweet potatoes-'

'It's got grooves to help me!' I said, defending my choice in knife.

The huge one he'd picked out for me was just not

cutting it. Literally. I didn't have the strength for it.

Henry shook his head, trying to take the knife from me so he could take over, but I wasn't having it. He only gave me one job a night to involve me with cooking and this was *mine.* I could chop a freakin' potato.

I waved the knife at him, threateningly, until he let me be.

'So, continue: Valentine's Day, you're in the restaurant and he says…' Henry said, getting me back to the story I'd been telling before I was rudely interrupted.

'Callum says: I think we're too busy to date. Like, he's speaking for me, too. Not just himself: *we're* too busy.'

I pushed a few blonde strands of hair out of my eyes as I chopped.

'He wasn't *wrong.* Doing four years in three was hard work and the final year was killing me, but it was like I'd never even considered us breaking up because I was *busy.* But here he was laying it out on the table right when my chocolate tort was about to arrive.'

'At least save if for after the tort,' Henry joked.

'But it wasn't like I could argue with him. Callum was really wracked for time. We basically said we'd get back together after graduation when everything had calmed down.'

'Only…?' Henry said.

'Only he'd been playing me like a massive asshole.' I stabbed my potato in frustration. 'We'd stayed friends and still met up once in a while for coffee – we both had lectures in the same part of the hall once every couple of weeks and we'd catch up after then.

'This one time he wasn't waiting for me outside our regular coffee place. He text me, telling me he was "stuck at home" so I thought I'd bring him a coffee to-go.'

My face heated up at the thought of what had happened next. Me, being let into his apartment by his roommate completely unaware. Callum and his psychology partner tangled up in the bedsheets together – naked. Me realising that the "lets stay friends and get back together when we're not busy" was just code for: the girl I swore I wasn't having sex behind your back wanted to go steady and I agreed because I don't want to stop having sex with her – but you I don't mind leaving behind.

I was never able to finish my sentence as Willa burst in through the front door. Her mama was soon behind her. Both of them looked like they'd been crying. Willa was waving her phone in the air like it was on fire.

'What's going on?' Henry asked.

'They've taken Kasey.' She shoved her phone in Henry's face.

'Who've taken Kasey?' Henry asked.

Henry took the phone from Willa and read whatever message was on there. He swore.

I wiped my hands on my jeans, walking over to them and peering around Henry to read what Willa was on about.

Unknown: Your girl, for our girl.

Henry looked up, our eyes meeting; asking me whether I'd read the message. Then his expression seemed to harden. It didn't take much for me to be able to read it. This was about me. Kasey was one girl, I was the other.

I didn't need to know who "they" were. There was only one *real* threat in this town for me. Henry didn't need telling, either.

'Lucas thinks Lilac's been staying with you…' Henry started, trying to rationalise why they'd target Willa and take her daughter.

'I don't give a *fuck* what they've been thinking!' Willa screamed. 'This is all your fucking fault! And you have to *fix this!*'

I didn't know who she was directing it to. Her eyes looked wildly between me and Henry. It didn't matter, really, whoever she meant. We were both culpable.

Henry for never discouraging Lucas and Trace when he could have – me for being a Montgomery and sticking around. Putting them all "in the cross-hairs" as Henry had called it.

I battled against the own sting in my eyes as tears threatened to form. I had no right to feel the pain Willa was right now as she suffered through Kasey's disappearance.

But I *loved* Kasey. And I couldn't help it. I couldn't stand to see Willa like this. Their family hurt because of me.

Henry didn't argue with her. He took her insults as she bombarded him with her verbal pain. He even took it when she slapped him. The crack was like the sound of thunder after lightning. Willa seemed to shock herself at her act of violence. Perhaps it was simply that Henry took it and didn't say anything afterwards, just nodded once like he accepted he deserved it.

Willa fell to her knees; her whole body just gave out, crumpling. She cried hysterically as her mama rubbed between her shoulder blades telling her that it was going to be okay. That Kasey was going to be okay.

'How'd it happen?' Henry asked, directing his question to her mama since Willa couldn't speak at all.

They'd already called the police, Willa's mama explained, and they were looking for Kasey now as they spoke. Willa mumbled about how they didn't think it was Lucas – that there wasn't any proof.

Henry became irate at that.

Of course it was Lucas. I was the "girl" they wanted. They hadn't been able to get to me since Henry had been protecting me, so they'd found a way to make us play into their hands.

Henry started to dial Rick's number, promising Willa they'd get Kasey back.

I backed away from them, giving them space. Henry mouthed to me, telling me not to go anywhere. I nodded, whispering that I was just giving them a little space. He seemed to know the guilt in my expression; possibly because it was playing out on his own. He let me leave to the edge of the kitchen where he could still see me, but Willa and her mama couldn't.

Willa's scream was ingrained in my mind. This was all my fault. If I'd just left town when Henry had told me to go back home to Texas…

No. This threat still worked then. They'd taken Kasey to get to me. If I was in Texas, it would have simply meant their demand would take longer to fulfil. And men who thought it was perfectly fine to kidnap four-year-old girls didn't have a patient or reasonable bone in their body.

Henry's voice raised and fell in angry tones as he spoke to Rick. I knew the sheriff hadn't been willing to step in to do anything for me, but this was Willa's daughter. This was a *child.* Surely, he'd put his old vendetta aside.

Weren't the letters I'd sent to the families informing them about the donation I was going to send over to them proof that I wasn't like daddy? That I'd do right by the people he'd wronged. Unless that's what had set this whole thing off? Lucas believing that I was going to get away just by throwing my money at the problem.

Henry was distracted enough with the call when I made my decision. I wasn't going to risk Kasey trusting in the judgement of men in this town who thought how they'd treated me was *sane.* I didn't have faith in the law in this bubble.

I grabbed Henry's keys and slipped out the back door, quickly putting his truck in reverse and driving as silently and quickly away from Henry's house as I could.

Lucas hadn't specified a drop-off place or whatever you called an exchange of hostages. But I knew there would be one place they'd have an eye on: the Manor.

If I turned up there, they'd have an alert sent to their phone. I just hoped that I would get there in time before Henry tried to be the hero and stop me.

22

DAWSON

I don't know what idiotic part of me thought that taking my eye off Lilac for a second would be a good idea. I'd thought the worst had already happened.

When I got off the phone to Rick – he had the whole sheriff's department put on alert, a unit were heading straight to the mine after I'd told them the plan the bartender at Side Street had overheard – and seen Lilac was gone, my stomach dropped.

My first thought was that she couldn't be that stupid. My second was that this was *Lilac*. She would risk anything and everything for those that she loved. She'd learnt that from me.

I immediately went to grab my keys. I didn't know where she'd go, but I knew Lucas was in the mine. If I got to him first, she wouldn't be in any danger.

'Fuck!' I swore, kicking over the chair at the kitchen table. She'd taken my keys and my truck. *Fucking fuck.* Of course she had.

'I'm taking your car,' I told June.

Willa looked at me with tear stained eyes, her makeup running down her face. She seemed to finally notice that Lilac was gone. Her mom passed me over the keys.

'She *went?*'

'She's gone to get your girl back,' I said bluntly. 'What else did you think she'd do?'

Willa stumbled over a few words before she settled on, 'where are you going?'

'To get them *both* back.'

I slammed the door behind me, leaving them in my house.

I drove as quickly as I could without breaking the limit too much. Since the sheriff's department were all busy with finding Kasey, I doubted I'd be pulled over for speeding, but mom's accident always made my mindful how I drove. Especially when I didn't have a clear mind. And with Lilac gone, my mind was anything but clear.

I headed for Miner's Mount, taking the road my dad used to drive every morning to get to the mine and the main site entrance.

Lilac's voice played on my mind every second I drove.

She was just chopping potatoes a second ago, it felt like. How could she be in danger now? How could Kasey be missing? How had things gotten so fucked up out of nowhere?

The car skidded to a halt on the old dirt path.

'They're not here,' the deputy said.

I'd slammed the door of June's car loud enough that everyone at the boarded-up entrance of the mine turned to look at me.

'What do you mean they're not here?'

Rory physically gulped. I could see his Adam's apple bobbling in his throat as he looked up to my six foot four. I tried to make myself more approachable in town since I'd gotten back from Iraq, but I knew I was an intimidating figure. It helped me on the ice. And it worked for me now.

'The entrance has been blocked since the mine shut. It's

not been tampered with.'

'There's more than one entrance,' I said. 'Check the other one.'

Rory nodded, telling the guys to do as I said. It was possible we'd gotten here before them. I told Rory as much.

Rory went back to the car radio and updated Rick. Rick had sent people to both Lucas' and Trace's homes, but they weren't there. And there was no sign that Kasey had been at either place.

I tried Lilac's phone for the billionth time.

'We could try tracking it,' Rory said once he'd come back.

'What?' I growled. I didn't mean to snap at him. But I couldn't help it.

'Her phone. Rick said the Montgomery girl is missing, too. That's who you're calling, isn't it?'

Willa or June must have called Rick to tell him what Lilac had done. That we were now in a situation where two girls were in danger, not just one. I doubted Rick would focus two brain cells on finding Lilac.

Rory hadn't lost anyone in the mining collapse. Even though he was part of the law enforcement who'd had their hands tied to stop Montgomery's parties, he was a good man. He didn't see Lilac as anyone other than one more innocent girl caught up in the hot-shit mess that was this town's drama.

'You don't have that sort of technology,' I said. It wasn't a question; just a fact. Grand Yutu's sheriff's department was old-school.

'No, but if she had *Find My Phone* turned on, we'd be able to see where it is.'

Lilac had exclusively *Apple* products; like she was fucking endorsed by them or some shit. I knew she had her phone connected to her *Mac* back at my place – and I knew her password.

I wanted to wait up at the mine, sure that Lucas would turn up here sooner or later, but that would mean just *waiting* and doing nothing whilst Lucas could have changed his plan on a whim. Lilac and Kasey could be being driven out of Grand Yutu for all we fucking knew.

If Lucas and Trace were high right now, they might not follow any sort of previous plan they'd set.

'I can get her laptop,' I said, going back towards my car.

'I'll come with you,' Rory said, getting in his cruiser, putting one of the other men in charge.

23

LILAC

Henry's truck was left abandoned at the Manor when the man who'd taken Kasey had turned up in a beat-up pickup truck older than Henry's by at least a couple of years.

He hadn't said much, simply: get in. He had taken my phone, throwing it out the window, then sped off.

I recognised him instantly as the guy who I thought had been hitting on me the first time I'd come into Willa's bar. At least now his interest in me made sense. I couldn't remember his name. But I knew enough that it was either Trace or Lucas. I guessed Trace as Henry had always said Lucas was the brains and Trace the lacky. You sent a lacky to collect the hostage, didn't you?

My whole body was shaking with adrenaline as I sat next to him. I wanted to demand to see Kasey. That since I had come to him willingly, I wanted them to let her go and give her back to Willa, but my mouth wouldn't say anything. It was as though fright had gripped my throat and the words were simply trapped just at my voice box, choking me.

I thought he was driving me out of town as the buildings became sparser, levelling out into abandoned farmlands and fields. A hysterical thought popped into my head reminding me that this was probably the land I'd inherited from daddy. The land he'd bought up like he had most of this town.

Did it do you any good, daddy, in the end? You lost mama. You lost me. You lost this whole town. And now you're gone, and still innocent people are suffering for your greed.

Miner's Mount watched as we approached. Even though we'd reached the beginning of summer now, the top of the mountain still seemed dusted with snow. It was probably an illusion, the clouds hung low today in the sky.

The woods at the base of the mountain were thick and luscious with greenery. Trace took us up a scenic path. Twisting roads that were smooth and pothole free, unlike the ancient roads that paved the rest of the town.

Eventually we turned onto a stretch of road leading to a grand entrance. A beautiful beige brick arch with a hand-crafted sign embossed with silver lettering: *Whistling Crest Resort.*

We had entered daddy's business retreat. The black heart of where the sickness that had infected the town began.

For all that Henry had said about what went on up here, the "village" looked perfectly innocent and homey. Like it wouldn't be amiss to see a family of four with a stroller walking down the street here. The cabins were spaced at a fair distance, each with their own huge driveway. From the outside, they had that rustic look; through the sparkling windows the luxury of the interior could be seen.

Trace drove us up to a cabin quite a way back from the main entrance. He pulled up in the drive of the only occupied house. I knew it was the only occupied one, because all the other drives had remained empty whilst this one shared the car parking space with Lucas' *Honda Ridgeline* pickup.

'Out,' he'd ordered.

I opened the car door and exited. He walked me up the path, a step behind me as though he were afraid I was going to run away. It wasn't like I would get very far if I did. Or likely find help up here. Daddy's resort was abandoned up here on Miner's Mount. No one would think to look for us here. Even me – the current owner of the village – hadn't thought about it since I'd learnt I'd inherited it from daddy.

I was surprised the town hadn't set fire to the whole place since they'd learnt daddy had passed away.

'Open,' Trace barked.

I pulled the handle of the front door. The metal was cold to touch and had that same expensive feel as the Manor door, only far less used than our family home.

We entered the foyer. The whole first floor was an open plan with a grand staircase leading to the bedrooms on the second floor. The room was a mix of white and greys – with accents of blues. I'd never cared much about interior design and yet my mind was picking up every detail.

It's the adrenaline, I told myself. *You're just scared.* It didn't help to rationalise the fear.

'Finally!' a male voice called out from upstairs. He made his way down.

Lucas was almost as tall as Henry, though in no way nearly as strong. His eyes were sunken and had that same dead-look Trace's did. Like he looked *through* me, rather than *at* me.

Whereas Trace looked like he could be attractive if he cleaned up a little, Lucas didn't have that same luxury. His face was sallow, his hair black and curling around the back of his neck like it hadn't been cut for weeks. His eyes were a little too close together and his mouth was a sharp slash of a thing, with a mouth of teeth that looked broken from one too many bar fights.

Part of me might have briefly recognised Trace from back in high school, though it was likely he'd been years ahead of me. But I certainly would have recalled Lucas if I had ever seen him before.

His brother and daddy died in the collapse, I reminded myself. Is now really the time to be cruelly cataloguing his appearance. But like with the décor – my mind simply couldn't stop.

Lucas had made his way down the stairs now and stood in front of me.

'Interesting that you came on your own.'

'She took Dawson's car,' Trace told him.

'Where's Dawson?' Lucas asked.

I didn't realise he'd been asking me until Trace grabbed my arm and squeezed, hard. I yelped. 'He's at home. With Willa.'

'He doesn't know you left?'

Trace squeezed me again.

'No,' I said.

Trace dragged me to the white couch in the middle of the living room. He pushed me into it. I righted myself quickly. He stood behind me, watching Lucas as he paced in the kitchen.

He muttered to himself, dragging his hand along the top of the marble surfaces. Toying with the taps on the sink before leaving the kitchen behind and entering the dining room that situated itself perfectly between the kitchen and the living room.

I looked around the rooms as inconspicuously as I could without taking my eyes of Lucas. Kasey wasn't here. I couldn't see her at least. She could be upstairs. I strained my ears, hoping that I'd hear some sign of her. She wasn't a very quiet kid.

'Where's Kasey?' the question slipped from my lips where the others had been choked in my throat.

Lucas slammed his hand down – hard – on the glass table. The vase in the centre shook, as though it might topple over. I flinched, though I tried not to.

'*You* don't ask the questions, you got that?' Lucas said.

I nodded my head.

'Speak. Tell me you got that.'

'I understand,' I said.

'Good girl.'

Trace laughed at the way I shook. I still wanted to know, but I couldn't ask again and risk upsetting Lucas. Not when he seemed so erratic.

Henry said that they'd used to get drunk together, even high sometimes. I knew he hadn't just meant weed.

I'd been to college, I'd seen a few of my classmates take party drugs – but I wasn't so oblivious to think this would be anything like that. I also knew that angry people didn't make good drunks. I could assume they didn't make good addicts, either.

'How do you like your dad's fine establishment?' Lucas finally asked me. He'd stopped muttering to himself now – my question seeming to focus his attention.

He went over to the wine bar and pulled out a bottle of red. 'You like red, yeah?' he said.

He smashed the top of the bottle off, rather than pop the cork. I jumped in my seat. The movement made me brush up against Trace who was standing oh, so close behind my seat.

'I *said*: you like red, yeah?'

'Yes,' I said.

He poured the contents of the wine onto the plush white carpet. The bottle glug-glugged until it was empty, and Lucas threw the bottle at the wall, aiming for the canvas painting hung in the middle. It hit the target, ripping through the centre of the picture.

'Such a fine place your old man had up here,' Lucas said, stepping into the puddle of wine and walking through, leaving a trail of bloody red prints behind as he paced.

'Much nicer than any home we've got down there. Besides your McMansion,' he sneered. 'And it's all abandoned. Waiting for more rich fuckers to use. Don't you ever get tired of *using?'*

'I… don't use,' I said. I didn't want to anger him by not answering the question.

He laughed at me. 'That was a rhetorical question, princess… and you might not have *before.* But you sure as shit will be starting tonight, princess.'

Lucas stalked towards me. Trace gripped my arms. I immediately started to fight at the reaction of being held down. He was nowhere near as strong as Henry was and I easily squirmed out of his grip.

Lucas hit me across the face. 'Don't *fucking* move,' he rumbled through clenched teeth. 'If you don't cooperate *fully* we'll make the girl pay for it.'

I slumped in my chair. It was the first mention that they still had Kasey. It figured that they would. Just like they'd planned on using me to get to daddy, they were now using Kasey to control me. Henry'd had it right when he'd realised using a child was the surest way to control a person's actions.

'Good girl,' Lucas praised me again. 'Now open your mouth.'

Being told to open my mouth was the surest way to lock my jaw. Trace anticipated it and held my nose. I struggled, trying to pull his hands away, but I couldn't. I couldn't breathe. I opened my mouth. In the second that I did, Lucas slipped something onto my tongue.

It felt like paper. As soon as it was in my mouth, Trace clamped his hand down over it so I couldn't spit it out. He then used his other hand to hold my nose once more. I struggled some more.

'I'll let go if you're a good girl and swallow.'

I felt my vision begin to blur. I swallowed.

Lucas grinned at me with those broken teeth. Trace matched that wicked smile.

'You lost the bet,' Lucas said to Trace. 'You told me rich girls would never swallow.' They weren't talking about whatever they'd forced me to ingest.

'There's always time for us to find out for real,' Trace said. His fingers ran down the red marks that had already begun to bruise on my arms from where he'd held me before.

'No,' Lucas said. 'There's not. We've only got thirty minutes before that starts to hit her. And we've got another drive to go on.'

Trace roughly dragged me back up from the couch.

'Aren't you going to ask where we're going, princess?' Lucas asked as Trace forced me into the back of the truck, climbing in after me.

'Where are we going?' I asked, obediently like he wanted from me.

Lucas just laughed. Refusing to answer the question he'd forced me to ask.

Trace's hands wandered as Lucas started the car. My legs clenched tight together as he pawed at my thigh.

Trace roughly turned my face towards him, tugging my hair hard. He then threw my ponytail to the side and licked up the side of my cheek. I wanted to throw up at the feel of his spit on my face. He gripped my hands hard to him, pressing them on his thigh and his – I wouldn't think where else – so I couldn't wipe it from my face.

'It's time for you to apologise for your sins,' he whispered in my ear. Then laughed once more, that dark and ominous tone that had no humour and only pain.

We didn't leave the resort. That much I was sure of. The houses became sparser and bigger: more like mansions than cabins.

The Ash Cabins were larger than Elm. These big luxury buildings that looked like they cost as much as your McMansion, Henry's voice came back to me.

Henry. He would be so cross with me right now for putting myself in danger. And for what? I hadn't even seen Kasey. I didn't know where Lucas had stashed her or what they'd done with her. If both of them were with me now, what did that mean for Kasey?

Watching her had been a full-time job stopping her from killing herself simply by being that unaware, carefree little kid. How would she manage if she was alone somewhere?

She could be in any one of these cabins. They could have stashed her in one of their shitty, drug riddled apartments or the trunk of a car. Tears silently fell down my cheeks as I thought of all the horrible scenarios that could have happened to her whilst she'd been taken.

Trace grinned at the sight, using one hand to collect a tear and popping it into his mouth, savouring the taste like my anguish was his favourite flavour.

Eventually, Lucas pulled up the car. Trace dragged me out, dropping me on the floor so hard I scraped my knees through the jeans I was wearing.

'Oops,' he chuckled. He yanked me back up.

I could feel the blood drip down my knees. They'd been skinned pretty badly. The pain stung, but I didn't have much time to think about it.

They led me to a collection of newly planted trees, possibly a few years old, up against the solid incline of the mountain. A couple of the trees had been snapped in half, like a car had rammed into them. Behind these trees, an adit appeared, one of the old entrances to the mine. Instead of being boarded up and blocked by metal bars, it was open.

'In you go, princess,' Lucas said.

Lucas and Trace used the lights of their phones to walk by. I didn't dare try to run, knowing that they were my only source of light. If I did, I would not only get lost down the many twists and turns they'd taken me, but I had no idea what they'd do to Kasey.

Every second we were here, I knew it wasn't safe.

Edie had Mr Lawson's old notes on the extent of how much damage there was down here through the ware of time and hard graft. The further down you went into the mine, the more unstable the walls were. I didn't know the exact location of the collapse, but I hoped Lucas and Trace had enough sense to stay as far away from that site as possible.

There were three entrances to the mine, that much I remembered from my childhood. The first was the largest and oldest near the very base of Miner's Mount – the one the old miners had used back in the day before daddy had opened Montgomery Mines. The second and third were the ones daddy had opened after they'd needed to find a new angle to get to the coal. This was one of those entrances.

People had been down here to investigate, so I knew it mustn't have been *that* bad as to be completely condemned, but that had been years ago. Now, we were entering a mine that hadn't been touched, hadn't been inspected but most likely *had* been tampered with plenty since Lucas and Trace both knew their way like experts around the awful tight tunnels.

'It's not safe down here,' I said, finally finding my words when Trace tripped up, stumbling over a rock he hadn't seen and slammed into the wall. I swear I heard some of the wall crumble under his touch.

Trace laughed manically at me. He scrounged to pick his phone up from the floor, the light illuminating his face making him look like a corpse for a moment before he had his phone back, secure in his hand.

'*Safe.* You're damn straight it's not fucking *safe*, princess! This is where they died! This is where they're *trapped.*'

My legs shook so much I found it hard to move.

'Walk,' Trace ordered, pushing me.

I couldn't move.

Lucas turned to see what the hold up was. 'I think little princess has figured out who we're taking her to.' Lucas moved close to me, so close I could feel his hot breath on my cheeks. 'You got to bury your fucking murderer of a father. We didn't get so much as a goodbye for ours or my brother. They couldn't take out the bodies in case there was a secondary collapse and the men trying to take them out got buried, too.

'But that didn't stop your daddy dearest from trying to keep the mine open. Fifteen *dead bodies* down here didn't stop him – but realising that he wouldn't get the profit he'd been banking on did. It's always about money with you people.

'Throw some dollar our way and you're absolved of your guilt. Paying us back isn't going to bring them back to life. There's only one way we can get true justice for our family. The only thing that would hurt him more than losing his money.'

'Daddy's already dead,' I said. You couldn't make a dead man pay.

'*Daddy* is watching this all from Hell,' Lucas whispered in my ear. 'And soon you'll be joining him.'

24

DAWSON

Lilac's phone was found outside the Manor. It made sense. Lilac was smart enough to know that Lucas would have alerts sent to his phone whenever the motion sensors picked up anything outside of her dad's house – waiting for her to come back.

Rory had stuck with me through the frantic drive back to my place, searching the laptop – with Willa and June pestering him for updates – whilst I located Lilac's phone and then driving to the Manor. I'd rode in the front with him, giving June her keys back.

My truck was there, too. As much as I'd snapped at him before, I was glad Rory was there with me. He was able to keep me up to date with Rick's, as well as the unit back up at the mine's, progress. Not that there was *progress.*

Lilac had already been gone for a couple of hours now. Kasey had been gone for more. There was still time to find them. It hadn't been that long. Two hockey games. But hockey went quick. This felt like it was dragging for years. And the longer Lilac and Kasey went without being found, the more impossible it seemed that we'd find them.

I'd watched enough shitty Crime dramas in college to know that it was the first 48 hours that made or broke a case.

Usually, you didn't already know who the fucking kidnappers were, or where they'd planned to take them. Which should have made this a whole lot easier and yet had we found them? Had we found a *sign* of them?

'*Fuck!*' I shouted the word as I kicked my truck. The door dented at the impact.

I had never been this out of control with anger and complete helplessness before. I was calm on the ice. I'd been calm in the middle of a fucking warzone. And yet here, in my own fucking town I was shitting myself and couldn't keep a thought straight in my head to figure out my next move and *find them.*

'I'm not watching that with you.'

'It's amazing!' I'd said.

Bloodsport had been one of my favourite films as a kid. Mom and Lilac had loved 80s rom-coms. I'd loved 80s action films. Van Damme was my go-to just as Molly Ringwald had been mom's.

'I've watched that film so many freakin' times,' Lilac said. 'Do you know that I can practically quote most of Jean Claude's lines by heart?'

'You can't.' I'd forgotten how she always called actors by their first names. She said if sports were for calling someone by their family name, then the arts were for first names.

Lilac clicked on the film, fast forwarding it to a random point. Then proceeded to quote – in time – the film. It was surprisingly hot.

'I learnt our school play lines by the second read through. Do you know how many times you made us sit through that crap?'

'Take it back!' I said, throwing a few pieces of popcorn she'd made at her head. 'This film is a masterpiece, not "crap".'

Lilac rolled her eyes at me and selected another film from her Netflix account.

'Just Friends – not happening,' I said. I didn't need to read the description; the title and movie poster was enough.

'Come on,' Lilac said, playfully. 'It's got everything you love. Ice hockey, girls with big boobs-'

'Old friends that get together in the end, it's not happening, Texas,' I told her reading the description.

She'd been teasing me non-stop since we'd fucked. I knew it was light-hearted. Her way to take the edge off me being home all day and her slogging through the legal minefield for the fifteen. The back-and-forth between us did help. But it was also annoying as fuck since my cock couldn't take a fucking hint that it was just teasing – there wasn't going to be any release here.

'Unfortunately,' Lilac said, stretching out in front of me so she covered the screen with her body, 'it already did.'

She pressed play, jabbing me in the ribs and stealing the popcorn at the same time.

This fucking girl, I'd laughed.

Memories of these past few weeks kept appearing at inopportune moments. It was like my brain was screaming at me, reminding me how much I had to lose if I didn't find her. As if I fucking needed a reminder.

I knew how much Lilac meant to me. Throwing in my face the innocent moments that had passed between us, reminding me how easily she fit back into my life, wasn't going to help me find her. She wasn't going to magically appear out of thin air just because I had some miraculous revelation that she was "the one" or some shit.

Lilac was the closest thing I had left to family. And I wasn't going to lose her. It was as simple as that.

I paced outside of Montgomery's mansion, staring at the camera like I was staring into the soul of Lucas' eyes. He could be watching me right now. That bastard could be seeing me break down in front of her house, laughing his fucking head off at how powerless I was – how clueless I was to where they both were.

'You fuckers!' I threw a rock at the doorbell camera. I had great aim. It smashed into the lens, knocking the thing clean off the wall.

'Urgh, Dawson…' Rory said.

Yeah, vandalising the place in front of a deputy probably wasn't a smart move.

'Fuck. Shit. I'm sorry,' I said, throwing up my hands to show I wasn't going to throw anymore shit. 'They have access to her dad's security,' I said, as though that explained it. As though he probably didn't already know since he worked under Rick.

'We have access to the mine security,' Rory said – as though what I'd said gave him an idea.

'The what?'

'Year before you came back, a few kids started trying to break into the mines. They thought it would be a good place to get high since we couldn't spot them there. Montgomery had cameras installed all over the place, when we told him, but he didn't want the hassle of hiring someone to watch the place – not like he did with the Resort. He left it to our department to keep an eye on it.'

'Have you checked the cameras?'

'I'm… not sure,' Rory said. Which probably meant that Rick had been in charge of looking over the footage since Lucas had planned on using the mines as part of his plot to get to Lilac.

'How long does it store footage, or is it just a live-time

feed?'

'Live-time, but it saves any footage which set of the motion sensors.'

'We're going to go look at that footage.'

'Dispatch would have called if any of them had been spotted up in the mines.'

'Yes, but the footage the cameras have saved will show us *where* abouts Lucas and Trace have been entering the mines. Since clearly, we've got the wrong spot.'

There was only Jane and Carolyn at the sheriff's department when we came in. Carolyn started to ask a million questions as soon as we walked through the door, but my look silenced her.

Rory took me to the archive room where they'd created an annex with a single computer. He logged onto the machine, sitting down at the only chair whilst I hovered over him. He must have felt my energy buzzing off me like a palpable wave. I could tell just by the tense way he sat in the seat and tapped impatiently on the mouse whilst it took a painstakingly long time to load.

Eventually, he was into the file and he pulled up the footage. The latest ones were useless. It showed him arriving in his cruiser, along with the other two cars and them checking out the entrance. A few minutes later, I appeared.

He clicked on the earlier files, but there was nothing more today. Not in the past few days. A week ago, had some footage of a few kids from the high school hanging around, but none of Lucas and Trace.

'Check the earlier ones.'

Howard's dad only heard Lucas mentioning the mine a week ago, but they'd been planning their revenge on Lilac since she'd come to town. Trace and Lucas weren't meticulous planners. It would be enough for them to check out the location once and decide that's where they'd do it. They wouldn't find the need to obsessively return to the area to make sure that it was still viable.

Their minds didn't work in logical time, either. They spent so much time high or drunk they could lose full days sometimes. I knew because I'd been the same those first few months of grieving for mom.

Rory still couldn't find anything. Fuck. What if Lucas had just been running his mouth at Side Street to throw me off the scent? I thought he was a stupid shit, but he'd been smart enough to hack into Montgomery's security. He knew I was with Lilac now – asking around town to see where he was, listening in to any clue about what he might have planned for her.

Throwing that little bit of information about the mines had been a stroke of genius. I'd obsess over that and wouldn't think to consider anywhere else. I'd been played.

Carolyn knocked on the door.

'Not now!' I shouted.

Where the fuck were Kasey and Lilac if they weren't at the mines? Would anyone else in town hide them for Lucas? Any of the thirteen other families? I might have doubts about the morality of a few of them when it came to Lilac, but I trusted the people in this town. They'd never do that to Kasey.

She continued to knock. Rory opened the door for her.

'I'm sorry,' she seemed flustered, her cheeks red. 'Rick called. He got a message from Benson-Arnold security.'

'Who're they?' I asked.

Rory answered. 'The people in charge of watching Montgomery's Resort.'

'They said they've had activity in one of the Elm cabins. They checked the footage. Kasey's up there,' Carolyn said. 'Rick and the unit from the mines have gone to retrieve her.'

I was instantly relieved for Willa, but it only lasted a moment. 'Did they say anything about Lilac?'

'No…' Carolyn said. 'Rick didn't mention her.'

'That fucking bastard-'

After everything, he was still going to let Lucas take Lilac. His cousin had kidnapped a *child* and he still thought that he could get off scot-free and finish his revenge plot as though paying back a dead man was the most important thing right now.

'It's not that,' Carolyn said, reading my expression along with what my words had insinuated. 'Lucas isn't going to be let off this time. Neither of them are. Rick didn't mention Lilac because the security footage shows Lucas and Trace driving away from the cabin with her. He doesn't know where they've taken her.'

I clicked back onto the folder Rory had selected. It belonged to a larger folder.

'Why'd you pick this footage?' I asked Rory.

'It's the only stable mine entrance,' Rory answered. 'The old mine was closed back in 2007 and the other was the site of the collapse. It's the only active adit.'

'It was the only active adit to the *miners*.'

I clicked out of the current folder and into the larger one, selecting the old mines. There was no footage – at least none of any interest besides a few elk that had set off the motion sensors. That area was largely overgrown now, returned back to nature. Lucas and Trace wouldn't have had the fortitude to hike to that area. It was why we'd all congregated to the mine that still had an entrance you could drive all the way up to.

That left the tunnels that had collapsed.

You're not that fucking stupid, I tried to tell the imaginary Lucas in my mind. *Tell me you're not that fucking stupid.*

I opened the folder for the collapsed mine. The footage

timestamps were regular and with large saved files with the sensors being tripped numerous times.

They began a couple months ago, though they got increasingly steady – the most recent twenty minutes ago. I clicked on that file.

The camera was positioned from an angle on the mountain face, looking out over the top of the mine entrance. Just on the edge of the frame, newly planted trees lined the perimeter, blocking the adit from the view of the dirt path that led up to it.

What if all that talk in town about Montgomery filling in the old mine entrance on this side of the mountain had been just talk? Could Montgomery really be that reckless to leave open an adit to the collapsed mine right next to his Resort?

I didn't need to remind myself that I'd already seen the activity on the saved footage to this particular file. Montgomery had let the mine kill fifteen people in the first place.

The footage began as Lucas' truck pulled up in front of the mine entrance. Lucas got out of the truck, followed by Trace. Then Lilac. Trace pulled her harshly from the car, dragging her down so hard she fell. When she got back up, I could see that she was limping towards the mine's entrance.

A small smear of blood was left behind on the dirt where she'd hit the ground. I growled. I think I must have sworn or said something more since Carolyn squeaked as though shocked by my language.

'They've taken her to the fifteen's gravesite,' I said.

Rory, who hadn't cursed a single time since I'd known him, let out a harsh curse.

He grabbed the keys to his cruiser, and we hurried out the door. We didn't need words. We just needed speed – and to make sure that we got to Lilac before Lucas and

Trace got bored of simply scaring Lilac and moved on to finishing the job.

25

LILAC

I'd thought daddy's ghost had been speaking to me back when I was alone in the Manor. When the songs had started playing on their own and the lights had flickered, I'd wondered if he was trying to communicate to me from beyond the grave.

I knew now that it had just been Lucas and Trace messing with me. I also knew what a real haunting felt like. Lucas and Trace left me in the dark, right at the mouth of the tunnel the fifteen were buried. When they said I was going to meet daddy in Hell, I'd been terrified they were going to kill me. But they hadn't needed to. In the depths of Miner's Mount, there was an entrance straight to Hell itself.

Mr Dawson was the first one who appeared to me. His face was caved in at the side, blood dripping out of his eye sockets. He didn't wear his work clothes. Instead, he wore what I'd usually see him in on a Saturday afternoon when Henry's hockey practice had finished.

His cold bloodied hands touched me, crushing my flesh between his bony hands. His mouth gurgled sounds that were like blood and mucus stuck in the back of his throat. I screamed and cried but he didn't stop.

I closed my eyes and told myself it was a trick of the light – but there was no light and still I could *see* him. The other miners then appeared. Their faces equally disfigured. They pulled and tugged at my skin, leaving my body wracked in cold, painful shivers.

The hands of the ghosts went into my skin, burying down deep. I could feel them with their tiny pickaxes mining into my bones. They wanted to take every last piece of Montgomery from this world and they would only succeed after they'd taken each bit of him from me.

I clawed at my flesh trying to get them out. Those tiny miners working deep in my veins. I could feel them prodding and poking inside me. Chipping away one bit at a time.

'Run, Lilac,' daddy's voice said. 'You've got to get out of here. They can't hurt you once you leave the mine.'

'Daddy?' I called out.

'He's wrong,' Mr Dawson said, his mouth bubbling with blood. Flecks of it fell on my face as he spoke.

'He just wants you to run like he did. He never faced his mistakes. He left us trapped. All we want to do is to be free.'

I sobbed, but the feeling of the miners inside my skin had paused for a moment. I listened to Mr Dawson's words like I were a snake and he were a charmer.

'You promised to help us, Lilac. You promised to get us justice. Can't you help us now?'

The other miners surrounded me, urging me towards the collapse. I knew what they wanted. They wanted what they always had. To be free.

I began clawing at the collapsed rock, digging as deep as I could into the mine: to rescue the men daddy had abandoned in Hell.

I dug for days. My arms had turned into pickaxes: the first Montgomery to mine in the Montgomery Mines. Daddy would have rolled over in his grave. Nervous laughter bubbled up from my lips.

I kept going. I had endless energy. I could save them. Since I'd begun digging, the ghosts had disappeared – like they knew I was doing what they wanted, and they didn't want to distract me.

I sang as I dug. I don't know what made me start. *Frozen 2* was imprinted into my mind from the endless times I'd sat watching it with Kasey. I sang through the list of songs, until I got to *Do the Next Right Thing.*

I got stuck on that song. Like a CD player stuck on repeat. The song became an endless repeat that I sang for hours until my voice got hoarse.

'You're a terrible singer, Texas,' Henry told me.

'I'm just rusty,' I told him back as I dug.

'You're not rusty – you've been singing for hours, you're just plain untalented.'

'Not everyone can be a great singer.'

'What are you good at?' Henry asked me.

'I've got a good memory,' I said.

'Yeah, and how does that help?'

'I can memorise facts easily.'

'Facts…' he didn't seem impressed.

'I finished college in three years. I graduated this month.'

'Impressive,' he said. 'How does that help you now? You don't need a college degree to dig in the mines. You just need to be strong enough to lift an axe.'

I showed him my pickaxe hands. I could mine. I was strong. Just because he'd never wanted to be a miner didn't mean I wouldn't be a good one. That's what I was doing down here, wasn't it? I wondered when my shift would finish. It was impossible to tell the time in the darkness. Had I been mining for a while already – or had my shift just started.

'You've barely even begun,' Henry told me. 'You've not made any headway at all. How will we fill your daddy's quota with slackers like you?'

I put my back into it. I would make daddy proud.

26

DAWSON

Rory couldn't drive fast enough for me. I regretted not taking my own truck, but with how riled up I was, I doubted I would have been able to drive and not crash the car. The last thing Lilac needed now was me to total my car like she had. Plus, it was still back at the Manor.

It took us a while to get up to the Resort. I hated every second of that scenic drive. For all I'd told Lilac about what had gone up here, I'd never been. And my first time was now trying to rescue the daughter of a man who'd killed my dad.

Rory parked the car next to Lucas' truck. We'd tasked Carolyn with watching the live-feed and to message us through the radio if there was any movement. She hadn't contacted us, and with Lucas' truck still here, we could be pretty sure that they were all still in the mine.

'You know I have to say you can't go in there with me,' Rory told me.

'Like fuck are you leaving me outside to watch whilst you go after those fuckers and get Lilac.'

'I know. But I had to at least say it.'

Rory passed me one of the two hardhats he'd somehow picked up when I hadn't been looking. They had a flashlight on the top which we could switch on and see by as we walked through the tunnels.

I'd once hated the thought of donning one of these hats and going to work down the mines like my dad so much I'd run away to the army to escape that fate. And now, here I was. What a stupid fucking irony.

Rory pulled out his gun as he walked. 'We don't know if they're carrying so try to stay behind me.'

'I'm ex-military,' I reminded him. 'I know how to handle myself,' I snapped.

It would have almost been impossible to know where they were in the tunnels of the mine – but this wasn't the first time I'd had to track fugitives in a cave system. Little signs of human movement could be read from unassuming things that would mostly go overlooked by someone who hadn't been trained. Plus, Lucas and Trace were clumsy as fuck and didn't know how to hide their movements for shit. Not that they'd tried at all.

I could see the story of how they'd moved through the tunnels like I was reading a book. There was a sign that almost looked like a struggle part way through the tunnel – like someone had fallen. It wasn't Lilac, but one of the guys. If it had been her, the impact zone would have been smaller with flecks of blood from her cut-up knees. They'd gotten back up and moved at a quicker pace from the length of their strides.

Rory's hand was resting on the trigger. Even if I had the option to bring a gun, I wouldn't have. Not in these close quarters, and not in the part of the mine where the unsound structure had already failed once and collapsed. I told Rory as much, but he wasn't listening. He felt safer with a gun in his hand.

Well, I felt fucking safer when we weren't in an area

where my hardhat was touching the fucking roof; the tunnel we walked down was barely big enough for us to stand side-by-side and my dead dad's body wasn't trapped beyond one of these unstable fucking beams.

We heard them before we saw them. There would be no element of surprise, not unless we switched off the lamps on our hardhats, but that would put us at a disadvantage and the last thing I wanted was to get into a fight in the dark with Rory's finger on the trigger and fuck knows what – if anything – Lucas had brought with him down here.

I got to Trace first before any of them had seen me move. I incapacitated him quickly, with little fuss like you saw in the movies. For a dramatic effect, they would have prolonged this scene to last minutes with us grappling – slamming into the unstable walls, dirt from the ceiling falling around us as tense music played and the audience at home wondered who was going to come out on top, or if the mine was going to collapse before we reached the end of our fight.

But Trace was a lightweight punk who'd never won a fight in his life. It barely took a second before I had him pinned underneath me, his chest pressed hard against the floor, his face twisting up towards me in anger.

Rory passed me the handcuffs whilst he pointed the gun at Lucas. 'No funny business,' he said – like he was part of the movie I clearly wasn't cast in.

Trace kicked from under me, but he didn't have much room to move. I didn't hold back when I flipped him over and slammed his head into the floor, once. I didn't want to kill him. But I knew exactly how to inflict pain and damage without going too far. He blacked out for a moment or two – people didn't black out for long periods of time when they'd been hit on the head. That was simply dramatic licence they used in films. If Trace had been passed out for more than a few seconds – I would have known I'd definitely gone too far.

He was in pain and disorientated enough now that I felt comfortable enough to stand up.

'Where's Lilac?' I asked.

Lucas just laughed. I moved towards him. 'I'm not fucking around, asshole. Where's Lilac?'

'I can't believe you went soft for the bitch,' Lucas said. 'You hated her more than we ever did. She killed both your parents.'

'Lilac did fuck all to my parents. Where is she?'

I grabbed him by the front of his shirt. I couldn't slam him against the wall, not like I wanted to. Rory had his gun trained on Trace now, but I could see him twitching, wanting to point it at Lucas who was the bigger threat.

'Keep that fucking gun pointed away from me and at him,' I growled. The last thing I needed was to be shot by some deputy who'd never had to shoot his gun before in the line of duty. I was never keen on being someone's first.

'Where the fuck is Lilac?' I asked again.

Lucas laughed at me. He wasn't high. I knew the signs enough. He was a little drunk, but that was a permanent state for him.

'In Hell.'

Lucas and Trace believed in the afterlife as much as I did. The only "hell" they'd ever known was a bad trip. Oh fuck. Oh fuck, no.

'Tell me you didn't.'

Lucas grinned like a Cheshire cat. I punched him in the kidneys where I knew it would hurt the most. He doubled over, crying in pain.

Lucas and Trace had tried every drug there was – at least everyone that wouldn't get them hooked for life. LSD had been their drug of choice until their dealer had fucked them over and given them the worst trip of their lives. Lucas had ended up in hospital with two broken fingers –

that he'd purposefully snapped himself when he'd been certain they were snakes. They'd kept the three remaining doses of the five strip to fuck over someone who'd crossed them. I'd never been an expert in drugs, but I wasn't sure there was necessarily a bad-batch so much as a bad-trip when it came to LSD. But you could certainly condition someone into having a bad trip.

Like fuck with their brain, making them think they were haunted whilst trapped alone in their dead parent's house. Or take them to a mine that had killed fifteen people, leave them alone in the dark and feed them stories about the ghosts of the men who had never been able to leave.

I punched him again, but Lucas was ready for me this time and tried to get in one of his own. I was easily able to deflect it and snapped his arm as it passed me. He wailed, the sound more animal than human. Rory flinched at the sound of bone cracking. I kicked Lucas' legs out from under him; he landed next to Trace.

'Call for back up. Don't let them move,' I said, as I made my way deeper into the mines to rescue Lilac from her own personal hell.

It took me longer to find Lilac than it had done me and Rory making our way to Lucas and Trace. I knew where I'd find her. It was where Lucas would have figured would scare her the most. Right at the site of the collapse.

Getting to her took on a new urgency since we'd found Lucas. The danger she was in having a bad trip *as well as* being trapped in an unstable mine was a thousand times worse than simply being trapped or suffering through an awful trip. Lilac high on LSD wouldn't know the difference between what was real and what was a hallucination. She could harm herself in a number of ways even if she wasn't in a mining tunnel that was unstable.

Some people believed that a mine was more stable after

a collapse because the weakest point had already been exposed and the worst had already happened. Those people were fucking idiots. Especially when it came to mines where the fault was in the barrier pillars or the girders that supported the roof. As was the case here.

It wasn't the case as it had been with Lucas where we'd heard them before seeing them. With Lilac, one minute I was rounding a corner of another tunnel, and the next I came up against the fallen debris that had killed my dad.

Lilac was curled in a ball besides the wall. A small hole had been dug out of the side – barely noticeable, but for the blood caked into it.

I rushed towards her. I scooped her into my arms, her head lolling over my arm. I held her like you'd hold a sleeping baby, protective of the head; mindful of those fragile limbs that seemed so delicate and loose like they had no tension in the muscles at all.

'Lilac.' I resisted the urge to shake her awake.

She was bleeding from her arms, her legs, even her face was pretty scratched up. Her hands were the worst of it. Her nails ripped from their beds; her fingertips scraped raw. I couldn't tell in this light if it was mud or blood dried black all over her body. From the tang of metal in the air, I had a fear it was blood.

'Lilac, baby, open your eyes.'

She twitched in my arms, but she didn't move. Her breathing was light, but her heartbeat was going insane inside her chest. Her eyes moved from beneath her eyelids like crazy.

'I'm getting you out of here. You're safe now,' I told her.

I picked her up, carrying her back down the tunnel that I'd travelled. The damage was self-inflicted. That much I knew. But I couldn't look at her too much without wanting to rip the hearts out of Lucas and Trace who were responsible for every minor cut to the larger injuries she'd need stitches for.

Eventually, I made my way back to Rory. Lucas and Trace were still on the floor, sitting now, not writhing in pain.

When they saw the state Lilac was in, they laughed manically. They'd left her alone in the dark, possibly feeding her lines to fuel her trip. Not that she would have been able to hear them. The worst trips isolated you in your own mind, blocking you off from every sense.

'Shut them the fuck up,' I hissed at Rory. 'Did you call for backup?'

Rory shook his head. 'The radio won't work this far underground.'

'Lilac needs the hospital,' I said. 'We need to get out of these mines and call for backup to pick up those two fuckers.'

Lilac stirred in my arms – and that's when everything went to shit.

Rory's inability to call for backup might have stopped them from pulling anything, as he still had a gun on them. But seeing me occupied with Lilac in my arms, and knowing that as soon as we got out of the mine they wouldn't be getting away with this as they'd once hoped, made them desperate.

They rushed Rory together, knocking him to the ground. Lucas' ability to work well with his arm broken as it was meant I'd either misread the signs and he *was* high, or I'd misjudged how much mental fortitude that asshole actually had.

Rory barely struggled for a moment before Trace had pulled the gun from him. Trace pistol whipped him, and Rory crumpled to the floor. Trace then turned to me, making sure the safety of the gun was off before he smiled manically.

Without looking at Lucas for direction, Trace said, 'here's how it's going to work. You're going to load her into the truck and you're gonna let us drive off. No hassle.'

Like fuck was I going to do that.

I didn't say it, but Trace could read it in my expression.

'Ah-ah. I really wouldn't fucking test me right now,' Trace said.

I was so sure that I'd handcuffed the prick behind his back. How was he... *fuck.* Double-joined slimy fucker. I'd forgotten he'd used to brag about that shit.

Trace awkwardly grabbed though Rory's pockets, finding the key to the handcuffs and unlocked himself. I would have been able to take advantage of that moment if I didn't have Lilac in my arms, to take the gun from him. He smirked as the handcuffs fell to the floor and he held the gun steadily again, as though he knew what I was thinking.

He then picked up Rory's hardhat and put it on his own head. He'd lost his cell at some point – probably when I'd tackled him. Still pointing the gun at me and Lilac, he bent to pick it up and shove it in his back pocket.

Lucas held out his hand – the one from his non-broken arm.

'What?' I asked him.

'Your hat.'

I raised an eyebrow at him. 'You're going to have to take it off my head. My hands are a little full right now.' I lifted Lilac a fraction to remind them of her presence.

Lucas didn't seem to pay any attention to her at all, but Trace's eyes were unnervingly fixed on her chest.

Lucas took the hat from my head, putting it on his own. Trace gestured with his gun, making me walk in front of them where I couldn't rush them from behind.

I tried to make sure not to jostle Lilac much as I moved at the quick pace Trace and Lucas set behind me. We left

Rory behind in complete darkness, which was probably the point so that when he woke up he wouldn't be able to follow us and call for backup.

I ran through possible solutions of how I was going to get Lilac out of this whilst apprehending Lucas and Trace at the same time. Lilac was my main priority. If it came down to it, I'd let them drive off as long as Lilac was still with me and could be on the way to the hospital as fast as possible.

Adrenaline was still pumping through my whole system, but I was struggling to come up with a solution. I'd always prided myself in being able to work out of a tight spot, but Lilac clouded my rational mind.

'Okay, here's far enough,' Trace said.

We were just at the mouth of the mine. The sun was beginning to set; light oranges and reds burning through the trees that obscured our parked cars.

'Give me the girl,' Trace said.

Lucas started. 'You've got to be fucking kidding me,' he said. 'We're not *taking* her with us.'

'I'm taking the girl,' Trace said.

'We take her and they come after us now,' Lucas said. His teeth were gritted. He wasn't used to being challenged. 'If we leave her, then he has to go get help. It gives us time to get away.'

Trace took a few paces then shot into the distance. I heard the sound of one of the tires from the vehicles outside pop as the bullet shot through it.

'There. He can't follow at all.'

Lucas shook his head. 'What else are we going to do with the bitch? She's not even fucking conscious.'

'She doesn't need to be,' Trace said.

I growled. Lucas shook his head. 'You sick fuck. *That's* the type of pussy you-'

His next sentence was interrupted as Lilac woke up. She

didn't notice she was in my arms. All she saw was the damage of her body: bloody and bruised, her fingers practically worn through to the muscle. I didn't know how long she'd been under the effects of the drugs, but it was likely that she was still partially tripping; perhaps not enough to keep the pain at bay.

Lilac's ear-piercing scream filled the tunnel, echoing down the mine and out into the dusk air.

Lilac's scream seemed to scare the shit out of Trace. He jumped, accidentally shooting the gun up in the air. The bullet hit the beam directly above us.

The fear in Lucas and Trace's eyes was instant. We'd shared many a nightmare together about what it would be like to be trapped like our fathers. What if the collapse hadn't killed them right away, but they'd suffocated or starved?

Forgetting their argument over Lilac, Lucas and Trace ran to the exit. The beam still seemed stable enough, but I wasn't going to risk it. I was wary of collapse, *before* that bastard had shot at a beam holding up the fucking ceiling. I said a prayer for Rory as I carried Lilac out towards the light.

Lilac struggled in my arms as I ran. She wasn't speaking, just wriggling around as though she were trying to move out of her skin – like her blood and pain was just an outfit she could slip out of.

We made it out. Lucas and Trace were arguing by their truck. I put Lilac down just outside of the mine, behind one of the snapped trees hoping to keep her out of sight enough that Trace forgot about her.

'Get in the car and drive already!' Trace shouted at Lucas, waving the gun around feverishly.

'I've got one arm! I can't drive a stick with one arm!'

'You're *always* the driver.'

'I know I'm always the fucking driver, but I can't drive

this time-'

They were going around in circles, almost as if they thought they had all the time in the world. As though I wasn't coming up behind them. Trace put a lot of stock in the protection that gun could afford him.

Treading lightly on the dirt path, I kept myself out of their eyeline as I came up behind Trace. With the gun, I'd considered him the one most likely to cause me damage, but I should have remembered Lucas was always the more dangerous of the pair. He'd spotted me but allowed me to sneak up to Trace because he knew that he had the better of me. He'd seen where I'd stashed Lilac and motioned towards going to her.

In the last minute where I should have incapacitated Trace like I had done before, a second of indecision cost me as I considered whether I should go back to Lilac and protect her from Lucas. Lucas got what he wanted and was able to give Trace a warning.

Trace whipped round, shooting once before I was able to grab the gun from his hand, twist upwards and take the firearm from him. I didn't register the sting of the bullet wound I'd sustained until I shot a bullet into Trace's kneecap.

Trace howled falling to the floor. Blood quickly began to pool through his pants.

'Hands on your head, chest on the hood of the car unless you want kneecapping, too,' I told Lucas.

He took one look at Trace before complying. I opened Rory's car door and grabbed the radio. I didn't know police codes, and I wasn't going to try and bullshit.

'This is Dawson, I'm at the collapsed mine entrance, west on Miner's Mount. I have Lilac Montgomery; Lucas Olson and Trace Toft who all need medical assistance. Deputy Rory Gibson is still in the mine, possible concussion. I need police backup to contain Lucas and

Trace.'

There was more that I had to say, but my vision was slowly starting to ebb away from me. I touched my shoulder and realised that I was bleeding out pretty fast. It was a through-and-through. Blood was equally pouring down the back of my jacket as much as my front. That was good. The through-and-through, not the bleeding fast. That was bad.

Dispatch on the other end of the radio started to reply to me, but my hearing wasn't working as well as I wanted it to. Instead, I heard nothing but a ringing. The sounds of Trace's swearing and grunting fading out into the same abyss my sight seemed to be going into.

I tried to reach over to the radio, ask them to repeat it, but I couldn't grab it. Fuck. I was going to pass out. I slapped myself in the face, trying to get back that adrenaline to keep me awake. I held the gun steady in my hand.

I think I must have blacked out for a second. Lilac was in front of me the next time I blinked. I was slumped into the driver's seat of Rory's cruiser.

'I'm sorry I got you into this mess, Lilac, you know that right?'

She didn't say anything to me. I wasn't entirely sure she was here with me, or still trapped in her own world.

'I love you, and you're going to be fine,' I said. 'You're my family and I won't let anything happen to you. I love you,' I said again. 'You're my… family.'

I remember saying those words again one more time, until the darkness finally took me. The last thing I remember was the feel of the gun slipping through my fingers and Lilac's voice. But I never quite heard what she said.

27

LILAC

The world was covered in blood and Henry was dying in front of me. That's how I knew this was all an awful nightmare.

I'd had the same dream a thousand times when I was fourteen. Thinking about what was happening to Henry in the army; the horror stories of the men who never came back, and the broken ones who did. I'd dream Henry was bleeding out in front of me and I couldn't do anything to stop it because I wasn't really there, I was just a ghost who was visiting him in those final moments. The power of my love drawing me to him.

When I'd moved back to Texas, those nightmares had still followed me, but over time they'd disappeared until eventually I'd gone to college and I'd almost forgotten the danger Henry was in overseas.

But here it was, once again. The drugs that Lucas had given me were causing me to hallucinate. Blood on my arms. Blood pouring from Henry…

Henry spoke, but his words were muffled. The gun he was holding slipped from his hand.

Sounds began coming back to me. The crackle of the police radio. Then the moans of Trace on the other side of the car. Lucas with his chest pressed against the hood of the vehicle Henry was currently bleeding out in.

This wasn't a nightmare. At least not the type I could wake from.

Kasey. Meeting Trace at the Manor. The cabin. The mines. *Oh, Lord.* The *miners.* The ghosts.

I threw up just outside the cruiser. The ghost of the miners' picks inside my arms made them feel like metal vibrating with a current of electricity through them. The feeling of the deep gouges on my arms and worn nubs of my fingertips couldn't quite reach my brain yet.

Lucas looked up from the hood of the car. Henry was slumped down in his seat, unconscious. A spark of an idea flared in Lucas' eyes.

I pushed through my sickness and grabbed the gun. My hands were numb as they held the weapon. Phil's lessons returned to me, though it wasn't as if I'd been any good at the range. I pointed the gun at Lucas. Trace was slumped on the floor now, almost out.

'Stay there,' I said. My voice was hoarse, like I'd been screaming for hours.

'You're not going to shoot me, princess,' Lucas said.

He stood up, ignoring me.

'Where's Kasey?' I asked.

I had to focus on the here and now – otherwise I'd get sucked into the mines and the awful Hell I'd discovered down there. But there were more important things than the dead at stake now. I needed to know where Kasey was – whether she was safe, where they'd put her.

'She's the least of your troubles now, girly,' Lucas told me.

'I said stay where you are.'

Somehow, I kept my voice firm and kept myself upright. All I wanted to do was collapse and wake up Henry. I just wanted to curl up into his arms and have him tell me that we were safe, and that Kasey was fine and we were going to be okay. But that wasn't going to happen. Sometimes the princess had to save herself. My shield was down. But I wasn't.

'Tell me where Kasey is.'

Lucas rolled his eyes at me. 'She's in the cabin, having a nap.'

'Did you drug her, too?'

It would explain why she was so quiet – why I hadn't been able to hear her when Trace had taken me there. If they'd given her something… they wouldn't have thought to lessen the dosage – or if they had, how would they have been able to calculate what would knock a four-year-old out? She could be dead.

Bile rose from my stomach once more, but I couldn't take my eyes of Lucas. Tears were streaming down my face, but that was the only weakness I would allow myself.

Lucas made his way over to the pickup truck we'd driven up in.

'Don't… leave me,' Trace said, wincing through the pain, fighting the blood loss that was threatening to pull him under.

Lucas went to open the car door. He wasn't going to get away. I couldn't let him. I pulled the trigger.

I'd forgotten about the kickback once you shot a gun. I almost hit myself in the face. The bullet hit the truck door and Lucas ducked, swearing.

'Fuck!'

'I said don't move.'

'Alright, alright,' he said.

'Go back onto the hood.' I didn't know what the position was called, but I figured he knew what I meant.

He was moving around to the hood when the other cars showed. Two cop cars. One with Sheriff Olson.

I hadn't seen him around town before – Henry had been

sure to keep me out of his sight, but I recognised him because he looked like a more put-together version of Lucas. The only perceivable difference between them (besides the damage alcohol and drugs had done to Lucas) was that Sheriff's Olson's hair was a little lighter.

'Put the gun down!' the sheriff demanded as he exited the car.

I should have done what he said immediately, but all I could think of was Henry's warnings about this man. How I wasn't to trust the police here because of him. If I put the gun down now, there was nothing to protect me and Henry with. Lucas and Trace would get away. And who knew what would happen to Kasey. Lucas could have lied about her being in the cabin. We couldn't let them get away until we had Kasey back. We shouldn't really be thinking about letting them get away *at all*, but with a corrupt sheriff, who was going to hold them?

My hands were shaking, the gun unsteady in my hands.

'She's crazy, Rick,' Lucas told his cousin. 'She shot Trace and Dawson. Nearly killed your deputy in there,' he motioned back into the mine.

There was someone still *in there?* What would the ghosts do with him?

'Dawson?' Rick called out.

Henry couldn't answer. He was still passed out in the police cruiser I was guarding with my body.

'Put the gun down, girl,' Sheriff Olson told me. 'And get down on the ground.'

I shook my head.

'Put the gun down.'

'Where's Kasey?' I asked Lucas again.

'Fuck. I already told you, crazy bitch. She's in the cabin.'

'We've got Kasey,' Sheriff Olson told me. 'Just put the gun down and we'll take you to her.'

'I'm not going anywhere with you,' I said.

'Gibson's in the mine?' Rick asked Lucas.

'She's a Montgomery – what does she care if she leaves another one of us to die in there,' he said.

He was lying. I didn't know of anyone inside the mine besides the ghosts from Hell. I trained my gun on Lucas. I could see the wisps of smoke around him, forming as he conjured the ghosts who worked for him: who toyed with me.

He was going to get away. He was going to call his ghosts and they were going to bring us all back down into the mines to Hell and we'd never find Kasey and they'd take Henry and he would die and I'd never see him again. I couldn't let that happen.

I shot the gun again. I missed Lucas. I'd always been an awful shot. But that wasn't the end of it.

The sheriff had seen me aim for his cousin, had seen me shoot, and he quickly whipped out his gun to stop the threat: me.

It happened so quickly: the decision in Sheriff Olson's eyes to pull the trigger and end my life. Unlike me, he would not miss. I was already covered in blood, so I didn't expect to be able to notice much difference besides the pain and then the emptiness Henry believed followed after death.

But that didn't happen.

Instead of being hit in the front, I was pushed forward from the back and a heavy weight pressed against me, protecting every inch of my body.

'I've got you,' Henry said, his voice in my ear. 'I've always got you.'

Henry was saying goodbye to me outside his home rather than letting me come to the airport with him. Mr Dawson was dropping him off and I'd asked whether I could drive up with them, but Henry didn't want me to make that drive. He wanted me to stay here with Edie.

'But I want to wave you off,' I told him.

'You need to say with mom,' he said again. 'She needs you. You need to look after each other whilst I'm gone.'

'I don't want you to go,' I said.

'I know.'

'I think you're making a mistake.'

Henry sighed. 'You're young, Lilac. You'll understand one day.'

'Only if you come back.' I grabbed his hand. I was never this forward. I never initiated contact, but this could be the last time that I ever saw him. I didn't want any regrets left between us. 'Promise me you'll come back, and I'll promise to try and understand.'

'You don't need me, Lilac,' Henry said.

'I know I don't need you, stupid,' I said. 'I've never needed you. I wanted you.'

Henry chuckled low and soft. There was always humour in his laughter, like he could find the light side of anything. Nothing ever seemed to get him down. He could face the end of the world and he'd probably still be able to laugh at something.

'The world doesn't need saving – not by you. Can't you let someone else do it?' I asked.

I knew it was too late. Henry was going. These were all words I'd said before and they'd made no difference. Edie's begging hadn't changed his mind. Henry wanted out of Grand Yutu and this was how he saw it happening.

Henry took me by surprise by pulling me into a hug instead of answering me.

'You've got to listen to me, Lilac, because the next few years are going to be tough and I'm not going to be there to help you through them, okay? Promise me you'll listen and remember what I say.'

He was still holding me close to him, whispering in my ear so I could only feel him pressed up against me, his voice in my ear, but I couldn't see him.

I nodded.

'There are going to be boys who want you to do things for them that you're not ready to. Don't ever let them force you into something you don't want to do. Never stay with a boy who isn't worth your time.

'And one day, when you're ready, only have sex with a person you love. Don't do it because you're bored. Make sure it's with someone who can make you laugh. The first time is always shitty compared to the rest, so it's good to have someone who can laugh about it with you.'

My face blushed a deep red at Henry talking about me having sex with someone in the future. In all my fantasies, I'd lost my virginity to Henry. However unlikely that was going to be, it was impossible now he was about to be shipped off.

'If people treat you like shit, don't let them walk over you. Tell them to their face they're being an asshole and you deserve better.'

'I can't use that word.'

'Like fuck you can't. Asshole.'

I scrunched my face up. Henry pulled back a little, looking down at me, staring at me in the eyes. His blue eyes bore into my brown ones.

I took a deep breath. Mama never let me swear. I got hit round the back of the head if I even said "damn" or "lord".

'Asshole,' I said.

Henry grinned. 'Yes. Promise me you won't just smile and let them treat you like shit.'

'I promise.'

'Even if you think you can get into their heads and understand – just because you can see why they're being

mean to you doesn't mean they get to be.'

I nodded. I understood.

'You're so fucking special. Don't ever forget that,' Henry said.

I shook my head.

'Lilac,' Henry took my chin between his thumb and forefinger, making sure that I kept looking at him. 'You'll always be my family. No matter what. You're it, you know that, don't you? I will always be your family no matter what.'

I knew that. To Henry, family was everything. It's why even though I knew he could never love me romantically; I knew I had a part of him that none of those girls at school did. He loved me with a love that couldn't be transferred to another woman. There would always be a part of his heart that had Lilac Montgomery etched into its surface no other person could claim.

'You'll always be my family, too,' I said.

'Nearly time to go,' Mr Dawson said.

'One more minute, dad,' Henry said.

'I'm going to write to you a thousand letters,' I said.

I'd already bought the stationary. It was quite fancy and grown up. I didn't want his new army friends to think that he was getting letters from his baby sister or something.

'You can't, Lilac.'

'What?'

Henry sighed. He looked sombre all of a sudden, like the light in his eyes had been extinguished. 'You can't write to me; you can't try and call me or contact me.'

'What are you on about? Of course I can. It's the army – it's not deep space.

'I need to focus on training – and after that I'll be in places that I can't be distracted, thinking about home and about you. If I know what's happening over here – what's

going on in your life that I can't help you with, I won't be able to concentrate.'

'Do you mean like with hockey?'

The first time I'd come to one of his games instead of just practice when he was seventeen, I'd been sitting next to a bunch of seniors. Edie hadn't been with me and the boys had gotten a bit rowdy.

When Henry had skated around the rink before the game, he'd seen me get pushed around a little and had banged on the plexiglass stopping the guys from being so rough around me in case I got hurt. For the rest of the game he hadn't been able to concentrate; his eyes always came back to me, skating towards the edge of the rink where I was instead of following the puck. I was his weakness.

Edie had always made sure to sit with me at any of the games I came to and not leave my side. Only then could Henry concentrate. If Edie couldn't come, then I wasn't allowed to go to a game. Henry's mind could never focus if he thought I wasn't safe.

'Exactly like that.'

'So... we just don't talk. For years?' My eyes were burning with tears.

He couldn't be serious. He was not only choosing to leave Grand Yutu, but he was choosing to leave me like this.

'You'll forget all about me!'

'I'll never forget you, Lilac.'

'But that's your plan. Leave me here and forget about me so you don't worry. Don't you think I'll freakin' worry every second you're gone? That's not fair Henry Dawson! You can't tell me I'm family and then say we can't speak again.'

'Mom will be able to keep you updated.'

'You're being an asshole,' I told him.

It was the first time I'd ever used that word. But I meant it. He couldn't do this. I loved him. And he loved me. He couldn't just leave me behind like this.

How was I supposed to live not speaking to him for months on end? I'd spoken to Henry Dawson every day for the past eight years of my life. How did you just cut someone out of your life like that?

'I am an asshole,' Henry agreed. 'You're gonna be fine without me, Lilac.'

'No, I'm not. Not if you leave like this.'

Mr Dawson beeped the horn.

'I've gotta go.'

'Henry – don't. You're just joking, aren't you? We're not really going to not speak? It's just a joke.'

Henry started walking towards his daddy's car.

'Henry, please tell me we're going to talk.'

Henry climbed into the car and closed the door. The window was still open. My hands grabbed through the open window.

'You promised me I'd always have you! For forever!'

'You always will,' Henry said. 'I love you.'

And the car pulled away.

True to his word, I didn't speak to him for another eight years until I came back to Grand Yutu to pack away my dead daddy's house.

28

DAWSON

The beep of the monitor was not unfamiliar. Nor was the pain of a bullet wound, fresh stitching, and the ache in my head like a pickaxe was working away slowly at my last brain cells.

But I wasn't in some military hospital. And despite the sterile smell of the ward, the lingering smell of coconuts had me thinking one word as I woke up: Lilac.

Unlike the mental blocks I'd been able to construct in the army to protect myself from distraction, I'd never had memory loss when it came to blacking out. Somehow, I was able to recall the last moments with a clarity that most people would be envious of in a sober, undamaged mind.

Fading in and out of consciousness as I fought the blood loss. Coming to just as Rick's gun pointed towards Lilac. Lilac realising she was about to be shot – and then I'd done what instinct told me to and protected her with the only thing available to me: my body.

But there was only so much I had the power to remember. And I wasn't superhuman. I couldn't know what happened once I was unconscious. Which meant I had no idea what had happened after I'd dived to save Lilac. Whether Rick had let Trace and Lucas go. Where

Lilac was now.

Rick wouldn't have given her over to Lucas, would he? He couldn't be that fucking corrupted in the head… but he had tried *shooting* her. What the fuck had that been about?

I pulled myself up into a sitting position. I couldn't rip the IV out without some serious pain and damage, so I swung my legs over the bed and grabbed whatever was attached to me to come for the walk.

I exited my room and out onto the main floor. The nurses' station was just a little way ahead.

COVID-19 posters and warnings were stuck on all the walls. The nurses and doctors were all in masks and gloves. We were outside Grand Yutu now; the protective bubble of isolation left behind. Couldn't the pandemic just be put on hold for one fucking minute so I could find my girl and make sure she was safe? The last thing I needed now was for us to survive a kidnapping, a shooting and then succumb to a virus when we were in a weakened state.

'Lilac Montgomery, is she in this ward?' I asked the first nurse I saw behind the desk.

Her brow furrowed in confusion. 'What room did you come from?'

It wasn't like I'd been looking at the room number when I left.

'Henry Dawson,' I told her, giving her my name. If I was here, then it was likely whoever dropped me off – Rick or one of the other officers – had given her my details. They'd need to know for the blood transfusion.

'I need to know if Lilac Montgomery was brought in with me,' I asked again.

'I can't give out information of other patients.'

'I'm family and I got shot trying to save her. I'm not asking what room number she's in. I'm not asking for private details. I'm asking to know if she's *here.*'

'I can't give out information of *other patients,'* she said again, emphasising the last two words again for me.

'Thank you. Now what room is she in?' I flashed her a smile that won over most women. I couldn't tell if it had any affect on her considering most of her face was obscured by her mask. That, and I was betting I looked like absolute shit.

'You need to go back to your room Mr Dawson. We currently have a no-visitors policy due to the coronavirus outbreak.'

'She was coming down from a bad trip. She was just kidnapped. And she's badly injured. She can't be alone right now,' I told her.

'You seem to really care for her, I can see that. But she's in the best hands right now. You've got to trust us to take care of her.'

I bit back my groan of frustration. At least she was here, that was one thing.

'Was there anyone else brought in with us?' I asked.

'There's a couple officers on the floor below guarding the men who came in with you. They're supposed to be transferred to the county jail by midday tomorrow morning.'

'Thank you.'

I started to walk away.

'Mr Dawson! I have to ask you to go back to your room! You can't be walking around the halls.'

'I'd prefer a set of pants to walk around in, too, ma'am, but I can walk just fine,' I said, being purposefully obtuse.

I grabbed a mask from the reception, slipping it on over my face, then continued over to the lift where I pressed for the floor below me. I spotted two officers from Grand Yutu at the same moment they spotted me.

'Dawson,' Davenport said.

'Did you find Rory okay?' I asked.

'Yeah. Had a bit of a fright being in the dark for so long,

but the deputy's doing fine.'

'Good. Trace and Lucas in there?' I asked.

Davenport nodded.

'Rick charge them with Kasey and Lilac's abduction?'

'Along with breaking and entering, defacement of property, reckless endangerment and assault of an officer.'

He pulled through. Perhaps my vote for Sheriff Olson hadn't been misplaced after all.

'Kasey?' I asked.

'She's home with Willa,' Davenport said. 'Scared, but no injuries.'

I paused. There were so many questions I had about Lilac I wasn't sure where to begin. Davenport seemed to read my indecision.

'We arrived at the scene ten minutes after you radioed in. Lilac had taken Rory's gun. Both you and Trace were bleeding out. Lucas had a broken arm. He was saying plenty of shit about a trigger-happy Montgomery.'

'Trace shot me,' I said.

'Yeah. I didn't think it was her – even though we found gunpowder all over her hands.' Lilac had shot the gun. Why had she? What the fuck was she thinking…? Well, she hadn't been. She was high. Fuck. She could have seriously hurt herself.

'She tried shooting Lucas. Sheriff Olson decided to shoot first. Only you dived in the way.'

'He missed.'

'I don't think he was exactly aiming for a kill-shot,' Davenport said.

His tone was reprimanding. I didn't give a shit. His sheriff might have pulled through in the last minute and done the right thing arresting his cousin, but he'd sure as shit not listened to me these past few weeks when I'd been telling him Lucas was up to something. And he'd tried to shoot Lilac. No matter if it was a kill shot or an incapacitating one. No one shot at my girl.

'Do you know where she is now?'

Davenport shook his head. 'A few rooms down from yours the last I knew. She was coming down from whatever drugs she was on. A nurse was staying with her, making sure she didn't try and scratch through to her bone again.'

'Thanks,' I said.

'How are you doing?' Davenport stopped me from getting back in the elevator with his question.

I was in a hospital gown, my right shoulder wrapped up heavily in gauze and bandages. I was attached to a drip and was pretty sure my ass was hanging out for all the world to see.

'Right as rain,' I said. 'Not my first bullet wound.' Probably wouldn't be my last.

The charts for the patients on the floor I returned to were hung on the front door. I scanned the names quickly, so that if anyone walked by it wouldn't be too obvious I was checking the rooms for someone.

Several doors away from the nurses' station, was "L. Montgomery." I swiftly slipped in through the door before anyone spotted me.

Whatever nurse had been sitting with her was gone. Instead, Lilac lay asleep with a thin hospital sheet covering her.

Her arms were wrapped in thick bandages. Her face had been cleaned of the grime and dirt from the mines, so the scratches on her cheeks looked pinker and more swollen. Lilac's hair was damp against the pillow.

'Lilac,' her name passed through my lips like a prayer.

At the sound of my voice, she stirred. I spotted some hand sanitiser that had been left by the wall. I'd not touched anything but the mask since I'd woken up, but I wasn't going to take risks. I lathered my hands in it, then I made my way over to the bed.

I'd settled down into the chair, the drip stationary next to me, when Lilac opened her eyes.

'Henry?' she asked.

'I'm here,' I said. I held her hand.

Tears began to flow freely from her eyes. Lilac looked at me helplessly, seeming tiny in the hospital bed, like she was drowning in a sea of white.

'You're okay?'

'Nothing a blood transfusion and a few stitches can't fix,' I told her.

Her face crumpled. 'I'm so sorry. I'm sorry – I didn't think. I should have tried to stop the bleeding-'

'Lilac, Lilac.' I sat on the edge of her bed. I pulled her to me, her head resting on my chest as I rocked her. 'It's okay. We're both okay.'

'Kasey-'

'She's home with Willa,' I told her.

'I was so worried,' she sobbed.

'I know. I know you were.'

When she was better we were going to have a huge fucking conversation about how stupid she'd been to run off and try and sort this mess out on her own – but that was for later.

'Lucas and Trace…?'

'They'll be in the county jail by tomorrow.'

I was glad I'd been able to get answers from Davenport. It helped that I could reassure her that everything was okay, not simply say that I didn't know.

'It's over?'

I nodded. 'Yes.'

'Don't leave,' Lilac said – as though I'd just come to visit her to keep her informed of the progress of the case and I was heading back to my own room to sleep it off.

'I'm not. I'll stay as long as you want me.'

Lilac moved over to the side of the bed a little more so there was more room for me. She turned to her side a little, resting her head on my chest, wrapping her bandaged arms around my chest, and holding me to her.

'I mean it this time,' Lilac whispered into my chest. 'You can't promise not to leave and then cut me out of your life for years.'

'I'm stuck in Grand Yutu now,' was the only answer I could give her.

I couldn't tell her that I'd follow her to Texas. But once she went, I wouldn't let it be like last time. I wasn't afraid I'd put myself or my unit in danger if I was thinking of her. I had a town to worry about – yes, but there wasn't a part of me that could shut out Lilac anymore. I would be worried more if I couldn't speak to her again.

'We're family,' Lilac told me.

'Yes.'

'And you won't leave me alone?'

'I won't leave you,' I said.

'Then I won't leave you alone, either,' Lilac told me, squeezing my hand.

I didn't answer her. I wasn't quite sure what she meant.

'You left, mama and daddy left – but I never had a choice to leave here. But I have a choice to stay now. I'm not going to abandon this town. Not when I have the means to fix it. And I'm not leaving you. I'm the only family you've got.'

'Lilac…'

She was more injured than me; had gone through an ordeal and her first thoughts after going through hell were how she was going to care for the town and me… This fucking girl.

'We're family, Henry Dawson,' Lilac told me. 'And we're forever. I'm not a little girl who's waiting for decisions to be made around me anymore.'

'You're staying – in Grand Yutu.'

Lilac nodded. 'I am.'

My heart felt like it was going to explode in my chest. She wasn't leaving. *Fuck.* She wasn't leaving. How did that work? How were *we* going to work?

'Henry?' Lilac asked, as though she could see the thousand thoughts running wild in my mind.

'Let's just focus on getting out of the hospital first,' she told me. 'And then we'll sort out the *forever* part. Can you do that?'

'I can do that.'

Lilac smiled, closing her eyes, and I listened as her breathing faded out into sleep on me.

JULY

29

LILAC

The end of May had seen America's COVID-19 death tolls top 100, 000. Outside the little nobody town of Grand Yutu, and in the states who'd had more intense lockdown laws than North Dakota, there were protests against the stay-at-home orders. Businesses were reopening, with new protocols that had to make sure there was a distance of six feet between customers.

As the world learnt to live a new life, balancing their health and safety between the phrases "social distancing" and "self-isolation", the small town I'd spent my childhood in was changing, too.

'Lilac… this, well, sweetie, this isn't what I was expecting from you,' mama said.

I hadn't spoken to mama for weeks after I'd found out what she had lied to Edie about. But my near-death experience had made me see sense.

Just like with daddy, though she had hurt other people with her actions, that didn't mean that she was *all* bad. Just as she wasn't *all* good. I was her shade of grey. I could never forget what she had done, and how that guilt had played into Edie's depression, but I could accept it and learn to move on. She would always be my family, and always part of my life.

'Daddy always said that property was a wise investment,' I told her.

'Yes, he did,' she said hesitantly. 'But it's one thing for you to own an apartment in Washington… quite another to own…numerous small-town businesses, a luxury mountain Resort, and three farms that haven't seen work in the last decade.'

She stated the list like she was reading from a sheet of paper. She possibly was as I knew she'd contacted daddy's old PA for a list of all the properties I'd acquired and was taking on.

With help from Lisa and a few of daddy's old contacts, I'd managed to secure the money owed to the fifteen families and pay them back every last cent. But like Henry had said, justice for the miners and the town couldn't be granted by throwing money at the problem.

'But are you sure Grand Yutu is the best place to be investing in?' Mama asked me.

She'd been expecting me to sell daddy's properties. But what use would that be? All it would do was add more money to the already absurd amount I'd inherited.

'I grew up here,' I said.

'Yes, I know, sweetie, and you always did love that place.' Mama paused for a minute. 'How *is* Henry?'

I knew she was convinced that it was my love of a man, not the love of the town that was the real cause of my change of plans for the future. Afterall, when I'd been younger my thoughts had mirrored her own: why did the people here not just run as far away as possible if they were so unhappy here.

She knew about how daddy had helped ruin this town. After what had happened down in the mines, I'd sent her daddy's journals. My daddy hadn't been a good man – but he had loved my mama and me. I wanted her to read in his own words how much he had tried for her. She couldn't hang onto the hate she felt for him forever, especially not for something for once that he *didn't* do. If I could forgive her, she could forgive him.

Once she'd read them, we'd talked at length about what had happened to the town since we'd left. Phil said Mama was attending some online therapy sessions to deal with the guilt of everything that had happened to Edie because of her selfish lie.

We both knew it hadn't just been mama's words that had pushed Edie over the edge, but whatever factor she'd had to play in her friend's death required therapy, and penance. She was apparently going to church more often, too.

That was fine for her – it was how she decided she would cope, but that wouldn't work for me. The only way I could see getting passed the guilt from how badly my family had damaged this down was to fix their mistakes. Daddy's legacy was me and his money. I was going to damn well make sure I did some good with it since he'd done so much wrong acquiring it.

'He's great. Still the un-official town mayor,' I said, answering her question about Henry.

'Mayor is a respectable job,' mama supposed. 'Why not make it official?'

'Because Henry doesn't want to go into politics. He loves being the town's hockey coach and handyman.' And farmhand, and stock-boy and taxi service for elderly neighbours – the list went on.

Though for a while, I'd worried he wasn't going to be any of those things again. Until we'd all be assured that his bullet wound wasn't life threatening or even that debilitating. Henry had joked that he'd had worse in the army and had recovered enough to become a semi-decent hockey player.

'Hmm…' was all mama had to say in response. 'You're staying safe, aren't you?'

'Yes, mama. Grand Yutu is probably one of the safest places I could be. We've not had a single coronavirus case.'

I'd never let her know what had happened in the mines two months ago. Her only worry for me was the pandemic – as though I hadn't survived other horrors in the meantime.

I still had nightmares about what I'd seen on the drugs Lucas had forced me to take; waking up in a cold sweat. I slept with the light on – having become afraid of the dark and the things that lurked there. Henry was my steady rock in those moments.

'I heard about a town like that in England during the Black Death… Eyam I think it was called. They had the plague and wanted to make sure it didn't get out, so they quarantined themselves.'

'Yeah, I don't think it's like that mama because we're protecting ourselves from the *outside*, not- it doesn't matter.'

Mama caught me up with the gossip from back home, asking the odd question about my own life until our weekly-hour chat was up.

'I love you, sweetie.'

'I love you, too, mama.'

I hung up the phone and settled into Edie's desk – my desk, rather, now that I'd taken over her little office in the library.

Jill and Kyle, the two part-time/volunteer workers who had been running the library at the reduced hours since Edie's passing had been more than happy to know I was planning on taking over Edie's old job; keeping them on to support with the events and activities I had planned with the re-opening of the rec centre that hadn't seen life since Edie's car accident.

The community library was looking fully stocked and re-furbished with the new books and bookcases from daddy's library. The walls had been painted a fresh egg-shell white as had the rec centre.

Hiring decorators and contractors for renovating the buildings I owned had been the first thing I did after locating each and every building I owned around Grand Yutu.

Since tourism had died down, a lot of the builders and decorators had struggled for work. Hiring them would not only give them employment so they could feed their families, pay for their homes, and put money back into the local community, it would also improve the town's aesthetic. Which was important since my main goal was to get Grand Yutu prepared enough so that after the quarantine, our small town was ready for tourists.

'*Liiiiilac!*' Kasey sang running into the library.

'Jesus, kid, slow down,' Willa called after her. 'She's not hopped up on sugar. She just had a nap,' she told me.

'Good to know.'

We'd all worried about how being taken would affect Kasey. Lucas had taken her straight from the garden at her meemaw's place to the cabins up at daddy's Resort. She didn't say she'd been mistreated. When Rick had found her, she'd been locked in one of the bedrooms, curled up under the bed where she'd taken a pillow and was clutching it close to her for comfort.

Willa had quit working for a month and simply stayed by Kasey's side every minute of the day. Henry and I had made sure that her bills still got paid and they still had groceries. Kasey seemed to be managing. She was still loud and bossy. She still loved *Frozen* more than anything in the world and demanded we role-play with her and sing.

The only change we'd really noticed in her is that she no longer liked to spend time alone, entertaining herself. She had to have someone with her and in her eyesight at all times.

The few times that they'd gotten out of the apartment, Willa said Kasey didn't like the look of a few of the men around town and would hold her hand extra tight as though she were afraid she would be pulled away from her mama. But if they were the worst things to come out of the ordeal, we'd all considered ourselves to have gotten off lightly.

'How's our resident Uncle Pennybags?' Willa had taken to call me that after she'd accused me of having a monopoly on small businesses in this town.

A lot of people were wary when they realised another Montgomery was investing in the town, but as I was temporarily living with Henry and had given back the money daddy had taken from the fifteen's families they'd come around.

I'd like to think that it was because they knew I was a good person and was trying to do right by the town. But it was more likely that they saw me as "Henry's girl" and that the good I was doing was his influence and since he had "control" over me, I wouldn't screw them over like daddy had.

'Busy,' I admitted to her.

'Not so easy running the town, is it?' Willa said, reminding me of Henry's taunts the first time I'd told him my plan.

'The planning part I'm acing.'

Henry putting me on bed rest for the first two weeks after the incident in the mines had meant I'd had a lot of free time to decide what I wanted to do. Everyone expected me to leave on the first flight back to Texas, but if anything, the one thing that stuck in my mind were Mr Dawson's words.

I knew they weren't actually his, now. Rather just part of the elaborate hallucination I'd been having on my bad trip from the drugs Lucas had given me. But whether they were spoken by a real person, or by the dark recesses of the mind, it didn't make them any less true.

Daddy had run from this town. Mama had, too. They'd left their mistakes for other people to clean up and I wasn't going to be the same.

'It's implementing it that'll be the problem.'

It required the town's cooperation and a whole lot of praying that COVID-19 would eventually have a vaccine and life could return to normal.

I planned on opening the Resort my daddy had built; giving the town back its idyllic charm Edie had fallen in love with. I knew this wasn't some short-term plan I could just throw a load of money at and hope by some miracle to improve the town. This was a long-haul investment that might take a decade to fully see some big, meaningful change.

Even after paying back the fifteen, I still had millions at my disposal, and it wasn't like I was investing unwisely. I was making sure that everything I did would eventually turn a profit and *number one* would benefit the community the most.

'Better you than me,' Willa said, plopping herself down on the couch I'd used to do my homework on whilst Edie worked at the desk. 'So… what are your plans tonight?'

I crossed my arms, not liking the suggestive tone she had on.

'Henry has a game,' I said – like she didn't already know.

The competitive nature of sports was something that I felt that this town lacked. With no local rival high school, the kids didn't have that same drive other high schoolers did, or competition to look forward to. To play against another school, they had to drive more than an hour way out into the city.

Henry had always done an amazing job giving them a place to get out their aggression and frustration on the ice – but I saw potential, and room for more.

The town now not only had a high school hockey team, but a local team for graduates (like Henry).

There'd been a local team before, but it hadn't amounted to much since they'd hardly ever seen the ice or had any sort of direction. Henry changed all of that. This would be a team for those new adults who would miss the teamwork, the rivalry and competitiveness of being on the ice once they graduated.

Eventually, the plan was to make two "rival" local teams that would work like they did in the big city. They'd each have their own coaches, managers, set times on the ice and they'd play paid games for the town to watch.

The idea came to me when I realised how much Henry missed out on the games he'd started getting back into in college. He admitted that it was unlikely that he'd ever go back: the town needed him too much – and he'd never had it in him to go pro. A lot of kids would be the same: never leaving, going pro not in the cards for them, but loving being on the ice like it was where they belonged.

The local matches would give something for the community to look forward to, as well as give high school kids an outlet, and graduates something fun to occupy their time.

There wouldn't be enough money in it for them to quit their day jobs and have a career as the local hockey champions, it would purely be a hobby. It meant that those that did apply had to really want it, either by loving the game so much, or the idea of small-town fame.

The money for the seats to the matches would go to funding more after school programmes for the kids and improving the town.

Tonight would be the first game between the high school team and Henry's new graduate team. *Nokota Horses vs. Black Larks*. They'd be pretty evenly matched, or so Henry said since *Nokota Horses* were still pretty young, but the *Black Larks* had only just gotten on the ice this past month and were a new team, though they'd had years of experience on the high schoolers.

As there were still social distancing rules in place, we'd decided to work like most of the professional teams and have an empty arena of fans but have the game online for people to watch. We'd "hired" some high schoolers to become our sports photographers and newscasters, creating a *Facebook* and *Instagram* page where we could livestream the first game.

'Yes, and as captain of the *Black Larks* he's going to want to celebrate when he wins tonight,' Willa said.

'What makes you so sure he's going to win?' I laughed.

'I'm not,' Willa admitted. 'But since he's the coach of both teams, it sort of means no matter who wins – he wins. And that means you get *lucky*.'

I laughed her off.

'Oh, come off it. This whole we're-just-friends thing is complete bull. No one in town is buying it. You live together for Christ's sake!'

'Mommy!' Kasey said, scolding her like her meemaw taught her whenever she used the Lord's name in vain.

'I believe you were the one who told me that Henry doesn't do serious relationships.'

'Yeah, but-'

'No buts,' I said. 'He's never asked me for anything more than what we have and I'm not expecting it from him. I'm living with him temporarily until I find the right place. He's even helping me look for apartments that might become available.'

'You're still fucking and I'm not buying what you're selling,' Willa whispered to me.

The truth was since the last time we'd had sex – after I'd become jealous over Viv's attentions – Henry hadn't shown an inkling towards wanting to get me into bed. I'd thought for sure when he'd rescued me from the mine that something would have changed between us. But it hadn't.

Willa never stopped nagging me about it, but she was as close to Henry as she was to me, so it wasn't like I could open up to her about how I really felt. She blabbed everything. She was not a subtle person.

Darci, however, I'd poured out my heart to. I'd known the moment I thought I'd lost Henry forever that I loved him. That whatever feelings I'd had for him as a child hadn't disappeared, only hibernated and grown over the months we'd spent together getting reacquainted.

Saving me and nearly dying in the process had made it easy to put things into perspectives. Actions spoke louder than words. He may have said some awful things in the past, but with his actions he'd shown that he'd never hurt me. And if I was honest, I had forgiven him for what he'd said long before the incident in the mine.

If I could, I would have him in every way possible: living with him, being his girlfriend, spending my life with him. But Henry was devoted to this town and whatever stopped him from having a girlfriend – whatever hang-ups he had about long-term relationships – that wasn't something I could change. And I loved him enough not to *want* to change him. I loved him how he was.

I'd take Henry however I could get him. Which meant being his friend – and nothing more.

There was no doubt in my mind: I would never find a better man in Grand Yutu, so like with the grand ideas of my plans for this town, I'd put my love life on hold.

Who knew – perhaps when tourism started to pick up

in a few years from now, and I had more time to focus on myself rather than this town, some tourist would fall in love with me and move to Grand Yutu to be with me like Edie had for Mr Dawson.

30

DAWSON

With the wound in my shoulder taking a month to heal and get the stitches out, I hadn't been sure that I would be playing the first game. I'd been slowly rehabbing my shoulder whilst coaching, but Lilac didn't want me to push myself and end up damaging my shoulder for good. Not that I wanted that. It was just difficult being on the bench.

In the end, I'd seen less than ten minutes of ice time and the kids had gone easy on me. Not that Lilac was able to tell – she was one of the only spectators at the actual rink rather than watching at home.

I swear I could hear her shouts at Miller for the body check he'd given me seconds after gaining the puck. With no one else around, she didn't distract me like she used to on the ice. I wasn't worried about her. Her presence was reassuring.

I spent the rest of my time on the bench viewing the game from the perspective of a coach. *Nakota Horses* ended up winning the game 3-2. It was a close game the entire way through. I could see that with more practice and having spent as much time on the ice as the *Horses* did together, that the *Black Larks* would eventually surpass most of the high school players. They'd simply been away from the ice too long and hadn't had the same training the teens had.

Calvin winked at Lilac like a cheeky shit when the final buzzer sounded. She blew him a kiss, probably just to piss me off. But I couldn't be angry with her, not even fake-angry. Not when it meant so much to me to see her smile.

Lilac always had this way about her to push her own fears and problems to the back of her mind. I'd known since she'd woken up in that hospital bed that she was doing it now: focusing on the town and fixing everyone else's problems whilst she let hers disappear into the background.

I knew there was going to be a point where she had to accept that she needed help herself. And she was one of those rich types who had access to the therapy bucket loads of cash afforded. For once, I couldn't be bitter about Montgomery's money because it meant that when Lilac was ready, she'd be able to get any of the help out there she needed. She certainly needed it.

Lilac had suffered through one of the worst trips I'd ever seen. Her arms were still badly scarred from the damage she'd done to herself and the tips of several of her fingers that had been stitched were numb. The doctors had said that she would likely never get that feeling back as the nerves had been so badly damaged.

She wouldn't sleep with the light off, and just like Kasey – she hated being alone now. But she still put on a brave face and acted like nothing was wrong. Still searching for an apartment she intended to live in all alone, even though most of the time I ended up having to come into her room at night because she couldn't fall asleep without me being there – the empty room and silence reminding her too much of what it was like down the mines.

'What's your poison of choice?' Willa asked at the bar, *Under 21*.

Tit Town was under new management: Willa's. Lilac had been going through her property listings when she realised what the "Blue Night Club" actually was.

Along with the renovation of the library and rec centre, Lilac's biggest project had been transforming the strip club into a bar for under twenty one's. A non-alcoholic bar with mocktails, loud music, dancing, and dancers.

Lilac didn't want to put the dancers out of work so instead had hired them in a different capacity. They didn't earn as much as they had done when Montgomery's summer business retreats had come through town, but they earnt a steady wage – and more than they'd been earning these past couple years since the retreats had dried up. They no longer took off their clothes, but still used the pole or the dance cages hung from the ceiling, that anyone could now get up in and dance.

Willa had quit her job at the other bar and had become the fulltime manager of *Under 21*. It gave her better pay, and work hours that would be better with Kasey starting kindergarten this fall. Plus, Lilac knew she could trust Willa to run the bar right. And she certainly could handle any of the punks who thought they'd try it on with the staff behind the bar and get them to serve underage kids.

Dismissing the old management had been easy since Lilac owned the club. They also couldn't sue for unfair dismissal since they'd illegally kept Tit Town open when the Governor had issued his lockdown order of all businesses to help stop the spread of corona.

With Tit Town gone, the general atmosphere of the town changed. But that was probably more to do with Rick making an effort now Lucas was behind bars. He'd seen how much he'd let slide when Lucas had taken Kasey. Lilac might have been an outsider and the town's treatment of hers could be understood somewhat. But Kasey and Willa were both Grand Yutu born and bred.

Protests against the police force abusing their power were happening across America. Rick didn't want to be part of that margin where people of this town considered him the enemy and not someone they could trust to keep them safe.

Lilac gave her order for some fruity drink and I declined; having a water myself. We stayed at the bar for a few minutes, shooting the shit – having people slap me on the back for my loss and offer to buy me a drink in consolation or congratulate me on being the coach of the winning team.

Lilac grinned the whole time from above her mocktail, occasionally rolling her eyes at whatever look Willa was giving her from behind the bar. (Willa still enjoyed tending the bar when it was busy like tonight. She loved the gossip and the atmosphere rather than being stuck behind a desk).

The DJ gave me a nod when I looked over at him. I subtly nodded back, taking Lilac's almost empty glass, and placing it on the bar.

'Dance with me?'

Lilac's face screwed up in confusion for only a moment before she accepted my hand.

The dance floor was packed. It reminded me of college and everything these kids would have missed out on if not for Lilac. A tiny percentage of the Grand Yutu population left and went to college. The majority went straight into jobs around town, which meant they missed out on all the fun college experiences of simply being a young adult letting lose for the first time.

An hours drive into the nightclubs in the city wouldn't exactly be safe for them – especially if they'd had a fake ID and were drunk when they returned home. Lilac changed that.

'I've found you a place,' I said as we settled into a place in the middle of the dance floor.

'What?' Lilac asked, the music too loud for her to have heard me.

'I found you a place,' I said a little louder this time.

'You have?'

We were standing opposite each other. Both of us uncertain where to put our hands – both of us focusing on the conversation rather than how close our bodies were pressed up against each other with everyone around us.

'Yeah. It's a pretty good location. Fully furnished, affordable rent.'

'I hear a "but" coming.'

'It comes with a roommate.'

'I'm not sure-'

'I've had them fully vetted. Everyone in town seems to think he's a pretty decent guy. I'm a bit wary, but you know I'm a bit overprotective,' I told her, my smile wide as I joked.

'*He?*' Lilac said.

'You don't want a male roommate?'

'*You*'re okay with me having a male roommate?' she asked me.

'Should I not be?'

Lilac pinched those little cupid lips of hers. Who we were to each other – those labels Willa seemed to intent on putting on us – had never been clear since we'd slept together.

Lilac had said sex had been a one-time thing and that it hadn't meant more than just two people fucking – but everything that had happened after that was one big contradiction. We knew we loved each other. We knew we were family – but we also knew that the chemistry between us hadn't faded since we'd first kissed. We'd simply ignored it.

I'd never believed I could have it all – have all of Lilac. I'd simply been content with getting whatever I could in the time that remained before she went back to Texas. I'd never considered asking her to stay because I wouldn't force her to be tied down: not to this town, not to me. But she had done that all on her own. She had *chosen* to stay here.

I didn't know if she still wanted me the same way she had as a little girl. She reminded me often enough that she was a grown woman now and had changed. But I hoped that part hadn't. I hoped when she asked for forever – she wanted it *all.*

The music took a decided shift. Instead of the dance beat that had currently been playing, Peter Gabriel's *In Your Eyes* began to play.

'What's going on?'

Lilac – 80s romance lover extraordinaire, wouldn't fail to miss the theme of *Say Anything.*

I pulled Lilac close to me, putting my hands on her hips. Her arms automatically slotted around mine, feeling them secure on my waist like they were meant to be there. A few of the winning hockey team wolf whistled me. Most of them already guessed what was going on.

'It's not a boombox outside your window or a flash mob or a kiss on the ice after I win a big game,' I began. 'But it is in front of everyone and I'm making a pretty big scene for you, Texas.'

Lilac started to notice that the dancers around us had stopped and created a small space so that we were stood in the middle of the dance floor – everyone's eyes on us.

'What are you doing?' Lilac asked.

'Lilac Montgomery, since you were five-years-old you've been a pain in my ass. I've never been able to walk anywhere without you stepping on the backs of my heels. For eight years straight you were the one person I talked to without fail everyday – and not just because I had to, but because there has always been something about you that drew me in.

'When I left Grand Yutu the hardest thing I ever did was say goodbye to you, but I thought that's what had to happen. You were always bigger than this small-town and I never felt like I could amount to much if I didn't get out.

'Blocking how much you meant to me was the only way I could move forward, and it wasn't until we kissed that everything we'd once been to each other came flooding back and I haven't been able to stop thinking about you since.

'You have meant – and still mean – more to me than any other woman on this earth. There is no one who can replace you and the thought of you not being in my life anymore kills me.

'I was willing to let you go because it was what was best for you, but instead of running you decided to stay here in this town. I would never have asked that of you. But since you're already here, I will ask one small favour.'

I knew the eyes of everyone in the club were on us, but all I could see was Lilac. Her eyes were shining with tears that hadn't fallen, but she was smiling and she hadn't let go of me. That was a good sign… right?

'Stay exactly where you are. Don't move out. Live with me.'

Lilac opened her mouth. Her smile dropped for a moment, like she was confused. 'Live with you?'

I nodded.

'Because I'm family?' she asked.

'Because you're everything,' I said. I bridged the gap between us, cupping the back of her head with the palm of my hand and bringing her close towards me.

'I love you,' I said, my mouth enveloping hers in a kiss. 'In every possible way there is to love someone, I love you

Lilac Montgomery.'

She melted in my arms; the kiss taking over. She wrapped her own arms around my neck, pulling herself up into the kiss.

Eventually, she broke from the kiss. 'If we do this, this is not just sex,' Lilac told me – as though her fears were that I was asking her to become my live-in fuck buddy.

'Lilac,' I chuckled. 'It was never *just* sex. It was sex with *you.*'

Lilac. My girl. The no one else had been able to contend with because they were competing with a woman I hadn't even known yet; just the girl she had once been and the potential of what she could become.

'You're the girl I gave my forever to,' I reminded her. 'Who else could compete with that?'

'Forever?'

'Like Allie and Noah,' I laughed.

Lilac scrunched up her face. 'You read my diary.' She knew my memory wasn't as good as hers.

'Yes,' I admitted. 'But that's the last secret I'm keeping from you.'

'Good,' Lilac said. 'Because my best friend once told me never to stay with a boy who wasn't worth my time.'

'Sounds like a smart guy.'

'No, he was pretty stupid,' Lilac laughed.

I could listen to that laugh for the rest of my life. I picked her up, spinning Lilac around on the dance floor.

And although she was gone and I didn't believe in the afterlife, in that moment, I swear I could feel my mom's eyes on me. And I knew that no matter how much work we had to put into this town, how much work we had to put into our relationship, it would all be worth it.

Because I had Lilac. And she had me. Forever.

Printed in Great Britain
by Amazon

44075563R00190